MERCILESS

STEEL DEMONS MC BOOK NINE

CRYSTAL ASH

SDMC series playlist

All American Nightmare - Hinder
Notorious - Adelitas Way
Hail to the King - Avenged Sevenfold
O Death - Ashley H
Joan of Arc - In This Moment
Radioactive - Imagine Dragons
Bad Company - Five Finger Death Punch
Love Me to Death - No Resolve
(Don't Fear) The Reaper - HIM
David - Noah Gunderson
Apocalyptic - Halestorm
Blue on Black - Five Finger Death Punch
Machine Gun Blues - Social Distortion
Wanted Dead or Alive - Chris Daughtry
I Get Off - Halestorm
You Shook Me All Night Long - AC/DC
Nobody Praying for Me - Seether
Loyal to No One - Dropkick Murpheys
Crazy in Love - Daniel De Bourg
Be Free - King Dude & Chelsea Wolfe
Raise Hell - Dorothy
Coming Home - Skylar Grey

Listen on Spotify at:
crystalashbooks.com/sdmc-playlist

Prologue

REAPER

TWO YEARS EARLIER

A pounding headache, a parched throat, and a queasy stomach. All three of which were becoming a lot more common these days.

Can't drink like I'm in my twenties anymore, I thought, rolling over slowly in bed so the room wouldn't start spinning.

I slid out of bed quietly so as to not wake up my flavor of the night. She wanted to get all cuddly last night and I was not having that. Most likely, she'd want to stick around once she woke up and I'd have to be an absolute asshole to make her leave. My hangover would help with that endeavor, at least.

A quick glance at the bed over my shoulder had me stifling a groan. Her makeup was smeared all over my pillowcases. I fucking just had them washed too.

I wasn't crazy about leaving her in my room with all my shit, but I sure as hell wasn't about to be here when she woke up. Somehow I managed to pull pants on without losing my balance or making a huge amount of noise. Grabbing yesterday's shirt, I held my breath as I opened the door. I didn't dare release it until I was down the stairs and out the front door.

The sun was already high on my short walk to the clubhouse, the sunlight damn near blinding. People were up and chatting, and the smell of food cooking on the grill had my hungover body salivating. I hoped Daren and Jandro pulled out all the stops for breakfast this morning.

"His Majesty graces us with his presence," my brother announced, white cigarette bobbing in his mouth as he pumped a lever on a citrus juicer.

I caught a whiff of menthol and turned my head, nearly gagging. While we had plenty in common, Daren and I couldn't be more different when it came to our taste in smokes. I liked my cloves and couldn't stomach that menthol shit. Why the fuck would I want to constantly suck on the flavor of toothpaste?

"Where you been?" Jandro turned some sausages with a pair of tongs while stirring up hashbrowns in a cast-iron pan with the other hand. "That girl wring you out?"

"Nah, I got so bored I fell into a deep slumber." I collapsed on a deck chair and threw an arm over my eyes to shield against that oppressive sun.

"You're an ass," Noelle informed me from some-where nearby.

"So what else is new?"

I felt a kick on my shin. "Kara's nice. She hooked me up with free shots at the Shady Lady."

"That doesn't negate the fact that she's a boring lay."

Something cold touched my forearm that was thrown over my eyes. "Drink this," Daren's voice told me. "You'll feel better, Grumpasaurus."

I took the drink with my other hand, not bothering to look as I brought it to my lips. "Fuck, Daren! Did you just give me something with *fruit*?"

"Calm down, it's a screwdriver. The orange juice will help with your hangover, dick."

"You're lucky he didn't put a little umbrella in it," Jandro chimed in.

"He knows I'd disown him, that's why." I sat up to down the rest of my drink, my stomach actually settling and my eyes adjusting to the brightness of day.

The jarring sound of glass breaking made me wince, although it wasn't a terribly unusual sound for a biker club. But it was the heavy thump of a body collapsing and Noelle's, "Daren!" that shot me to my feet.

He was convulsing on the ground. Noelle rushed to grab his head so he wouldn't smack it on the concrete floor. I went to grab his arms while Jandro went for his legs.

"Shit, it's a bad one this time." Jandro frowned, his worried gaze on my brother's face.

He was right. Daren's arms tore out of my grip, every muscle tight and contracted. Even his fingers had curled into claw-like hands. "Did he eat or drink anything?" I fought to restrain him again before he hurt himself.

"Yeah, we should put him on his side." Noelle already had his face turned toward the floor, petting his hair and flushed cheeks while she stared down at him. "We got you, baby bro. It's gonna be okay," she cooed at him.

Daren never recalled us talking to him during his seizures, but she always did anyway. It seemed to work, in any case. His movements slowed, reducing to jerks and twitches for a minute before he was still.

"Hey." Noelle placed his head in her lap, smoothing her fingers over his forehead. "You okay, bud?"

Daren rolled up to a sitting position, yanking his arms and legs out of my and Jandro's grips. "Easy," I told him, holding my palms up. "Take it easy, bro. You know how these fuck with you."

"Yeah." His face was pale, eyes looking away from us as he hurried to his feet. "I'm heading back to the house. I don't feel good."

"Do you need anything?" Noelle was quick to ask, doting on him like our mother had.

"Just for all of you to give me some space," he snapped before storming off.

"The fuck is his problem?" I muttered, tapping my pockets in the hope that I had my cigarettes.

"For real?" Jandro stared at me. "Dude deals with seizures all the time that give him weird visions, and you wonder what his problem is?"

"I'm just saying, it's not like him to stomp off like a toddler." I found a smoke and stuck it in my mouth.

"I wonder if he saw something bad." Noelle worried her lip between her teeth.

"Both of you leave him alone like he asked," Jandro huffed, returning to the grill. "Swear to fuck, I don't blame him for running off when his siblings are always pecking at him."

"We watch out for him, 'Dro," I corrected. "He's the youngest of us."

"Yeah, well I'm the youngest too, so I know how he feels." He pointed at me with his metal tongs. "And sometimes, having my siblings act like my parents is fucking annoying. So just leave him be 'til he's ready to talk."

"Jesus, what crawled up everyone's ass today?" I lit up and turned my attention to the bottles of orange juice and vodka on the counter, considering making myself another drink.

"If everyone around you's an asshole," Noelle hip-checked me on her way inside the clubhouse, "might want to take a look in the mirror."

"Takes one to know one," I grumbled.

She was just upset that the guy she had a thing for didn't stick around. What she didn't know was that he used her to try to needle his way into the Steel Demons. I took one look at the bastard and knew he didn't have it in him. He bailed on her once I wouldn't even entertain the notion of making him a prospect.

Noelle would get over it. There was a guy out there worthy of her, one who wouldn't try to weasel into my club like a little bitch.

I got my belly filled with food and another megadose

of vitamin C before heading back to my house. Hopefully Daren had enough time to cool down and the girl in my bed had seen herself out. Even in the stifling desert heat I walked slowly, biding my time and enjoying a post-breakfast cigarette.

Daren waited for me on the front porch—my mirror image in some ways but also my polar opposite. The outburst earlier was strange coming from him because he was usually so relaxed and easygoing, not a cantankerous hothead like me.

I tossed the butt of my black clove while he lit up a fresh, white menthol. "Hey, Reap."

"Hey." I paused before the first step on the porch. "You alright?"

"Yeah, sorry about that." He scratched his forehead with his thumb. "Told your girl to get lost."

"Thanks." I approached him and leaned against the side of the house. "Want to talk about…anything?"

He was quiet for a long time.

"I saw my own death, Reap."

That was fucking weird—both that he saw something so grave and also that he said it in such a concrete way, not in a riddle or random innocuous detail like usual.

"Oh. Shit, well." I ran a hand through my hair. "Is it cool, at least?"

He huffed out a mirthless laugh. "No. About as uncool as it gets."

Fuck, he was serious. And seeing it had obviously shaken him. His fingers trembled as he took a long drag off his cigarette.

"Well, we can prevent it, right?" I was no good at emotional support, so the president in me sought to figure out a solution. "What good is this fucking gift of yours if we can't use it to change the course of the future?"

"No, it needs to happen. It *will* happen." Daren tossed his cigarette and quickly fished for another.

"Bullshit. Says who?"

He smiled as he lit up again, like he was enjoying some secret I wasn't privy to. "It'll be okay, Reap. Just wasn't what I expected to see today." He went quiet again, now seeming peacefully resigned about everything, before his eyes bounced back to me. "I saw your death too."

"Didja now?" I pulled out a cigarette of my own. "Don't tell me—on the cafe racer in the desert with an Uzi in each hand. Wait, actually." I lit up before moving on to my better idea. "At roughly like forty-five or so. Older than now but not *too* old, you know? Please tell me I die from cardiac arrest while mid-stroke in the best pussy of my life."

Daren laughed genuinely this time, a bright sound that all the women loved. "That's a better guess than you might think."

"Yes!" I pumped a fist. "Tell me what she looks like. And seriously, do I actually die before I start having boner problems? Because that's what's *really* important."

"Sorry, bro." Daren smirked. "You're gonna be old as shit. A fucking grandpa."

"Aww man, seriously?" I huffed out a disappointed sigh. "I'm no fucking MC president worth his salt if I live to old age. We're meant to go out in blazes of glory."

"Shit's gonna change in the next few years." He got that faraway look again, tapping the ashes off the end of his smoke. "Some of it will be really fucking bad, but not all of it will be."

I snorted. "Now that's the cryptic bullshit I was expecting. But hey, listen." I walked up next to him and grabbed the back of his head for some brotherly rough-housing. "You're not fuckin' dying on my watch, okay? I mean it. If I gotta live to be an old fart, so do you."

My brother just humored me with that secretive smile again. "Fuck yeah, Reap. I'll be there for all of it."

ONE

MARIPOSA

PRESENT DAY

I felt haunted.

I floated around like a ghost haunting my house, even haunting my own body. I didn't feel alive, but trapped inside a vessel. And I haunted those who surrounded me, namely Jandro, Gunner, and my in-laws.

Reaper's parents, Finn and Lis, were staying with us temporarily, in order to *support us*. Whatever that meant.

Ever since Reaper and Shadow were taken, and Tash's forces disappeared from Four Corners like a dark fog, my father-in-law and two remaining husbands talked late into the night. They sat around the living room or at the kitchen table, talking over whiskey in hushed voices. When I asked about these talks, Jandro or Gunner would squeeze my shoulder and assure me vaguely that they were figuring out how to get our other two back.

By the third day, I'd had enough of waiting.

I opened the garage door and started up my dirt bike, not caring who heard at seven in the morning. Foghorn answered the roar of my bike with a crow, which prompted Jandro to come running from the backyard.

"Where are you going?" he demanded, immediately suspicious as he stepped in front of my bike.

"Where do you think?" I shot back.

His face hardened, then both of his hands fell to grip my handlebars. To stop me. "You're not going anywhere."

"Let go, Jandro."

"They'll take you too, if you go," he hissed back through clenched teeth. "Underworld, sky, and the thread that ties them together. They'll have all the pieces they need, and then where will we be?"

"If you don't let go, I *will* run you over."

"Mari," Jandro pleaded, his face cracking with emotion. "Why are you doing this? You can't help them alone."

"At least I'll be doing something!" I screamed in his face, my resolve breaking with the realization that he was right. "Not sitting on my ass here. Planning, talking, and not doing shit!"

A sob escaped my throat and my vision blurred. The next thing I felt was Jandro pulling me into him, his arms cradling my face and back as he pulled me into his chest. I was sick of crying, sick of worrying, speculating, and *waiting* for something to be done. Every second that passed felt a tiny step closer to losing Reaper and

Shadow. And that feeling only amplified the pain creeping into my system like a poison.

At some point, Jandro turned off the bike and led me inside. The sullen faces of Gunner and my in-laws in the living room indicated they'd caught on to what I was about to do. I didn't care. I'd happily throw myself in the path of danger if it provided even the slightest chance of getting my men back.

Jandro led me to the loveseat where Gunner sat, holding his arms open for me. I sagged limply against him, accepting his embrace with no enthusiasm, while Jandro sat down after me. The two of them wrapped around me, sandwiching me protectively between them. Under any other circumstances, I would have loved and enjoyed it. But I only felt smothered, even suffocated.

"Mari," Finn began in a choked voice, his hands clasped with his wife's from where they sat across from us. "Please believe me when I say we know how frustrating these past few days have been."

"Frustrating," I repeated in a flat voice. "That's an interesting choice of word."

"Mari." Gunner tried next. "We all want the same things. Any one of us would do anything to get Reaper and Shadow back."

These empty platitudes were sickening, literally. I felt on the verge of throwing up.

"Then why was I the only one ready to ride out of that garage just now?" I demanded, then turned to Jandro. "And why did you stop me? I thought we fought these battles *together*."

"Because the last time we were all out there, two of

us got taken away." Jandro's gaze burned into mine. "And I'll be damned if the same thing happens to you."

"He's right," Lis chimed in softly. "Rory and Shadow stepped up so you could get to safety. Your men will do anything to protect you, so please don't be reckless, Mari. You are brave and strong, but don't let their sacrifice be for nothing."

I gawked, dumbfounded at my mother-in-law's words. "How can you say that? This is your *son* we're talking about. Your last living son! And I'm not some helpless damsel, I will do anything to protect *them* too!"

"What she's saying is," Gunner voiced gently, "there are four of us and only one of you. We can't afford to lose you, Mari, because you are irreplaceable."

I wanted to scream at all of them. Why couldn't they understand? "So are all of you! I can't afford to lose any of you."

"That was an understood risk every time one of your men stepped onto a battlefield," Finn said. "You know as well as I, sweetheart, that there was some chance that not all of your men would return."

"So what's your brilliant plan, then?" I demanded. "Treat them as casualties of war and just move on with our lives?"

"No," Finn said with a firm shake of his head. "I will not consider them fallen until I see them with my own eyes." His face softened just a fraction, weariness settling into his features. "But this…force, whatever it is. We're even less prepared to deal with it than I initially thought."

"We've been hardly prepared during this whole

war," I argued, looking to Gunner and Jandro for support. "We've beaten incredible odds in previous battles, haven't we?"

"Baby girl." Gunner gave a sad, heartbreaking shake of his head. "You saw the size of those mind-controlled forces. They surrounded the whole city. The five of us didn't even make a dent."

"But if you mobilize the whole army—"

"We did have casualties, not to mention damage to property and equipment when they swarmed the town," Finn cut in. "And we're still recovering from the ambush in which Jerriton helped us. It wouldn't just be dangerous to send troops to New Ireland now, it would be a suicide mission."

I sank back against the couch. "Then what do you have planned?"

I was met with deafening, defeated silence. That terrible lack of any answers had me yearning to run out to the garage and hop on my bike again.

"We don't want to give up," Jandro said finally. "We just can't see how to pull this off in a way that isn't a suicide mission."

"There has to be a way," I insisted. "There just has to be."

"If you have a plan that isn't running in blindly to save them," Finn softened the remark with a small smile, "we're all ears."

Of course I didn't. I knew it was stupid to rush out on my bike, to pick fights with my loved ones and accuse them of not caring, but I didn't know what else *to* do. I had nothing to pour my worry into, no battles to prepare for. I was running in place, spinning my wheels like a motorcycle stuck in a mudslide. It wasn't just me dealing with this, but knowing I wasn't alone was a small comfort. I didn't want comfort anyway. I just wanted my men back.

And it wasn't just the fact that they'd been captured by the enemy that weighed on me, but the timing of it.

Shadow and I had just reached such a beautiful part of our relationship after struggling for *so* long. He no longer feared hurting me or being open and vulnerable with me. It was incredible to see his confidence, to see how his journey of healing had paid off. He deserved a lifetime of happiness and love, and to imagine him being tortured again, regressing to a point of constant fear and distrust, was a pain I could not fathom.

And Reaper…

A pang of regret hit me so hard in the chest, I had to stand up and leave the room. My chest, my whole body even, felt so constricted and tight. I needed space and fresh air. I made a beeline for the sliding door in the kitchen, pulling it all the way open and shutting it behind me. Being out here, without everyone's eyes on me, was only marginally better. It didn't help that I caught sight of Reaper's whiskey in the corner of my eye on my way out.

I sat on the edge of the stoop, a soft breeze and the light clucking of chickens my only background noise as I thought back to my last moments with Reaper. Before the battle, before he was taken from me.

He had been earnest and heartfelt with me. I knew the depth of his remorse without a doubt, and he was there for me when I was inconsolable after seeing my dad in the field hospital. After everything we'd been through, Reaper still hadn't given up. I leaned on him when I was weak and told him how much I still craved him.

Then my husband gave me exactly what I craved and I *still* pushed him away.

My fists clenched as I wrapped my arms around my legs, resting my forehead on my knees as my eyes squeezed shut. Hot, angry tears threatened to spill—the anger aimed entirely at myself.

How could I? Why did I? I tried to think back to my emotional state at the time but it was out of grasp, murky like a fog. Mostly I was heartbroken that my own father didn't recognize me, and I was so, so tired. But was I still angry at Reaper? Resentful of what he did to Shadow? My tempest of emotions had been so volatile, I couldn't pinpoint how I *actually* felt toward Reaper.

My last moment alone with my husband could have been spent turning over a new leaf, rekindling the passion that burned so hot when we first met. It could have given him something to hold on to while being captured, a renewed sense of hope.

I was less worried about Shadow in a sense because he believed in our future together with his whole being. He would hold on until the very end, if it came to that. But Reaper…his own well-being was so dependent on that of his loved ones. He had already carried so much guilt over his parents, his brother, and now us.

If he believed our relationship was still irreparable, I worried—no, I was scared to *death*—that he wouldn't fight for his life. Family was everything to him, his reason for living. If he felt cut off from his family, then…

"Hades," I whispered, my lips against my fists. "Don't take him from me, please. I need him. I love him. I can't let him go yet."

As if coming to answer me, the silent black dog approached me from the side. His head lowered, eyes large and full of sympathy. Hades only nudged the side of my leg, but the sensation I felt was like a heavy blanket being draped over my shoulders. A weight, a pressure in the air that was comforting, like being wrapped in a hug.

I released one of my knees to scratch his neck, searching those impossibly dark eyes for answers.

"Can you see him? Or feel him?" Desperate hope bled into my voice. "Is he okay?"

He lives, dear daughter. Hades licked my hand, releasing a sympathetic whine. *The pulse of Reaper's life has not crossed into my realm yet.*

That was a small comfort, but better than nothing. Something bumped into me from the other side, and I looked to see Freyja rubbing against my opposite leg.

Do not doubt the depth of his love, she told me. *He is not adrift, but still yours in every sense of the word. Love will strengthen him.*

The sliding door opened behind me while I absently pet the animal gods at my sides. Their assurances sounded like little more than platitudes, probably because they too did not offer any solid plan for getting Reaper and Shadow out.

Jandro and Gunner came to sit next to Hades and Freyja respectively, sandwiching me in the middle of a cuddle pile. To top it all off, Horus flew down from his perch on the roof, flapping to slow his descent so he could land in my lap and not stab me with his talons.

"Whatcha thinking about?" Jandro leaned over and dropped a kiss on my shoulder before leaning his head on me there.

"How I was such a massive bitch to Reaper right before he was captured."

"Mari…" Both of the guys voiced my name as if to reassure me, but I held up a hand to stop them.

"It's true, don't try to convince me it's not. I keep going over our last moment together and I just…" My throat closed up, choking off my words with a sob.

"You were processing your dad and everything." Gunner reached over Freyja to stroke a tear off my cheek with his thumb. "You had no way of knowing what would have happened next. None of us did." His hand fell to pet Freyja's back. "I don't think these guys even knew."

We did not, Horus confirmed from my lap. *Our guidance led you to this moment, but we cannot see beyond here.*

Gunner startled next to me, and I remembered that he never heard Horus speak until recently.

"I just…hate that I left him feeling rejected and like I still hadn't forgiven him," I said. "Because…I do. I forgive him for Shadow, for everything." Speaking the realization out loud made me feel even worse. What kind of wife was I? To want my husband back so desperately only after he was taken away from me.

Jandro slid an arm around my back, rocking me gently toward him. "When we get him back, you can tell him that. He'll be the happiest grumpy bastard that ever lived, and this will all be a distant memory. Okay?"

I wanted so badly to believe him. We'd overcome so much before, as a group and individually. More than anything, I wanted to believe this would end happily for us. All of us alive and together.

But I couldn't ignore the cold, gnawing fear that a happy ending was impossible.

TWO

SHADOW

Another day, another metal pipe slammed against my ribs.

I bellowed at the impact, squeezing my eyes shut as I slid against the wall to get away from my attacker. The pipe came down again on my forearm, my thigh, and then the other side of my ribs. I flinched and cried out with every hit, trying to protect my injured areas and make myself as small as possible.

It only encouraged my attacker to hit me more, which was just what I wanted.

He dropped the pipe with a metal clang, panting for breath as he reached into his pockets and slid brass knuckles onto his fingers. If my eyes weren't so swollen, I would have rolled them. What kind of pussy needed brass knuckles to hit a chained-up, defenseless man?

His punches had little power behind them, even with the extra weight on his hands. If my hands were free, I was certain I could break his jaw with a single punch.

But I cried out in protest, begging and pleading for him to stop as I tried to escape the abuse.

He punched me until he was completely spent, leaning with exhaustion against the wall. Sweat coated his skin, dripping down his smug face as he slipped the brass knuckles off and returned them to his pants pockets.

"We'll play again tomorrow, big bitch," he told me, turning to the prison door.

"No." I shook my head at him, putting a grimace on my face. "No more."

Relief made me sag in my restraints as he unlocked the metal-barred door to leave, then locked it again behind him. To him, I looked sad and pathetic slumped against the dungeon wall, but the day had been a good one as far as these went.

They hadn't touched Reaper at all today.

He sat against the adjacent wall, completely silent during the beating I took. When the guard was gone, he remained staring at the door. I started cleaning my wounds with the meager amount of water I had rationed, a skill I had never fully unlearned.

"You need to stop doing that," Reaper finally said, his voice raspy from dehydration.

I paused in my washing, then continued on. "No, I don't."

"Shadow." He looked at me for the first time, one eye normal, the other a swollen, purple bruise from his beating yesterday. His speech was also off, slurred, probably from a swollen tongue. "They'll kill you."

He wasn't wrong about that. My pain reactions may

have been fake, but the damage to my body was real. My muscles were seized up and stiff around my injuries. I was finding it more difficult to breathe.

But there were two of us. And if we both didn't survive, one of us had to.

I was built to withstand torture. The first twenty-odd years of my life had forged me into this. Pain had become a distant memory and abuse, my constant companion. I adapted to this because I had no other choice. Even after a much better quality of life within the last several years, my old survival habits kicked in like they'd never left.

Sure, I might die, but it wouldn't happen quickly. So far, these shitheads with their metal pipes and weak punches didn't hold a candle to the Bathory cult that raised me, nor the sadistic bitch who brought me into the world.

"Better me than you," I said, pressing a hand to my mouth to stem the flow of blood from my lip.

"Why?" Reaper demanded. "Why are you playing into these sickos' torture fetish so that they pile on you and forget about me? You think I like watching you get beat?"

"Because I can handle it."

"So can I!"

"I *know* torture, Reaper. And I can't feel pain. It just makes sense."

"So what? It doesn't mean you should. Fuck, man." He returned to staring straight ahead at the door of our cell. "You've been through enough, Shadow."

"And you shouldn't have to go through it at all."

"Why the fuck not? Am I not in the same fucking dungeon as you?"

"Because you're the president!" I had never truly spoken to a child before but it felt like I was arguing with one right then. "The club needs you more than it needs me. Mari needs you."

Reaper huffed out a defeated laugh. "Everyone says that, but no, she absolutely fucking does not. You, on the other hand..." He glanced at me with his good eye. "You need to get back to her. And she will be pissed to find out you're taking all the hits to save my ass."

"She'll understand, I think." My bloody lip was finally clotting, so I pulled my hand away. "And we both need to get back to her."

We were both silent for a while. There was nothing to do except talk, sleep off injuries, or stare at the walls. Meager food and water rations were brought once a day like clockwork. No one spoke about any plans for us, about the Sha, or whatever it was.

"Do you think Four Corners is still standing?" Reaper asked.

"I don't know," I admitted. "Mari and the others haven't been thrown in here with us, so I hope that's a good sign."

"Yeah, I think we'd know if she was here." Reaper's throat worked in a swallow, like he wanted to say more. "I'm sorry, Shadow."

My head had started to droop with exhaustion, but it lifted back up at that. "For what?"

"Everything." He was looking at me with both eyes again. "You were there when we first formed the club, and I never took you seriously as a brother. I used your assassin skills, and your art for all of our tattoos. But when you needed friendship and guidance, I just let Jandro deal with you. I should have respected you more from the beginning, and I'm sorry that I didn't."

"Reaper, it's—"

"And with Mari." He faced forward again, closing his eyes. "I handled that so wrong. I fucked it up so bad."

"It's really okay, Reaper," I insisted. "That whole time away was actually something I needed badly. And it all worked out in the end." My eyes shifted around our cell. "Current circumstances not included."

He laughed bitterly. "No, I get it now. I deserve to be in here."

"No, you don't." I pulled at my restraints, wishing I could go to his side. "No one deserves a life of torture, Reaper. I wouldn't even wish it on the people who did it to me."

"Well, you're a better man than me."

"That's not for me to judge."

"Who, then?" he scoffed. "The gods?"

A thought occurred to me with that last question. "Have you tried your ability from Hades since we ended up here?"

"Yeah, there's nothing."

My eyes narrowed. "What do you mean?"

"There's nothing for me to see through, no death."

"We killed lots of Tash soldiers back at Four Corners. You can't see through any of them to assess the situation over there?"

"No. I've tried and they're…not empty vessels. It's not life, but there is something *in* them. Something holding on that won't let go."

I sat back against my wall, even more confused. "But you saw through the ones on the battlefield."

"Those weren't fully zombified, I don't think. Not under complete control like the black swarm that came for us."

"Why should that matter?" I wondered aloud.

"I don't know, Shadow. All I know is that it feels like I'm trying to crawl into a slab of solid concrete like it's a sleeping bag. It's just not happening."

"What about Hades?" I pressed. "Has he told you anything?"

"If he did, you'd be the first to know," Reaper said bitterly. "I'm sure you know by now these gods only intervene when it suits them."

Well, fuck.

Worse than the torture, than being separated from Mari and everyone else, was not knowing anything that was happening outside these four walls. Was Mari safe, alive? Was there still a home for us to return to? If I wasn't so exhausted from all the beatings and lack of food, it would keep me awake.

I scooted my legs to the side to lie down as comfortably as I could with a bunch of chains and restraints attaching me to the wall.

"In case it wasn't already clear, Reaper…" I started to drift off right away, my head resting on my hands.

"Hm?"

"I forgive you. For everything."

Neither of us said anything after that, but I was certain we both felt it—the finality of what the other man said. We were unburdening ourselves, making peace.

Just in case neither one of us made it out alive.

THREE

MARIPOSA

"I've had enough of this."

Freyja had the gall to look surprised as I scooped her up from Shadow's bed. Once I had her secure against my chest, I darted out of the room in search of Hades. I couldn't bear to spend any time in Shadow's room since he was taken. It was too painful being in the room without his large presence filling up the empty space.

Hades was in the living room, belly on the floor and paws stretched forward as if waiting for me. I deposited Freyja down next to him and, after a moment of thought, decided against looking for Horus. The falcon was probably miles high in the sky, and at least I had two out of three here now.

"You all have been dead silent since Reaper and Shadow got captured, and I'm not having it anymore." I looked back and forth between the two animals, both of their ears flattening down at my confrontation.

"Humans alone are no match for this thing, so tell me what you know. What is the Sha? How do we beat it?"

The Sha? Hades repeated the name in my head with a tone of surprise. *You are certain that's what this manifestation of chaos is?*

"I think so." Doubt filled my head as I thought back to when I was almost taken, and Shadow had stepped between me and a gun. "One of the controlled soldiers said the Sha wanted us alive to begin with, when he was going to take Shadow and me."

A beat of silence passed before the gods responded.

It's as we feared, Freyja said mournfully.

"What is?" I demanded. "What is it exactly?"

The Sha is the physical embodiment of Set, the brother of Horus, Hades explained. *They are direct antagonists of each other. Opposites in every way.*

"Okay, but we don't just have Horus. We have you two," I pointed out. "Doesn't that tilt things in our favor?"

The natural order has been slipping toward mindless violence and suffering for generations. The collapse of your civilization has allowed for the Sha's energy to thrive, Hades said. *The Sha exploits and weaponizes humanity's weaknesses for its own gain. It has likely been waiting for this moment to consolidate such immense power since ancient times.*

The death god's voice was so grave, so serious, but without any conviction behind it. It sounded like the fight had gone out of him, and that scared me more than anything I'd seen so far.

"Can anything be done?" I asked, fearing the

answer. "Can the Sha be stopped? Or even…reasoned with? Bargained with?"

There is no reasoning with chaos, Freyja said. *No mercy to be found in pure violence, and no bargaining with a force that will never compromise. The Sha's power can only be diminished by severing its bond to humanity and the physical realm.*

"How do we do that?"

By killing its physical form, Hades answered. *Just as killing the dog, cat, or falcon we inhabit would sever our bonds with you.*

However, it's not easily done, Freyja cautioned. *As you have seen, we enhance these animal bodies just as we've enhanced human abilities for you.*

"Well, what kind of animal is the Sha? It can still be wounded, right?" My gaze drifted over Hades' flank, knowing he had a scar under that short, dense fur. He'd been in bad shape when I dug that shrapnel out of his thigh way back when I first got caught up with the Steel Demons. If I hadn't been there, the dog might have died. And then would Hades, the god, have been able to guide Reaper and the Steel Demons through all of their trials since then?

That is another concern, Hades answered after a long quiet moment. *The Sha is represented by no true animal that has ever walked the earth. In that sense, it is completely unlike Freyja or me.*

Puzzled, I stared at the stern-faced Doberman. "What do you mean?"

The Sha is a creature not known to humanity, Freyja cut in. *If it is not truly an animal that exists, there is a possibility that it cannot be killed.*

"That's impossible." I rocked backward, still floored by this information despite finding it completely unbelievable. "Everything that's alive can be killed."

Gods cannot be killed, Hades said with a slight huff. *We can, however, fade into obscurity. It is humanity that creates and sustains us, after all.*

We are known to inhabit animal vessels and forge tangible bonds with humans before that happens, Freyja added. *It is often a last resort, such as during the onset of a collapsed society.*

"So if we can't kill the Sha, we have to weaken it," I mused aloud. "And the way to do that is by reducing the belief in Set?"

It is more devotion than simple belief, but yes.

"And how would we do that? Kill his devoted followers?" I couldn't even pretend that I was disturbed to talk so casually about killing people now. Murder was the lowest crime I would commit to get Reaper and Shadow back.

That is one way, Hades remarked just as casually. *Devotion needs to be given freely, willingly, to be a true source of power. The Sha's true followers are not those he forces into battle, but who he keeps closest. Those who believe in his cause with their whole being.*

"The general's council," I blurted out, remembering the transcription from Andrea's first letter. "If the Sha is the one in power, the ones who carry out his orders are the ones closest to him."

All of which are in the fortress in New Ireland, Freyja was quick to point out. *You have seen the extent of our abilities, dear daughter. Horus' sight reaches far, but we cannot get you past the Sha's army undetected.*

"Well maybe we can lure the council out." I stood up from the floor to shake out the numbness settling into my legs. "They still need the rest of us, right? What if we set a trap?"

Hades growled irritably. *I would not advise that.*

Your husbands would never allow it. Freyja was quick to agree.

I stabbed my fingers through my hair with a groan of frustration. "Well it seems I'm the only one coming up with ideas, so if you have anything, I'm all ears."

Silence stretched on for much longer than I was comfortable.

If it is any comfort, we are still bonded to Reaper and Shadow, Hades said. *We can feel the force of the Sha's power threatening to unravel our bond so that it can penetrate their minds and control them. However, it has not yet succeeded. As long as Reaper and Shadow remain bonded to us, there is hope.*

"You can...feel them?" I fell to my knees, eyes locked onto the ancient depths of Hades' gaze. "Are they okay? Can you talk to them?"

They are holding on for now. But no, communication has not been possible. The Sha is not controlling them, but he may have cut off that aspect of our bond.

I closed my eyes, my whole body feeling heavy as my gaze lowered to the floor. "Is there anything...anything at all that we can do?" Wearily, I brought my gaze up to plead with the gods in front of me. "Please. They are bonded to you, bonded to gods! Doesn't that mean anything?"

I'm sorry, Hades said. *We have lost many bonded humans*

over the millenia, to other gods or even simple human violence. It's always painful on a cosmic level.

"No." I shook my head and even let out a soft humorless laugh, I was that firmly in denial. "Not you too. You are *gods*, you can't be giving up on them!" My eyes widened as a sudden idea hit my brain with a bright spark. "Can you possess humans like you do animals?"

Hades growled, baring white teeth before he snapped, *No.*

He hesitated long enough in answering that I knew it wasn't as cut-and-dry as that. "Why not?"

We simply don't. It is not done.

"But you *can!*"

Hades barked a warning. His whole body was in warning mode—ears back, hackles raised, and low growl rumbling from his throat. But it was too late. Now *I* was the dog with a bone.

We will not inhabit you or the others. It is out of the question.

"But why?" I demanded. "If there's no chance of it helping, then fine. But it doesn't sound like that's the answer."

Inhabiting human bodies is incredibly dangerous to those we possess, Freyja explained. *It has not been done for nearly a thousand years. Such an occupation has grave consequences.*

"Like what?"

Like losing your humanity, Hades snapped. *You will turn into an empty, used-up husk like those the Sha has discarded. Is that what you want for you and your men?*

My chest deflated, the initial rush of a new idea gone as quickly as it came. "So that's what the Sha is doing?"

In a sense, Freyja said. *He is not possessing vessels in the exact same way we would. Think of his method as reaching with hundreds of thousands of hands. Each hand grabs someone by the mind and forces submission. That is how he is able to control so many.*

I perked up slightly. "So the way you possess is different? It doesn't have to be harmful?"

It still is. Hades turned his head to direct a growl at Freyja, who arched and hissed in response. *We inhabit animals because their brains are instinctual. They are simpler, and do not object to our occupation.*

"I would not object to you if it meant saving Reaper and Shadow," I insisted. "Neither would the other two. You'd have our full permission."

That does not matter, Hades growled irritably. *Human minds are too complex to house another being for long. It doesn't matter if you knowingly permit us, your brain will unravel itself trying to process that a foreign entity is occupying the same space. We are meant to guide humans, not control them.*

Thousands of years ago, Freyja added softly, *gods would possess human prophets to communicate their commands. They could only do so for short periods of time, and the human would be wrung-out, never the same again after multiple instances of this.*

It was an abusive practice. Hades' tone softened. *Humans are not ours to be used. This is why Reaper is an instrument to me. I've had to force his hand before, yes, but I never have or will possess him to carry out a task myself.*

I slumped back, feeling more defeated now than ever. "So that's it? There's really nothing?"

We are sorry. Freyja bumped her head into my hand

but I pulled away, not in any mood for affection from the cat. *We've seen many civilizations rise and fall. We hoped with all our hearts that this one would survive.*

33

FOUR

REAPER

The days became a blur of pain, hunger, and debilitating thirst. Not even our tally marks on the dungeon walls were accurate anymore. Shadow and I both drifted in and out of consciousness from our injuries, the exhaustion, and for me, excruciating pain on a level I never knew before.

The tips of my fingers were throbbing and extremely sensitive, bleeding stumps from where my fingernails had been ripped out. I couldn't even pick up a bowl of water to drink without intense pain throughout my whole hands. I had to drink from it on the floor, like a dog.

It hurt to breathe. Hurt to swallow, to blink my eyes. Hurt to stand up or sit down. I took it head-on at first, playing the stoic, unaffected one while Shadow kept our abusers entertained with his cries and yelps. Then they started getting more creative with me, trying new methods to get a reaction. That was when I lost my fingernails and the molars in the back of my lower jaw.

They left my teeth on the floor, just out of my reach, as if to taunt me. And they got a reaction alright, albeit still not as dramatic as Shadow. It wasn't that it didn't hurt. The pain just never stopped.

Even with Shadow taking the brunt of the torture, I was nearing my breaking point. Only that scared me more than the pain. Any more of this, and our captors would have their broken-down shell to do with as they pleased.

"Reaper," Shadow muttered hoarsely from across the cell.

At the sound of something metallic scraping on stone, I cracked one swollen eye open as far as it would go. He was pushing his water bowl toward me with his foot, the container with less than an inch of water in the bottom.

"Drink some more," he urged me.

"No…you need it." I didn't even know if he could understand me through my swollen, aching mouth.

"I'm okay. You're worse off than me, so have it. Even a little bit helps you stay alive."

I couldn't see him well enough to gauge that for myself. He sounded better than me, so he probably hadn't lost teeth yet. I knew they took some of his fingernails too because I had to listen to him screaming about it yesterday.

Or was that earlier today? I didn't know anymore.

My mouth did taste awful though, and the thought of just rinsing it out sounded more luxurious than a feather bed right then.

I inched my hand gingerly toward the bowl, my

fingertips already screaming in protest at grazing over the stone floor. Before I could fully turn my body and lean down to take a drink, footsteps approached from outside our cell.

"Again?" Shadow was quick to put on his pathetic, simpering voice. "Already?"

The guards unlocked the door with no comment, and several sets of footsteps quickly crowded our cell. I counted five pairs of boots and one pair of…feet?

I tried to squint but my eyesight was terrible after all the hits I'd taken. Five people definitely wore boots with dark pants tucked into them. The figure in the middle wore some kind of dress or robe. Loose fabric grazed the floor around their legs, and as the group walked toward me, my fucked-up eyes thought I saw a glimpse of *paws*.

"Stand up, both of you," barked one of them. When neither Shadow or I rushed to move, the speaker thumped the butt of a long rifle on the ground. "You will stand before the great general, prisoners. Or you'll lose more than teeth or fingernails." He cocked a round into the chamber and I knew that was our final warning.

I couldn't use my hands to press up, so I painstakingly tried to use the wall. From the rattling of his chains, Shadow was also putting in a massive effort and getting nowhere fast. A new voice spoke, and from the eerie shiver over my spine, it could only be the robed figure in the middle.

"Here, allow me."

The voice was strange. Ancient like Hades' but with an odd cadence that sounded…wrong. Almost like a foreign person speaking English, but that wasn't it either. I didn't dwell on the voice any longer than a fleeting second because all of the pain was suddenly *gone*.

I gasped at the relief. The absence of pain felt so blissful and sweet, I thought for a moment I might have died. I looked at Shadow, I could see him now! We were still chained up in this dungeon and therefore not dead yet. I stared at my hands, turning them over in fascination. My fingernails were intact, and gone were all the lacerations on my palms and fingers. My jaw, head, ribs, everything felt normal.

"Now you may stand," the strange voice commanded.

Shadow and I rose to full height, and my eyes met several looking back at me. Before I could closely inspect the strange person in the middle, the guard to the right slammed his rifle on the floor again.

"You will not gaze upon the great general!" he hissed.

I recognized the guy, even though his head and mouth were covered in black cloth. Only his eyes were visible, brown eyes with dark, bushy eyebrows. I had met those eyes before, shook those hands that now threatened me with a rifle. He was dressed entirely in black rather than a general's uniform, but I never forgot the one man who'd betrayed me and eluded me for so long.

"General Tash," I said, my tone full of contempt. "Or his impostor, rather." Keeping my gaze averted as he instructed, I angled my head toward the strange, cloaked person in the middle. "And the *real* general, I presume."

"Ahahaha…"

The laughter was soft, nothing more than an amused chuckle, but it made every hair on my body stand on end. That was the exact same laugh we all heard, the oppressive force in our heads that tried to break our sanity, and had succeeded in so many others.

Forgetting all decorum, I stared directly at the black hood in front of me. "What are you?"

I *felt*, rather than saw, the thing smile. Like Hades, its power seemed to fill the room like it's own atmosphere.

"I am the Sha. General Tash is simply the moniker I use when necessary. When I must be perceived as…human."

"And I'm supposed to know what the fuck that is?"

Only then did it pull back its hood.

And the face underneath…didn't make sense.

I stared at a long snout, somewhat like a dog's. So that was why it sounded so weird. Black lips pulled back in a smile, revealing canine-like teeth. Its skin was a dark gray with black fur in some areas. Eerily human eyes sat below two pointed, triangular ears that were narrow where they attached to the skull and widened at the top. The creature pulled back its sleeves to reveal long, black claws at the ends of its hands, and those were indeed paws instead of feet that I saw earlier. A tail flicked forward in an almost playful manner, forked in the middle to create two shorter tails at the end.

"I don't…" My eyes drifted all over this thing, trying to make it make sense in my brain, but it just wouldn't. "I don't understand. Are you a god?"

"I am the physical manifestation of Set." The Sha

grinned. "I do not make sense to you because I am no true animal that has ever existed. Chaos, by definition, does not make sense."

"Set?" Shadow repeated in a whisper, speaking up for the first time.

"Yes." The creature turned to him. "Has my brother ever told you about me?"

"Brother?" I remarked.

"Horus and Set are brothers, according to the mythology." Shadow looked just as unnerved at the sight of the Sha as I was. "They battled for nearly a century. Horus lost his eye, but he won." Shadow's features hardened as he stared down this thing in front of us. "Because the chaos, the violence you represent, it destroys everything. Even you. Do you realize that? If you win, you will annihilate humanity, the very source of your power."

The Sha turned its eerie gaze to him. It was smaller and not as broad as Shadow, but there was no mistaking the heaviness and concentration of energy that radiated from this animal-person-thing. It made Shadow suck in a breath and press flatter against the wall.

"Do you really think I'm bound by the rules of the tangible universe, human? You believe the laws of physics apply to *me*?" The Sha's lips pulled back in an unnerving smile. "If they did, then I would not be standing here. I am not meant to exist, but I do. Do *you* understand that?"

The Sha turned its snout toward me, pinning me with those creepy eyes. "Your companion gods all have real-animal counterparts and roles compatible with humans. But I," the Sha brought a clawed hand to its chest, "am not the same as your pet gods. Disorder and violence flourish in the *absence* of humanity." The Sha lowered its hands to its side, angling its gaze to Shadow. "So you are incorrect, I will not be destroyed. I will thrive."

"That's…impossible," Shadow whispered.

"Of course it is." The Sha grinned. "I *am* the impossible, in the flesh. Also," the Sha tilted its head in a curious, dog-like gesture. "I can see the attempt at repairs my brother has made on *your* fractured mind, human. It's stapled and knitted together so crudely, it's no wonder your madness escapes in your dreams. But don't worry," the Sha assured him with fake cheer. "Let me in and I'll undo all of that. Your thirst for violence will be set free, no longer caged up like you once were."

Shadow paled, and for the first time since I'd known him, he looked genuinely frightened. Not his normal nervous-because-women-were-around, but actually fucking terrified.

And then it was gone, his face morphing into a cold mask as he stepped away from the wall, pulling on his chains. The restraints stopped him six inches away from the Sha's snout, and Shadow snarled, "Release me now and I'll show you how violent I can be."

"In due time." The Sha appeared unfazed by Shadow's bulk towering over it.

"Why are you torturing us?" I blurted out in a quick demand. "You want us all gone, why not just kill us and get it over with?"

"Because you, the leaders of the resistance against

me, will be more useful to me in my army." The Sha leveled its gaze at me and I felt a sensation like a rough jabbing in my brain. "The bonds with your pet gods offer some protection against my methods, but the best minds always take time to break. And it will be *so* satisfying putting you on the front lines against your own people."

I tried to hide the shudder up my spine at that. So this instance of being miraculously healed wasn't likely to last. He would start up the torture again, bring me to the brink of death, heal me, and start the horror show all over again. At least, that's what I would do if I wanted to break someone's spirit.

Even knowing that, my own self-preservation wasn't the only thing on my mind.

This thing seemed to enjoy talking, so I wondered how best to ask about Mari. Did it have her captured and imprisoned somewhere else? Seeing her suffer would be the fastest way to us losing our shit, so I wanted to believe she was still free.

"I *can* still read your thoughts even though I haven't broken you yet, human," the Sha sneered. "We do not have your woman because she is not needed to sever the protective bond of your gods."

"Not needed?" Shadow repeated. "You gave the order for the sky, the underworld, and the thread that ties them together."

The Sha grinned smugly and spread its hands out to the sides. "If I destroy the bond with the sky and the underworld, what is left to tie together?"

Fuck.

Any hope I had left was snuffed out in that moment. We were done for from the moment Shadow and I got captured. And I hated nothing more than the sinking feeling that nothing could be done to stop it. Dad and Gunner could march in with an army of millions and it *still* wouldn't be enough. The Sha would just cast its net even farther and come back with an army twice as big.

"By the way." The Sha turned to address Shadow. "Your performance of extreme pain has been most entertaining but I'm bored of it now." Shadow's face slacked in shock as that creepy stare returned its focus to me. "Guards, you will now concentrate your efforts on Reaper. High pain, low fatality." The Sha turned toward the door with a smug grin. "And make sure Shadow is watching. One more week should be enough."

The Sha's split tail brushed over my feet as it turned to leave while the guards drew knives, brass knuckles, and even a small torch.

"No, don't!" Shadow cried out in a panic from across the room. "Leave him alone and come at me!"

They ignored him and closed in tightly to surround me.

FIVE

MARIPOSA

I couldn't place what brought me here now. I'd been avoiding it over the last several days, but something pulled me to Shadow's room today. Some desperate impulse to maintain hope maybe, or the simple need to feel my husband nearby.

My walk into the room was slow, deliberate. I looked at the beam in the ceiling, the one he could touch with his fingers and stretch his upper body forward. He looked so hot when he did that, I wanted to run my nails over him every time.

I moved my gaze to the bed, running my hand over the neatly made comforter. We made so much love here, both alone and with Jandro. We talked and laughed about nothing and everything. I wanted to burrow under the sheets and curl up, to feel some illusion of Shadow holding me, always wrapped around me in a protective embrace. If I imagined hard enough, I could feel the light kisses he would leave on my skin.

The bed dipped as I sat on the edge. Maybe Jandro and Gunner and I could sleep here tonight. I didn't know, it just felt so wrong that Shadow wasn't here.

My eyes lifted to his desk, the simple flat surface only holding a lamp, a sketchbook, and a small case of pencils and pens. I followed my feet to stand at the edge of the desk, staring down at the sketchbook's cover. The edges were worn, the cover scuffed slightly, well-loved by his large, beautiful, creative hands. I stared down at the book for what felt like minutes, wrestling with myself.

Don't. He didn't want you to see everything in there. It should be his decision what you get to see.

The dissenting thoughts were weak, powerless as I reached out to touch the cover. I choked back a sob at the feel of the thick, sturdy cardboard. Shadow loved this thing. How often had he held this book, flipped it open, and turned the pages? He touched this sketchbook almost as much as he touched me. His life was documented in here, the good and the bad.

It was heavy as I picked it up, returning to sit on the edge of the bed in a daze. I just held the sketchbook between my hands, felt its weight on my lap for a few moments before flipping open the cover.

Small doodles greeted me on the first page—simple sketches, mostly of subjects in nature like plants, flowers, birds, and reptiles. In the lower right corner, he drew a highly detailed animal skull, a fox or coyote from what I could tell.

Flipping through the pages, I felt a small sense of relief that this was Shadow's 'safe' sketchbook. It was mostly rough tattoo ideas and practice sketches. He must have had a different book for the things he preferred to keep private.

I smiled at one page entirely dedicated to Freyja as a kitten. He sketched her in various poses—sleeping, hunting, and playing. The pencil lines were loose and fluid, no doubt moving fast to keep up with the boundless energy of the kitten.

As I flipped toward the back of the book, I noticed an increase of portrait sketches, rather than symbols and animals. A smiling, upper body portrait of Jandro with a chicken perched on his shoulder made me pause and run my fingers over the pencil lines. He captured everything, from the playful mischief in Jandro's eyes, to the texture of the bird's feathers. *Mi amigo,* Shadow had captioned the portrait in small, blocky letters.

I turned a few more pages, spotting the familiar faces of Reaper, Gunner, and even a few self-portraits. I spent several long minutes looking at those—it was fascinating seeing how Shadow saw himself. One portrait even seemed to have been traced over, the same mirror image as on the opposite page, the only difference being the absence of scars.

Shadow looked like a different person without scars, still strikingly handsome but in a crisp, refined way that didn't seem to suit him.

I let out a soft gasp, my heart accelerating at the sight of the next spread of portraits.

It was me.

The sleeping faces of Mari, Shadow had titled this page.

These sketches were quick, rough studies, but his pencil lines were much softer, lighter when he drew me. One was a close-up of my face while sleeping on my side—my eyelids, eyebrows, lashes, nose, and mouth, all in exquisite detail. Like he had been lying right next to me, drawing me as I slept.

Another showed my bare back with my hair spilling out over the pillow and the sheet draped low over my hips. He copied my tattoo into the drawing as well, but his focus was on the contours of my body—the lines of my hip and waist, and even the tiny sliver of my face that was visible.

The next drawing showed me sleeping on a man's chest—Jandro's, I realized from the rib tattoos. Jandro's head wasn't in the frame, but his arm wrapped solidly around my back. My mouth was open slightly, cheek resting on his sternum and a hand over his heart.

I couldn't stop bouncing my gaze from each of the drawings, fascinated at all the little details Shadow saw and brought to life on paper. Every time I looked, I saw something new. The freckle on my shoulder, or how he made my lips curve to give me a slight smile in sleep. I felt vulnerable looking at these, realizing how Shadow's eyes truly missed nothing. They were highly intimate, these portraits. And although I was nude in every single one, they were not at all explicit.

That was not the case for the image when I flipped the page however.

My face heated at the sight of myself, laid out and bare from head to toe, with a man's head between my legs—Jandro's again.

Ecstasy was Shadow's chosen title for this piece.

My head was turned to the side, mouth open in a scream and brows pinched with tension. One hand gripped the back of Jandro's head while the other fisted the sheets next to my head. My back arched off the bed in one long, curving line. As I took in all the details, it dawned on me how realistic this portrait was. It was like going through a checklist in my head. *Those are my breasts, yep. My hips, my belly, my legs.* Shadow even drew my appendectomy scar, the one he loved to kiss so much.

There was no altering in this artwork, no ridiculously huge boobs or unrealistic waist-to-hip ratio. You would think a guy's erotic drawing would contain plenty of fantasy in there, but no.

There's nothing for him to alter, some voice whispered to me. *Having you was more than he ever dared dream of.*

Turning the page once more confirmed that, this last portrait pulling a sob from my chest. He drew me from the waist up, dressed in my medic jumpsuit complete with my red cross armbands. My face was serious, determined, with my arms crossed in front of me like I was about to tell some medics to get off their asses.

And he gave me wings.

Large, intricate butterfly wings spread out from behind me, making me look like some kind of ethereal fairy from another world. At the bottom of the page, Shadow wrote, *Mariposa, the love of my life and healer of my soul.*

A tear fell onto the page, then another.

The tears were coming faster and I had to shove the book out of my lap to not further ruin the drawing. I couldn't stop, curling up onto my side as I sobbed loudly. Just when I thought I couldn't cry over my men anymore, my well of sorrow turned out to be bottomless.

SIX

MARIPOSA

I had no memory of drifting off to sleep, except for waking up with sore, puffy eyes and the heavy weight of an arm draped over me.

"Hey baby girl." Gunner curled around me tighter and nuzzled a kiss into my hair.

"Hey." My voice was scratchy and hoarse and I felt unusually warm. It took a moment to realize that was due to a blanket draped over us both.

Gunner was thankfully quiet as he squeezed me protectively, peppering kisses into my hair and on my face. None of my men would offer empty platitudes as comfort and I was grateful for that. They knew how I felt. That I wasn't okay. If anyone could understand my pain, it was them.

"You tired of being sad?" he asked after several long minutes stretched on.

"Yes," I answered automatically. I wanted this heavy, crushing despair to be gone.

"Good. Let's go." Gunner sat up behind me,

pushing the blanket back as I looked at him in confusion.

"Go where?"

"The garage." He was off the bed now and grabbed my pant legs to slide me closer to him. Then he scooped under my knees and back to carry me.

"Why the garage?" I didn't resist, but just hung limply against his chest. All of my strength had been cried out.

"Because Jandro's in there."

"Okay?"

Gunner looked down at me with a wry smile as he carried me out of Shadow's bedroom. "He's been with you a little longer than me. He knows what you want when you're sick of being sad."

"And that is? Whoa, Gun!"

He did some crazy maneuver with my body that was too fast for me to follow. I thought I was going to fall for a second when he released one of my legs, but then he grabbed it again while turning me in his arms so that I was facing him. Gunner now held my legs around his waist in a straddle, barely missing a step as he walked us to the garage.

"Gunner, what is it that I supposedly want? Besides, obviously, Reaper and Shadow back."

He nudged the garage door open with his shoulder while placing a long, lingering kiss on my mouth at the same time. For the first time in days, my heart fluttered at the affection. It wasn't much, but that tiny response was the most alive and good I'd felt in all that time.

"Us," Gunner whispered sensually. "For your men to make you feel better."

Behind me, I heard the metallic clang of tools being dropped into a box. "She said it?" Jandro asked.

"Yeah." Gunner kept walking forward until he perched me on the back edge of the bike's seat that Jandro had been working on.

Jandro rolled up from the creeper he'd been lying on, white tank top smudged with black grease. "Alright, I should probably shower first though."

"Nah dude, right now." Gunner wedged his hips between my thighs, his steadying hands on my waist. "You're the only one she hasn't fucked on a bike."

"Guys, wait." I brought my palms up against Gunner's chest. "I actually don't think I'm in the mood right now."

"'Course you're not." Gunner stroked my cheek, his gaze warm and loving. "But you don't want to feel sad anymore, right? At least for a little bit?"

Oh, *now* I saw what he was getting at. Jandro told him about how we had sex right before I left to find Shadow. I had told Jandro I was tired of feeling miserable then, and it was true. A good fucking seemed like the perfect distraction, a release of all the misery I'd been absorbing for weeks before. In my exhausted, heartbroken state, I probably even thought it would make for a nice goodbye.

The sex had been wonderful, but it made leaving so difficult.

I nodded at Gunner, pulling my lip between my teeth. Like back then, I barely felt like myself, being so knotted up with fear and worry. Fuck, I barely felt human, or alive. My men knew that, and this was an attempt to give me a little bit of life back.

"Then will you give us a chance to get you in the mood?" Gunner's fingers trailed to my neck, his eyes remaining fixated on mine. "We'll stop if it's not doing anything for you." His thumb dragged over my dry, cracked lower lip. I must have looked like shit, but he was staring at me and touching me like I was the only thing he wanted. "I just want my baby girl to feel good."

I bobbed my head in a tired nod. "Okay, we can try." That was probably the most un-sexy thing I could say to get things started, but Gunner only smiled warmly as he leaned down to kiss me again.

His tongue probed gently at the seam of my lips and I opened up to him, closing my eyes and returning the sweet presses of his mouth. The light fluttering in my body returned, but it didn't grow stronger as Gunner's hands slid around my waist to stroke my back. Nor as his tongue surged deeply into my mouth and he touched me in all the right ways. He wasn't doing anything wrong, but I couldn't bring myself to feel *into* this.

Our kiss ended and I didn't find myself reaching for another.

"I'm sorry, Gun," I whispered. "I just can't."

Before he could answer, the bike shifted slightly as Jandro climbed on behind me. Warm fingers, slightly damp from just being washed, skimmed over my hips. Jandro's chest came to support my back, his form solid and smelling lightly of motor oil.

"Lean on me," he ordered gently, hands spanning across my hips and lower back. "Let us care for you."

I allowed my head to tip back, finding Jandro's shoulder there to catch me. Gunner took the opportunity to kiss down the column of my throat, and a small gasp escaped me when his teeth closed to take a sharp nibble of my flesh.

I barely had a moment to take another breath when Gunner's mouth returned to mine, his kiss biting and rough. The sting of his teeth in my lip made me squirm against the hot, solid wall of Jandro behind me.

Gunner broke away, his eyes bright and pretty lips smirking. "I think I know what our girl needs."

"Yeah?" Jandro's breath fanned over my ear and neck in a light tickling sensation that was nowhere near enough.

Gunner's hand closed around the front of my throat and my pulse immediately fired up. He felt it thrumming under his firm grip on the sides of my neck and grinned at my resulting ragged breaths.

"She needs it hard. She needs us to fuck her until she's sore and bruised and can't feel anything else that hurts." Gunner adjusted his grip on my neck so he could brush his thumb tenderly over my cheekbone. "Isn't that right, baby girl?"

His filthy words, his bites, and the weight of his hand on my throat made me feel more alive than any of the warm hugs or sweet kisses I'd received in the last few days. My pulse throbbed in my pussy, the need to be taken roughly already making me ache.

"Yes," I whimpered desperately. "Make me feel nothing else but you."

With that, Gunner returned the pressure to both sides of my neck, squeezing just a fraction tighter as he took another rough, bruising kiss from my mouth. A hard, sucking bite on the nape of my neck stole my breath away. Jandro's hands dove under my shirt as his mouth attacked the back of my neck, pawing and groping rudely on his way to my breasts.

The guys got me topless and Jandro's hard pinch of my nipples had me crying out. Already I was so sensitive and it made me crave even more sensation. Gunner got to work on removing my pants and then it was Jandro's hand on my throat, holding me in place while he sucked and gnawed on my earlobe.

"You want me to fill your little ass?" he asked in a harsh growl, his free hand still groping roughly over my breasts. "Want to ride two cocks on this bike, *Mariposita?*"

"Yes! Yes, please!" I was squirming hard against him, both to get away from the intensity of his rough touches and to lean into him for more.

Jandro released the nipple he was plucking, bracing his other forearm between my breasts to hold me still. His grip on my throat wasn't hard, but it was solid and unyielding.

"Open your mouth," he commanded.

I obeyed, sticking my tongue out while my eyes focused on Gunner, just a few feet out of reach and stripping slowly out of his clothes. I wanted his cock in my mouth, the thick bulge calling to me as Gunner rubbed a hand over the front of his jeans.

I got Jandro's fingers instead, tasting clean and lightly soapy as I closed my lips around them.

"Suck," Jandro ordered. "Get them nice and wet for me."

I did so happily, a small amount of my despair already melting away. I knew it was temporary, but it felt so good to be commanded, to be touched and taken with abandon. It was a relief for my mind to be pleasantly blank instead of racing at a mile a minute. The ache in my heart was still there, but right then it was outshined by the ache in my cunt, and the rough, buzzing friction on my skin from all the manhandling.

"Good, stop." Jandro seemed to enjoy giving me orders just as much as I enjoyed obeying. "Put your legs over mine."

He released my throat and we shifted in our rear-facing position on the bike until my thighs splayed open on top of his.

"That's right." Gunner watched us from where he stood, stroking his thickening cock that was now out of his jeans. "Spread that pussy open for me."

Jandro's fist wound in my hair, yanking my head back with a firm pull as the fingers I just sucked on trailed down the cleft of my ass. I let out a small whimper as he started to push inside. It had been a while since I'd had a man back there.

Gunner was on me in a flash, hand gripping my jaw and eyes burning into mine. "I said spread it open for me." His voice was low with warning. "Let me see you play with yourself."

A small part of me wanted to pout and refuse, to tell

him to go down on me instead. But this wasn't the head-space for that. I didn't want to make this a game, I just wanted to feel. I needed a distraction from this black hole of hopelessness threatening to swallow me up. My guys were hurting too--they probably needed this control as an outlet just as much as I needed to let go.

I trailed a hand down my body, Gunner's eyes following with rapt attention as I brought my fingertips to my clit. "Like this, love?" I asked in a high, breathy voice as I began to circle and stroke.

Gunner leaned down in reply, drawing a nipple into his mouth with a heavy groan. He bit and sucked at my flesh hard, the sensitive peak feeling like it was being teased by the edge of a knife.

"Don't stop playing with that pussy," Jandro ordered. He was still working his way into my ass, adding liberal amounts of saliva as he patiently stretched me.

Gunner moved on to my other breast to continue the same treatment. My skin was already red from Jandro's manhandling and now my nipple looked bruised from Gunner's mouth.

And yet it was so good and freeing. The pain brought on a rush of adrenaline that fueled a need for *more*. More rough handling of my body, more bites and bruises until I squealed, and please, please, please, a rough fucking.

My clit came alive under my own instinctive touch, amplified by Gunner's treatment of my nipples like they were directly connected. He angled his mouth lower, sucking the sensitive underside of my breast as he forced my knees apart. He gripped the flesh of my inner thighs--hard, commanding, and perfect as his mouth trailed down. I thought he'd want to taste me and slowed my own touch, but he returned a hard pinch to my nipple that made me yelp.

"Don't stop," Gunner ordered. "Your first orgasm's on your own, baby girl. You know why?"

I shook my head, my teeth sinking into my lip.

"'Cause it's for Jandro to feel, once his cock is nice and snug in your ass." Gunner held my jaw again. "And not before then. Got it?"

I whimpered, feeling like I was in over my head. It was bad enough when they denied me, now I had to deny myself? I was already close. If I kept up my current pace, it wouldn't be much longer.

Jandro tugged on my hair wrapped in his fist, the tingling pain in my scalp a sweet reminder of his control.

"Relax," he ordered with that sinful mouth against my ear. He was fucking my ass with his hand in earnest now, the pinching discomfort easing away as he prepped me for his cock. "The sooner you relax and can take me inside, the sooner you can come."

I groaned in wordless frustration. It wasn't enough! I wanted both of them inside me *now*. My breasts were a bit sore, but I craved more pain. Spanks on my ass, more hands on my throat, or--

"Ah!" I yelped, jerking against Jandro as a hand slapped down on my clit. Gunner's hand. It was just hard enough to hurt, to overload my senses for one split second.

"You stopped touching yourself." Gunner's hand

returned to my throat and now my body was absolutely buzzing. Despite the pain, or maybe because of it, that slap to my clit brought me even closer to orgasm.

"Bad baby girl." Gunner shook his head, clicking his tongue in disappointment, but his eyes flashed excitedly. "What am I gonna do with you?"

I didn't dare voice any suggestions but mentally I was begging him. *Do it again. Bite me. Choke me. Tie me up. Anything.*

"How about my cock down your throat?"

The moment my lips parted, Gunner guided me down, bending my body forward with his unforgiving grip on my neck. I took him in my mouth eagerly, my hand returning to my clit as if on instinct. Gunner waited for me to get a rhythm going first, dragging my lips and tongue over his hot, solid length, before he took control again.

His hands closed around my throat as he started to thrust his hips. He went slowly at first, then started to fuck my mouth harder. I moaned louder to encourage him and rubbed myself harder, letting his hands hold me up as I took his dick down my throat—gagging and choking and never getting enough.

When I felt a wide cock spreading me apart as it pushed into my ass, it sent my pleasure soaring. I pressed back onto Jandro, pushing away from Gunner with a great gasping breath just as my furiously rubbing hand finally released an orgasm that hit me like a mini-explosion.

"Oh fuck, she's squeezing my dick so hard. Holy fucking shit..."

A rough tug on my hair brought me upright again and sat me all the way down on Jandro's cock.

"Ohhh fuck," we said together. Jandro's forehead pressed to my upper back, squeezing a hand around my arm as he sucked in ragged breaths.

"You okay back there?" As breathless as I was from my throatfucking and my orgasm, there was still a bit of smugness in my voice.

"Almost forgot how fucking delicious your ass is." His forehead lifted away and he got back to business, swatting the right side of my ass hard as he sucked a rough kiss on the back of my shoulder. "Now bounce on this dick and let's see how bad Gunner wants that pussy."

My feet found purchase on the sides of the bike, my legs splayed open and on display for Gunner. I braced my hands on Jandro's thighs as I started to lift up and down. The foreign sensation of him sliding in and out of my ass felt better as I found balance and a rhythm. And even more so as Gunner watched me.

Jandro slapped my ass as I rode him, and I knew each side would be decorated with his handprints before we were done. With each whimper and moan as he filled and stretched me, I hoped it would entice Gunner to come take his fill.

"Please Gunner," I begged when the watching became too much and one cock became too few.

"Please what?" he rasped, his gaze focused hungrily on my pussy.

"Please fuck me. I need you too."

"You need me, baby girl?" He drew closer with an

outstretched hand but instead of a throat grab, it was a gentle caress of my cheek. "You really do?"

"Yes!" I gasped, nearly in tears with how badly I needed him. "I need you so fucking bad."

And I realized this was what *he* needed, to hear those exact words from me.

Gunner leaned in, connecting our mouths in a fierce kiss. He held my cheek in a gentle hold, but the way his cock drove through me was anything but.

My head dropped back to scream as the two of them filled me, the sensation intense and overwhelming but exactly what I needed. Jandro resumed holding my throat, crashing up into my ass while Gunner pulled back.

"More…yes…" I begged with breathless pants, eyes squeezed shut as I sank into the best feelings that bordered on too painful.

Gunner splayed my legs open wide, holding the inside of my knees with a punishing grip that I knew would leave finger-sized bruises. He kissed me roughly between his thrusts, biting lips and cutting off my gasps for air with his tongue. With Jandro holding me in place, I could do nothing but take it all and plead for more.

They were merciless in how they fucked me, using me and giving me a purpose after I had felt so useless for days. I was used to some roughness, but their hard grabs, slaps, bites, and punishing thrusts took me to the edge of my limits.

And still they watched me carefully, easing back at my yelps of pain until I begged for more. Jandro's chest was slick with sweat at my back and his sexy groans of effort grew labored as he snapped his hips up against my ass. Gunner took some of my weight off of him, the long muscles in his arms flexed and tight as he held my legs. Sweat was beginning to bead on Gunner's skin too, one running down the ridges of his abs as he fucked me.

"Is that all you boys got?" I taunted when Jandro's hand began to slip from my throat.

Jandro growled in reply, squeezing tighter than before as he began to fuck my ass wildly. Gunner closed my legs, bringing them against his chest, and that dialed up the intensity to the point where my screams filled the small garage. To turn it up even more, Gunner hugged around my legs with one arm and slapped the backs of my thighs as he fucked me.

Jandro's palm crashed against my sore, stinging ass. His other hand on my throat had me seeing bright dots. The culmination of it all, the constant strikes against sensitive flesh while they both fucked and filled me was almost overwhelming. The crazy thing was, I couldn't tell anymore if it was too good or if it actually hurt too much.

I opened my mouth and my hand flailed, trying to signal for some reprieve, when one of them grabbed my hand and placed a soft kiss on my palm. That small touch of sweetness was the final piece that sent me crashing.

I came hard, seizing and clenching around both of them to the point of making their thrusts stutter, and then wringing their releases from them forcefully.

"Oh God, oh...fuck..." Jandro's arms wrapped

around my middle, his forehead against my back as he shuddered and pulsed through his orgasm.

Gunner could barely stand, his hands ending up on Jandro's knees splayed on either side of the bike seat. His forehead rested on mine, strands of golden hair mixing with my dark strands.

"Baby girl," he huffed, face flushed as his eyes searched my face. "Did we hurt you?"

I took a moment to answer. I felt *everything* now that it was over. The stretch and ache in my skin and limbs rose to the surface now that the adrenaline was ebbing away.

"Yes, but," I touched a finger to his lips when his brows knitted, "it's okay. I wanted to hurt and I feel… okay now. Not good, but better."

"Hot bath," Jandro grunted against the back of my shoulder. "You're gonna be sore for a while."

"Shit, I think *we're* gonna be sore." Gunner pulled me off the bike and folded me up carefully in his arms. "You just about killed us."

"But it was good," Jandro added, sliding gingerly off the bike. "I think we all needed that."

I couldn't agree more. It didn't fix anything but the release of tension, of frustration and helplessness, made me feel lighter. After a bath to soothe my aches and pains and a few decent hours of sleep, maybe then I could think of a way to get Reaper and Shadow back.

SEVEN

SHADOW

W atching Reaper get tortured was infinitely worse than receiving it myself. Like with the men who shared my cage with me growing up, I was powerless to do anything to save him.

Only this time, I had to watch it all happen to my president and friend. No amount of pulling on my chains and yelling at them did any good. Every time they left him in a limp, bloody heap, I fought like hell to escape my own bonds to help him. But not even I could loosen the chains that were bolted to the ground. With the lack of food and water, every day left me weaker.

And every day, Reaper's breathing got quieter. He moved less after every beating, and I was getting increasingly worried whenever several seconds would pass without him taking a breath.

A few times, the Sha had returned and miraculously healed him, only to have the torture start all over again. Even those days were becoming few and far between. I was afraid to fall asleep in case Reaper stopped breathing altogether.

"Reaper."

I talked to him as much as I could, just to let him know that I was still there. That we still had a life outside of this dungeon worth going back to. When I was alone in my own dungeon, I would have killed for someone to talk to other than my mother. Even when I knew they'd be going to their death, I yearned for the men who'd be thrown into my cell with me. They weren't always friendly, but they didn't hate me and they told me about an outside world that sounded wondrous and imaginary.

"Reaper." I repeated his name until I got a pained groan in reply. Metal scraped on stone as I pushed my water bowl toward him with my boot. The water was dirty and only half an inch deep, but if it would extend his life another minute, I would make sure he drank it. "There's water about a foot away from your left hand. Drink it."

A wheezing, rattling breath answered me and my skin crawled with the sound. It sounded like he had fluid in his lungs. He had a bad cough two days ago. Now it seemed he didn't even have the strength to cough.

"Drink the water, Reaper," I insisted. "I need you to hold on. Our whole family does."

His bloody fingers twitched on the floor at his side but he didn't move for the bowl. I swallowed, my own throat as dry as a bone, but Reaper needed that water more than me. His hand looked wrong too—swollen, bruised, and probably broken in several places. The guard had taken turns stomping on it this morning.

"Hey," I called when the cell got too quiet. "You with me?"

"...Yeah..."

It was little more than a huff of breath, more weak and defeated than any sound I'd heard from him before. Fuck, he would surely die without medical treatment soon. How far was the Sha willing to go to break into his mind? Had that not already been accomplished yet? I wanted to ask Reaper these questions, but more importantly, I didn't want to waste what little remained of his strength by making him talk.

The Sha had tried to pry into my head a few times since being here, but whatever protection our companion gods had over us didn't allow the Sha inside. It felt like an outsider was pounding on my door every day but never making it inside my house. I could only hope the case was the same for Reaper.

I had a sense the Sha was growing frustrated at being unable to mentally break us. But even if he didn't succeed, he could kill us even easier. Able bodies were apparently disposable and easy to replace. That was all humanity was to this thing—a means to an end.

Our cell door opened with a series of metallic clanks and a guard walked in, carefully holding a metal bowl with both hands. I was guarded, alert and tense as I watched him approach Reaper, who was painstakingly trying to move away, but there was little movement anymore that didn't hurt him.

"Look at this," the guard said with a smile I did not like at all. "A full bowl of fresh water. Just for you, puppy."

A smell hit me that I couldn't place. Something sharp and bitter that definitely was not water. Reaper's cracked, bloody lips parted with a soft pant. He knew better than to trust our captors, but he was also badly dehydrated. His brain heard *fresh water* and now he wouldn't be able to think of anything else.

The guard stood in front of him, waving the bowl from side to side in front of Reaper's face. Of course Reaper couldn't smell it when his nose was broken in several places.

"Reaper, don't drink that," I warned. "It's not water. It doesn't smell right."

The guard clicked his tongue at me. "Sounds like your buddy just wants it for himself. Can you imagine how good a drink of clean, filtered water will taste?"

"Don't listen to him," I said. "He's messing with you. Reaper, please don't drink it."

But Reaper's instinct to survive was stronger than anything else. He leaned his head forward, dried tongue out to taste. When his mouth touched the liquid inside, he jerked back with a hiss at the pain. The guard's raucous laughter echoed off the brick walls as he threw the bowl's contents onto Reaper's face.

I had to look away as Reaper shook and screamed, his throat already so raw that it was a whispery, aching sound. He reached up instinctively to wipe his face, but the stuff only transferred to the open wounds on his fingers.

The recognition of that smell hit me too late— distilled vinegar. It looked exactly like water if you couldn't smell it, and it burned every open wound that it touched.

The guard walked out, chuckling amusedly to himself at his little prank. He didn't have his mask or hood on for this visit, so I focused my gaze on memorizing his features as he locked the door. If we escaped, he was mine.

I also noticed that this particular guard didn't appear to be under the Sha's mind control. His eyes were bright with plenty of life there. He wore his expressions clearly, from the conniving smirk when he first walked in, to the peals of laughter from throwing vinegar on Reaper's face. So the Sha didn't place everyone under its control, but why?

Maybe they joined its cause willingly, I thought with disgust.

I took a mental tally of the guards the Sha always surrounded itself with. One was the vinegar-thrower, and I recalled a few more that didn't have that blank, zombie look in their eyes. It was hard to be sure with their faces almost completely covered, but it made sense for something like the Sha to have a few dedicated followers with no need to break into their minds. Not to a normal person maybe, but the leaders of my cult did it without mind control at all.

The Sha was infinitely more powerful. People would align themselves with that thing out of self-preservation, to end up on what clearly looked like the winning side. The Sha probably didn't even need to offer salvation, riches, or whatever cult leaders promised. All he had to do was not turn them into zombies.

Reaper quieted after several minutes, and I pulled as far away from the wall as I could to get closer to him. "Hey, Reap. Are you okay?"

His head was bent low, chin nearly touching his chest. Blood dripped from his lips, which meant he must have bit the inside of his cheek again.

"Reaper, please say something."

He didn't answer with words, but with a slow, barely noticeable shake of his head from side to side.

"Okay, I know. I shouldn't have asked if you were okay. I know you're not." My teeth ground in my jaw at the sheer unfairness of it. Saying sorry or wishing I could help him did nothing of use. Neither did the pep talks, but at least maybe those turned his mind to something besides the pain.

"We're going to wipe this plague off the earth," I said. "We're going to get out. Mari's going to fix you up and when you're good as new, there'll be hell to pay."

Reaper rolled his head up slowly, like it took every ounce of his strength to do so. He turned his head toward me, both eyes bruised, swollen, and unseeing.

"It's going to feel so good," I went on. "We'll kill the Sha. Kill everyone who followed him willingly and allowed him to get this powerful. Then we can just live. Go on rides every day, spend time with our wife, our family. We just have to get through this."

Reaper's lips moved in a shaky whisper and I leaned into the chain around my neck to get closer.

"What did you say?"

He repeated it and I had to hold my breath to hear his weak, whispery voice.

"…I'm…not gonna…make it…"

"Yes, you are." Desperation bled into my voice. "You have to, and you will."

"…Sorry…Shadow…" His head lolled to the side before he brought it upright again, an enormous task for a man so beaten down. "…Love…Mari…"

"Stop. You're the fucking Steel Demons MC president. You're the instrument of the God of Death. Your work is not done, Reaper. You *need* to live." He stopped talking and moving, which made my panic spike. "Reaper? *Reaper.*"

I held my breath again and listened hard for his. Finally, there it was. The weak, sick sound told me he was still clinging to life. Exhausted, and not nearly relieved enough, I leaned against my wall and allowed my eyes to shut. I needed sleep, but my desperation to make sure that Reaper was alive kept jolting me awake whenever I drifted off.

I didn't tell him the real reason I couldn't lose him in this place, but it rattled through my mind right then.

If you don't make it, then I won't either. Because I can't live as a man who sat here and allowed you to die.

———

I JOLTED awake to the sound of Reaper's pained groans, my eyes snapping open to see one of the guards kneeling in front of him.

"Get away from him!" I jumped up, pulling on my chains as far as they would allow me in hopes of scaring this person off.

The black-clad figure gave me an impassive look over their shoulder that stopped me in my tracks. *That's a woman,* I realized at the sight of blue eyes and long, dark eyelashes. The mask on her lower face covered a delicate nose bridge. Her stature and overall features were smaller than the other guards, and yet I remembered her from the Sha's personal guard detail. She'd stood in the back, shorter than everyone else. But I was too distracted by the otherworldly creature talking to Reaper and I to pay her much attention.

In any case, woman or not, she was here to enact her personal brand of torture on Reaper.

"Stop touching him!" I yelled again when she ignored me the first time. "You want to fuck with someone, fuck with me."

Her next glance at me was narrow-eyed and annoyed. "You don't have to take my help, but I'm your best shot at living if you do."

"Help?" I couldn't have heard her correctly. I was hallucinating.

The woman returned to her task, which I realized was washing Reaper's face. His sounds of pain were quiet, more discomfort than anything else. A bloodied rag was discarded on the floor next to her, while she dipped a clean rag in a bowl of actual water and wrung it out before wiping it over Reaper's face and neck.

Her passes over his skin were light, intentionally being careful of his injuries. I found myself feeling envious as I watched her tend to him. Fuck, water over my skin would feel so fucking good.

"Who are you?" I asked, settling back against my wall. "Why are you helping us?"

"He has a fever," she said by way of answer, placing the back of her palm against Reaper's forehead. "A lot of his wounds are already infected. I made him swallow Tylenol before you woke up, but it might not do much. I'll do what I can to bring water and better food, but it may not be for another day."

"You're not under the Sha's control." If she was ignoring me, two could play at that game. "You have your own mind and are on the Sha's personal guard, but you're working against him. Why?"

The woman collected her rags and now-empty water bowl, then headed for the door. She adjusted her hood as she unlocked the door, and I thought I caught a glimpse of dark brown hair. "If I tell you now, the Sha may be able to extract the information from your mind and compromise both of us." The woman let herself out and paused on the other side of the door. "But you'll know when the time is right."

She turned to leave and, with my keen sight in the darkness, I caught something with a bright and glossy pattern hidden under her hood.

A pattern that looked like snake scales.

EIGHT

MARIPOSA

The hospital was where I always used to go to get my mind off things. Being busy used to help me cope.

Now, seeing Robert Anderson and some of the others who recovered from the mind control, only reminded me that my husbands were now captured by the source of that abuse. I could barely function at home, I couldn't focus at work. I was just a mess.

I had ridden out alone into the unknown for one man once. Every cell in my body wanted to go out and find my two, but Jandro and Gunner stopped me every time I attempted. They stuck to me like velcro, making sure I didn't run out and do anything stupid.

Jandro was in the day room across the hall now, spending time with patients as they recovered, but I knew he was also there to keep an eye on me. I couldn't get a single moment alone and hated how stagnant everything felt. The army was planning, strategizing supposedly, but *nothing* was being done. And every time I had enough and got off my ass, someone made sure to stop me.

I had screamed and cried and hit so many pillows over the lack of action to get my men back. I was exhausted, and nothing would release the rage at what had taken them from me.

Medics and patients alike barely talked to me anymore, so I was surprised to hear the door to the break room open. The Pop-Tart in my mouth tasted like cardboard as I turned in my seat to see my dad standing in front of the door.

He was looking better. His eye was healing and the staples in his head wound had been removed. Still, my chest cracked at the sight of him. He'd been one of Tash's victims and couldn't remember me or the second language he was fluent in.

"Buenos dias," I said absently to him before turning back around. Technically, he wasn't allowed in this room, but fuck if I cared about hospital protocol anymore.

He was silent for several long seconds before I heard a soft, "Morning, *mijita.*"

I froze, my pulse shooting up to pound furiously as I processed those words. When I turned around again, it was with the heartbreaking fear that I had misheard him. "What did you say?" I whispered.

My dad's lips trembled and his dark eyes were filled with unspent tears. "I said good morning to my daughter."

I stood shakily from my chair, unable to believe what

I heard as I gripped the armrest until my hand ached. "You…you…"

"Yes!" My dad rushed forward with his arms out. "I remember you, Mariposa."

Emotion burst so hard from my chest, I was barely aware of what my body was doing until we crushed each other into the hug I'd spent years yearning for.

I thought I couldn't cry anymore, but his thin hospital shirt was soaked through after moments of being pressed to his chest. He felt thinner and more frail than I remembered, but this hug was exactly the same as all the other ones we shared before. When he'd come home after weeks of fighting, Mom and I would cling to him like we'd never see him again. Then he'd leave again and we held onto him like we'd never let him go.

"Oh my daughter, I'm so sorry." He kissed my hair and rubbed my back. "I should have recognized you the moment I saw you."

"No, it wasn't your fault." I sniffed against his shoulder. "None of it was your fault."

"It all came back to me today," he explained, just as sniffly as I was. "It felt just out of reach for the last several days, but it all finally came back to me. I remember *everything*."

"What's better, *reposado* or *añejo*?" I asked in a shaky whisper near his ear, hardly able to believe it. If he could tell me his favorite type of tequila, I knew it was true.

A peal of laughter burst out of him. "Always *añejo*, you silly girl."

Our bone-crushing, tear-filled hug stretched on,

neither of us prepared to let go. The only sounds we made were laughs and sobs. When I finally felt a bit lighter, my hold on him loosened and my dad pulled back to hold my face in his hands.

"Look at you." He beamed, eyes bouncing all over my face. "My beautiful daughter. Are you a nurse now?"

"No, that's still not allowed," I laughed, wiping my nose. "Just a medic."

"*Just* a medic," he repeated with a scoff. "I've seen you running around and working your ass off. I'm so proud of you, *mijita.*"

"Oh, Dad…" I reached for his face. He was still the same but had changed so much. A weariness had settled into his eyes, I couldn't begin to fathom what being under the Sha's control had done to him.

"Mom." I remembered suddenly, my pulse shooting up. "Did she ever find you? Has she been in touch with you at all?"

Dad frowned, his brow wrinkling. "I…I don't know, *mijita.* That part of my memory still isn't all the way there. I remember seeing her face, I'm just not sure *when.* If it was the last time I left home or…"

"It's okay." I smiled at him through the tightness in my chest. "Do you want to sit down? Maybe have some breakfast? I could have Jandro bring us something."

"Ah yes, Jandro." Dad smiled teasingly at me. "He's certainly been helpful. How long have you two been a thing?"

I put a finger on my chin as I thought back to the beginning. "Seven or eight months, I think." It felt like I'd known all of my men for years already. Our time spent together might not have been long, but circumstances had forged our bonds deep.

"He seems like a good guy, but what's with that vest he wears?" Dad headed for the small break room table to sit down. "He's not part of an actual gang, is he?"

"Well, kind of." I followed him to the table, my feelings somewhere between nervous and amused. "But that's not the most shocking part about our relationship."

My dad's eyes narrowed, lips pressing together into a frown. "What do you mean?"

"I'm with him and three other men." I swallowed and stifled a laugh at my father's wide-eyed, scandalized expression. "We all consider ourselves married. I have four husbands, Dad."

"What?!"

I spent the next hour explaining the nature of my relationships and answering his many probing questions. Time slipped away and it was just like catching up with him on his weekends home on leave. Only this time, he'd never have to step foot on a battlefield again.

"And General Bray, the leader of the Four Corners Army, is Reaper's father," I explained. "I think you would like him. He and his wife are really sweet."

"So they get one amazing daughter-in-law, and I get four *very* different son-in-laws," Dad laughed. "Who's really getting the better deal here?"

A soft knock on the break room door interrupted us, Gunner sticking his head in moments after. "Hey, Dr. Brooks is looking for you, baby—oh! Hello." His blue eyes widened and he backed out toward the lobby. "I'm sorry, I didn't mean to interrupt."

"No, Gun! Come in." I waved an arm, ushering him inside. "Come meet my dad. I just finished telling him all about you guys."

Gunner's eyes bounced back and forth between my father and I as he slowly re-entered the room. "*All about us?*"

"The important parts, anyway." Dad smirked as he rose from the table, sticking his hand out toward Gunner. "I'm Javier."

"It's a pleasure, sir." My husband grinned broadly as he shook my father's hand. "Gunner." He looked at me next, warmth shining in his eyes. "I bet you're happy his memory's back."

"You have no idea." Tears welled up in my eyes as Gunner pulled me into a hug, dropping a kiss in my hair. This was the good news I needed that I never imagined I'd receive.

"You deserve this, baby girl," Gunner whispered, as if he knew what I'd been thinking. "This and so much more."

"I've heard only good things about you so far," my dad remarked, inspecting Gunner with that critical dad-eye.

"Let's try to keep it that way," Gunner joked, squeezing an arm around my shoulders.

Dad looked back at me. "So when can I meet the rest of your...husbands?" He tried out the plural form of the word like it was foreign to him.

My smile dropped. "That's the thing. Two of them

have been captured by the Sha. Gunner and Jandro are the only ones here with me now."

"You met Reaper," Gunner told him. "Shadow, I don't think you've met yet."

"Oh no, you did!" The memory came to me suddenly. "Shadow was the one who carried you out of the field hospital when we evacuated everyone."

My dad's eyes widened. "You're married to *that* guy? Jesus, *mijita*, you're gonna kill me."

"He wouldn't hurt a fly. You'll see when you meet him properly." *When, not if.*

Dad squeezed my shoulder, noticing my downturned face. "If these guys are as great as you say, they'll find their way back to you."

I leaned into him, silently grateful for his support. That was my dad. It didn't matter if I had four husbands or made questionable choices in high school. He had my back no matter what.

"Thanks, potato."

The ache around my heart eased a little more when he snorted with laughter and hugged me tighter. The Spanish word for potato was *papa*, so calling him that had been a longtime inside joke. His reaction proved that he remembered it too.

"Don't think I'll be a useful soldier anymore, but let me know if there's anything I can do to help."

"There might be, actually." Gunner stroked his chin thoughtfully. "Do you remember anything inside of the New Ireland fortress? A general layout or where certain things were located?"

Dad squinted and started rubbing his forehead.

"Maybe? I dunno, I can kind of remember flashes of things. Every time I try, I get a hell of a headache."

"Get some more rest," I said. "I'll take you back to your room. The rest of your memory probably still needs time to return."

"Or I'm just old," Dad chuckled.

"That too." I took hold of his elbow. "Come on, *viejito*."

"Some things don't change," he sighed with a parting smile to Gunner.

"It was good to meet you," Gunner offered politely. "I'm glad you're on the mend, sir."

"I'll be right back to see what Dr. Brooks needed," I said, leading my dad out of the break room.

"I'll let him know what's keeping you." Gunner planted a quick kiss on my head before skipping backwards with a bright grin. "He'll be overjoyed to hear the news, I'm sure."

"Nice *gringo* you got there," Dad said when Gunner was out of earshot.

"They're all nice." I nudged him with my arm. "In their own ways."

"Four of them, huh? You really need that many?"

My laugh filled up the corridor as we walked and, damn, it felt so good to *really* laugh. "I didn't *need* that many, it just kind of happened that way."

"I trust you, *mijita*. You've always been smart. I just, fuck." He shook his head. "I never thought I'd wake up one day and see you again, all grown up and married."

"Someone's looking out for us." I squeezed his arm, steering him gently when I noticed his balance wasn't completely stable. I'd have to see about getting him a cane, if his pride would allow him to use it.

"Yeah, the snake is."

"What?"

"Huh?"

"What do you mean, Dad?" I stopped walking, peering at his face curiously. "The snake is looking out for us? What snake?"

"Oh, I don't know." His face had been relaxed, if even dreamlike, but right then, he was frowning. "I'm not sure why I said that." His expression turned sheepish. "Ignore me. I'm just a silly old potato."

Something inside me was going off like alarm bells. This was important. Gods inside animals had brought us too far for me to just ignore what he said. But my dad's already-limited strength was waning for the day, and he gripped the railing next to us.

"Let's get you to bed," I said, gently urging him forward. "I'll bring you something for your headache. Are you hungry?"

"No. No, *mijita*. Thank you."

The hospital was still overcrowded and understaffed, so his bed was wedged in a room where three other patients slept. "When you're discharged, you're coming to live with us," I announced, deciding right then.

"Mari," Dad sighed. "No, I couldn't—"

"You will," I insisted. "We have plenty of room, and you're family. Plus, when we find Mom…" I paused, focusing for a moment on that instinct inside of me that *knew* my parents were alive this whole time. Both of them.

"When all this is over, and we find Mom," I repeated, fighting to keep my voice steady. "They're building lots of houses here. You two can live with us until you have your own place."

My dad smiled tiredly as he settled into bed. "Sounds real nice, *mija*." His eyelids fell slowly, the exhaustion taking over him. "My beautiful daughter, it's so good to see you again."

"You too, Dad." I squeezed his hand. "I'll be here when you wake up."

I watched him as he slept for several minutes, battling the urge to shake him awake. What if he didn't remember me again when he woke up? Time slipped away as I just watched my dad breathe.

When a warm hand dropped to my shoulder, I looked up to see Jandro beaming down at me. "Gunner told me," he said in a hushed voice. "I couldn't be happier for you, *Mariposita*."

I stood up, allowing myself to be wrapped up in a hug by him.

"He's back," I whispered into his chest in disbelief. "I really have him back."

"You do," Jandro affirmed with a loving squeeze around me. He brought his palms to my cheeks and touched his forehead to mine. "And you'll get the rest of them back."

For the first time since Reaper and Shadow were taken, I felt the tiny spark of hope that he was right.

NINE

REAPER

P ain was my constant companion. It woke me up, it knocked me out. It fed me and drained me. The only time it wasn't with me was when I was unconscious. Every time I got used to one kind of pain sensation, the Sha's guards would switch it up and do something new to shock my system.

The Sha never entered my mind, and from what I could tell through my pain haze, he never entered Shadow's either. Shadow was always with me too, I guess. Although I was never constantly aware of him like I was with the effects of the torture in my body.

"Drink more water," he told me. "It's safe. She brought a whole bowl for you."

I was pretty gun-shy about sticking my face in a bowl full of clear liquid after the distilled vinegar incident. Shadow insisted there was a woman among the Sha's guard who was working against him and helping us. I never saw her, I figured he had to be hallucinating. But then why would he still be in the dungeon with me if his mind was breaking down?

Maybe I was still sane, but I couldn't make sense of anything anymore. I still remembered Mari, my club, my home, everything I was fighting for. Mentally, I held onto it all for a while, but it was starting to slip from my grasp at this point. I didn't know if they'd been captured or killed by the Sha's forces or someone else.

The only thing I knew for sure was that I'd be a changed person if I ever made it out of here. Maybe I'd be a better person, or maybe a shell of the man I once was. But day after day of torture loosened my grip. Not on my sanity necessarily, but the willingness to endure. My wife's face, the happiness I once knew, was fading into a distant memory, and all I knew anymore was burning, stabbing, aching, blinding pain.

"Reaper." Shadow was starting to sound far away too. "Tell me one word. Just let me know you're there."

"…hurts…"

"I know. Can you do me a favor and drink some water? It will help you heal a little bit."

I would have laughed if I had the energy. What did he know? He couldn't feel any of it. They didn't even bother with him anymore.

"…Mah…ri…" It felt like I hadn't said her name in so long. My broken, swollen, bleeding mouth could barely form the syllables.

"She'll find a way to come for us." Shadow used to sound so optimistic, so gung-ho. Now even he didn't seem convinced by his own words. "You should go to

Gunner's hot spring with her when we're back. It's a beautiful, secluded little place. It'll be perfect for you two to reconnect."

That did make me laugh, which quickly turned into a wracking, wet cough that felt like knives dragging along the inside my lungs. I probably had pneumonia. And, fuck, probably cancer from all my damn smoking. Just as well.

"Be quiet!" A guard smacked his rifle on our cell door.

"He really needs a doctor," Shadow answered.

"You think I give a fuck what *he* needs?"

"…don't…" I tried to warn Shadow, but the guard had already decided. I heard a metal clang as he began to unlock the door.

"The Sha wants him alive, right? He won't be for much longer, he's in bad fucking shape." Sweet, innocent Shadow, still thinking reason applied to these people. Still thinking he could save me, that we'd reunite happily with our family if we just kept the hope alive.

"The Sha can bring him back if he dies."

Boots scuffled across the stone floor toward me, then one snapped up to kick me in the face. The slap of cold, filthy stone hit my temple as I slumped over.

"Stop! Come hit me, you fucking coward!"

As usual, Shadow's pleas went ignored as the guard whistled for more to join him. The blows pelted down, my body already too beaten-down and exhausted to react anymore. Sliding into unconsciousness felt different this time.

I might not make it back, was my last realization before it took me under.

———

THE STRANGEST SENSATION woke me up. I couldn't place it as I squinted against the bright sunlight. The feeling was so jarring, it didn't occur to me until a moment later how strange it was to see *sunlight.*

I touched my abdomen, face, and arms frantically in disbelief. I could *move.* The endless blue sky above me nearly brought me to tears as I figured out what this feeling was.

I wasn't in pain anymore.

Which meant I had to be dead.

I rolled up to sit, my surroundings even more shocking than the lack of pain in my body. I was home, in the community where I grew up. My old neighbors' RVs and cabins surrounded me on either side, with the steep canyon walls of Yavapai Point in the distance.

Taking a glance behind me, I saw *my* house exactly as I had left it. Everything looked pristine, not like an abandoned ruin like when I brought Mari here to tell her about how I grew up. It felt like I could walk around the back to find Carter lifting weights, or Nolan tilling the soil to grow vegetables. Or even Daren.

I scrambled to my feet, suddenly eager to reunite with the family I'd lost.

"They're not here, Reaper."

I whipped around at the sound of a voice I knew all

too well, to see a man I didn't recognize standing where there had been no one before.

"Hades," I said.

"Correct."

The God of the Underworld looked like…a normal guy. If I passed him in a crowd, I probably wouldn't look twice. He had brown hair and eyes with a clean-shaven, unremarkable face. He walked toward me at an unhurried pace, like he expected to find me here.

"Why isn't my family here?" My eyes bounced around all of the surrounding structures. "Why is *no one* here?"

"Because you're not dead." He shoved his hands in his pants pockets, an oddly human gesture for someone who spent so much time as a dog. "Not yet, anyway."

"So why am I seeing you?"

"You're on death's doorstep, as the saying goes." Hades said it easily, even lightheartedly, like we were two strangers chit-chatting in line for food. "You're in a coma. And if you don't receive medical attention soon, you *will* die."

"Let me guess." I crossed my arms over my chest. "Mari and the guys aren't anywhere near close to breaking us out, are they?"

Hades didn't say anything, which was enough of an answer for me.

"So how long do I have here?"

"That depends." The god removed his hands from his pockets to clasp them behind his back. "You can enter your childhood home now." He nodded at the cabin behind me. "And you will no longer be on the doorstep of death, but in its realm completely. Your mortal soul will leave your body, and there is no coming back."

"And if I don't?"

Hades looked at me gravely. "Then you have until the damage to your body becomes too extensive to repair."

"So probably not long," I concluded.

Hades shrugged. "You have surprised me before. I wouldn't rule it out again."

I looked back at my front door, the flood of memories pouring in more clearly than ever. Mom got so mad when my siblings and I ran in and out of the house and left the door open when it was hot. I tried to sneak girls into my bedroom a couple times, but that damn door always had a loud creak in a certain spot.

"Will I see them again?" I asked Hades, still staring at the door.

"You may," he said as a non-answer.

I looked back at him. "Care to elaborate?"

"The underworld is not a *place*, Reaper. It is a state of being." He walked up to stand next to me, his gaze on the door. "I can assure you rest and peace in your next phase of existence. But whether you see your past loved ones again, or if you even remember them?" He turned to face the canyon behind us. "That I have no control over."

"Wait…what?" I followed after him as he began his leisurely walk toward the horizon. "What do you mean by that?"

"You may pass by your father Nolan one day,"

Hades said, tilting his face up toward the sky. "But you may be a seed carried by the wind, while he may be a spine on a cactus. Now, does a seed know it's a seed?" He looked at me over his shoulder, his expression amused. "And does a cactus know it's a cactus?"

"What the fuck?" I raked my fingers back through my hair. "Are you telling me that all that hippie bullshit about becoming trees and shit is real? Ugh." I scrubbed my hands down over my face. "Fuck it. I don't wanna die after all."

Hades returned his gaze to the horizon. "What you want doesn't matter."

"Right, it's all inevitable. The circle of life or whatever. Everything happens when it's supposed to. Just let me come to terms with the disappointment that there's no hell for me to throw beers back with my fathers."

"I used to think everything happened as it was meant to," Hades scoffed. "I believed that for millenia. It's different when you're a god coming to terms with your own demise."

"Oh, you're gonna die too? Perfect."

"Everything will. Even the Sha." Hades started to look wistful. "Ideas and concepts don't exist if there's no one left capable of thinking them."

"Well, that's not comforting at all." I gave him a hard look. "What'll happen to my family?"

"If the Sha is not stopped soon, all of humanity will perish in the violence it brings. You, the ones we've bonded, were our last stand against the chaos coming for us all."

My mouth went dry at his declaration. "And we're losing."

"It appears that way." Hades' tone was even, although it carried more than a hint of sadness. Maybe even regret. "We may have acted too late. A generation ago, maybe our odds would have been better. I watched over your father Finn, and almost chose him as my instrument at one point." He gave a small shake of his head. "But there's no use in wondering what could have been."

"The Sha believes it won't die when it wipes humanity off the earth. At least, that's what it told us."

"Naturally." Hades didn't sound surprised. "The Sha believes anything that favors itself."

"Hades." I gritted my teeth. This place suddenly felt wrong. If I couldn't just die to be with my fathers and brother, then what was the point? "Can you wake me up?"

"No." He angled his head toward the cabin behind me. "If you choose to cross the threshold, I'll handle it from there. But I cannot force any being toward life or death."

"They need me. I need to...fuck, I can't just *wait* here."

"I believe this is similar to what the Christians call purgatory." Hades stroked his clean-shaven jaw. "Only instead of being cleansed for heaven, you're caught between life and death."

"And you really can't do anything to move the needle in either direction?"

"No," Hades repeated. "It's not my place to interfere."

"Right," I scoffed. "That's what you use me for."

"You've been grasping for control your whole adult life," the god mused. "Now, that control is completely out of your hands. What better time to reflect? To think about how you would go through life differently if you return. Or, should you choose to move on, the impact you had with this life."

"No control, huh?" I felt claustrophobic, despite being out in the open. An itch crawled up my skin, some instinct pulling at me.

I looked back toward the cabin, at the door that would send me to the underworld. Immediately the itch stopped, replaced by a soothing, peaceful feeling. *I have to go,* I thought.

"Reaper." Hades' voice was hard, carrying a note of warning as I turned to face the house. "Do not go through that door unless you are absolutely sure it's what you want."

"I don't know. I just..." One foot stepped closer, then the other. "I don't like it here. It doesn't feel right, and that's my home."

"If you go, there is no coming back. Do you understand?" Hades stepped closer to me. "You may not see Mariposa again for a very long time."

"Fuck, Mari." The urge to walk through that door felt magnetic now, and resisting only made it worse. "What's happening, Hades? Why is it pulling me?"

His brow furrowed the tiniest amount, the only

change in his otherwise calm, neutral face. "Your body must be failing. You're getting even closer to death."

"Shit." I slapped a hand to my chest, feeling like there was a fist inside my chest cavity physically pulling me toward that door. All my instincts were telling me that that place would feel much better than here. "I want to go, but…but not yet. I need to work things out with Mari. I want to become a father and watch my kids grow up—fuck!"

Calm.

That single word rumbled through my senses, lifting the hairs on my skin and echoing through my mind.

Be calm and stay. We are here with you.

"What is that?" I looked all around me. "*Who* is here?"

"Well." Now Hades had some amount of surprise in his voice. "I didn't know anyone else could be here."

I whipped around again to find another man standing in front of my parents' cabin, effectively blocking the door. Like Hades, he looked like a normal guy, but with warm brown skin and glossy black hair that hung straight past his shoulders.

"There seems to be much you don't know, old god," the stranger said to Hades, almost in a playfully chiding way.

"Leave it to a young god to still have an ego," Hades responded with a huff.

"I'm sorry, who are you?" I asked the newcomer.

"The companion god of a friend," he answered, leveling his dark gaze on me. I thought Hades' presence was heavy. This god made my knees want to buckle under some invisible weight. "Don't be afraid," he added. "I'm only here to encourage you to not choose death. At least, not until there is no other choice."

"You cannot interfere with his free will," Hades said with a snarl.

"His failing organs already are," the new god retorted. "I cannot heal as others can, but I can hold him closer to life for a short while longer." His gaze returned to me. "Until you are rescued or you die, Reaper."

TEN

JANDRO

Mari's dad was cleared to leave the hospital the next day, and all three of us welcomed the distraction of getting him set up in our home. I felt my old caretaker instincts kicking in from when my aunt and uncle started getting old and they needed more help around the house.

Gunner and I hovered, eager to help but also not wanting to be overbearing. Mari knew her dad best and it was heartwarming to see them bantering and cracking jokes. She had more brightness in her and smiled like she hadn't in days.

"Are you hungry, Dad?" Mari was darting around his room now, checking and rechecking that he had everything he needed, while us three guys just watched her movement like the cutest tornado.

"No, *mijita*. I don't have much of an appetite lately."

"You're skin and bones, *viejito*." She poked his cheek. "You're gonna have eggs for breakfast every day. You need the calories."

"Quit your fussing, you're not my wife." Javier smacked her hand away but he was smiling. At least he was, until a deep frown settled on his face and Mari took a seat on the bed next to him.

"Do you remember her?" she asked gently. "When you last saw her?"

Javier rubbed his forehead while Mari took his other hand. "I don't…I don't know. I'm sorry."

"It's okay," Mari assured him, though it only seemed to make him more frustrated.

"It's not okay! It's, shit, it's like she's right there but I can't reach her."

"It'll come to you," I said from the doorway, trying to be helpful. "Don't force it."

They both glanced up as if noticing us for the first time. Gunner thumped me once on the back before turning away from the room. "We'll be right out here if you need us."

"Shit, good call," I muttered, following him out to the living room. I got so wrapped up in taking care of Mari, and by extension, Javier, that I didn't stop to consider what they needed most was to be alone.

"They need their time together," Gunner said, confirming that he was following the same train of thought. "And I'm sure our hovering doesn't help him remember any faster."

"You're right." I collapsed onto the couch with a sigh. "If he *does* remember the inside of the compound, you really think that'll help us?"

"Fuck, anything is better than what we got now."

Gunner settled into an armchair, the one Reaper usually sat in, and stretched his long legs out toward the coffee table.

The front door swung open moments later, General Finn Bray coming through like a bull in a tea shop. He was disheveled lately, miles away from his usually clean-cut and polished appearance. His hair was mussed, his jacket wrinkled and buttoned incorrectly. Like us, he was barely sleeping and fraught with worry. The general paused at the sight of us, leaving the door wide open behind him.

"Well, I'm glad you two got some time off to relax," he growled irritably, eyes narrowing at us. The stress and lack of sleep also contributed to him having less of a filter. He and Reaper had the same scowl and temper when things were this tense. Like father, like son.

Gunner started to sit up, but I got to my feet faster. "Mari's dad is here," I said, lowering my voice. "He remembers her now, and we just got him settled in. We're giving them space, that's all."

Finn's expression softened. "He does? Oh, that's good...great, even." A weak smile wobbled onto his lips. "I'm glad. That's something, at least."

Mari and her dad came out of the bedroom then, probably alerted to the noise Finn made when he got home. The prickly general softened even more at the sight of his daughter-in-law. "Hey, sweetheart."

"Hi, Finn. I'd like you to meet my dad, Javier." Mari stepped to the side, keeping a loose hold on her dad's arm. "Dad, this is my father-in-law, General Finn Bray."

"It's a pleasure." The two older men shook hands, with Javier throwing a teasing smile in his daughter's direction. "You runnin' an old folks home out of here, girl?"

Mari glared and slapped his arm that she was holding while Finn released a bright laugh. It seemed like everyone was put in a better mood now that Mari and her old man were reunited.

"So is one of them yours?" Javier nodded at me and Gunner.

"Thankfully not," Finn chuckled, but the brief happiness left his eyes at that moment. "My son is Rory —Reaper. One of the captured ones."

"Oh, right." Javier rubbed his forehead while glancing at Mari with a sheepish look. "You told me that. Sorry, General, my memory isn't all there yet."

"That's alright. It's a lot of new information to take in, I'm sure." Finn straightened a little, a bit of the poised general returning. "And if you don't mind me saying, Javier, you've raised an incredible young woman for a daughter."

"She made it easy." Javier nudged Mari with his elbow. "Most of the time."

"Well, don't let me keep you from getting settled in." Finn started up the stairs toward his own borrowed room, which was Reaper's personal bedroom.

With Mari, Gunner, and I never wanting to be apart for long, we spent most nights in my room, which freed up the rest of the bedrooms. Now that we had Javier staying with us, it was nice to have a somewhat full house again, even if it was under the worst circumstances.

Moving in and getting up to greet Finn seemed to zap most of Javier's energy. He started leaning heavily on Mari as she guided him back to bed. Now alone again, Gunner and I exchanged a quick look.

"I really, *really* fucking hope he remembers," Gunner confessed quietly, reaching up to stroke Horus' chest feathers.

I nodded, choosing to keep my thoughts to myself. Javier's memory of the New Ireland compound might be the one thing that could save Reaper and Shadow.

It was all we had and barely, at that.

———

"AHHH! YOU MOTHERFUCKING...COCKSUCKER!"

I examined the line of blood growing thicker inside my forearm. Fucking Foghorn caught me with his spurs *again* while I was trying to collect eggs. If the rooster was so determined to not have his children become breakfast, maybe it was time to throw *him* in the pot.

"Fucking asshole." I kept grumbling on my way into the house, heading for the kitchen sink to wash the cut. I was so preoccupied with cursing out the rooster that I didn't notice Javier at the kitchen table until he spoke.

"You can trim back their spurs," he told me in flawless Spanish, raising a mug of tea to his lips.

"Oh yeah?" My native tongue flew from my mouth without thought as I turned to face him, keeping my arm under the running tap water. "You know much about roosters?"

"I come from a family of farmers in Mexico," Javier said with a nod and a small smile. "You can trim the spur with nail clippers or grind it down to the quick." His eyes shifted toward the backyard. "The challenge is not getting sliced up while you hold him to do it."

"Sounds like it would be a two-person job."

"Or three or four," he chuckled, looking back at me. "They're crafty sons of bitches. Especially when they've got a brood to protect."

"Don't I know it."

I took my eyes off of Javier to turn off the water and stem the flow of blood on my arm with a towel. When I looked up again, his elbows were braced on the table and he held his head in a white-knuckled grip.

"Javier!" I hurried to his side and placed a hand on his shoulder, but he flinched and pulled away from the contact. "Mari!" I called toward the bedrooms.

"No, don't yell," Javier wheezed painfully, hands moving over his ears. "It's too loud."

"What's going on?" Finn and Lis poked their heads out from the living room.

"Get Mari, something's not right."

I hovered protectively over Javier, not wanting to touch him or leave his side. A few drops of blood had fallen onto the table's surface. I didn't know whether to be relieved or concerned that they came from his nose rather than his ears.

"What's happening?" Mari darted in moments later,

rubbing her eyes and blinking. Her face had lines in it and her hair was mussed like she'd been napping hard. Reaper's parents and Gunner were right on her heels.

"I don't know," I told her. "One minute he was fine, we were talking. And then…"

"Everybody back up. Give us space, please." Mari went into medic mode like the flip of a switch. She placed her hands on her dad's shoulders, holding firm when he flinched at the touch. "Dad, I need you to talk to me. Tell me what—"

Javier began muttering in a long stream of gibberish. I picked up some Spanish words that didn't make sense in the context, and it sounded like there were some other languages garbled in too.

Mari's face went white. "Oh no. No, no, no, no."

"Babe, what is it?" I went to her side despite her earlier request for space. She looked like she was about to fall to the floor at any moment.

"I think…he's regressing." Her gaze was locked onto her father's face, which was still propped up by his hands, mouth moving rapidly without saying anything. "He's losing the ability to speak. Or retain language, or something."

"Oh, Mari…" I was shattered on her behalf. She had just gotten him back and now…

"No." Javier's hand snapped out, grabbing one of hers. "It's not that, not that, not that…" He sounded like a malfunctioning robot.

"Baby girl, step away from him." Gunner had come up beside me, his posture defensive like mine had become. If this was the Sha trying to regain control of one of his drones, Mari was in danger. Shit, we *all* were.

"Dad, let me go." Mari's attempt to yank out of her dad's grip went nowhere, so Gunner and I stepped up to help her.

"Sorry, Javier," I muttered before forcibly breaking his hold on Mari's wrist.

Gunner and I each restrained one of his arms, pulling him back against the chair he sat in. More blood trickled from his nose, his lips still moving rapidly while his voice was at a frenzied whisper. His eyes stared blankly at nothing in front of him.

"I think we should take him back to the hospital, sweetheart," Finn broached gently.

"Not yet." Already past the shock of her father grabbing her, Mari wiped at the blood under his nose with a napkin.

"But if he's regressing as you say," Gunner began, but Mari cut him off with a sharp wave of her hand.

"It was just a guess, I could be wrong. Give him a minute."

"*Mariposita,* I'm gonna have to agree with them." The regret was heavy in my voice. Fuck, Javier and I were just having a nice chat. What the fuck happened?

"I said, give him a minute." Mari's eyes snapped up to mine. "Just trust me, please."

"Okay." I glanced at Gunner, who nodded his agreement. But both of us tightened our grip on the man's arms.

Mari continued tending to her dad's nosebleed while also checking his pulse and focus of his eyes. She asked for her penlight, which Lis scurried off to find for her. Feeling something near my pant leg, I glanced down to see Freyja winding around the chair legs and Javier's feet. The cat jumped into Javier's lap, purring up a storm as Lis returned with the light. When Mari shined it into her dad's eye, the response was immediate.

"Ah, fuck! You trying to blind me, *mija*?"

The light fell to the floor with a clatter, and I felt every bit of relief that took over Mari's face.

"You're back!" she cried, reaching forward to hug him. "Holy shit, I thought I lost you again."

"Is that why your husbands got me in a headlock?"

Mari laughed, quickly wiping tears as we released him. "Don't be dramatic. Now what the fuck was that?"

Javier rubbed his eyes. "I don't know. Feels like I blacked out." He glanced up at me and Gunner on either side of him. "You guys look like a couple of bouncers about to toss me on my ass, so it couldn't have been good."

"Dad." Mari touched his face to bring his attention back to her, carefully inspecting around his eyes, nose, and mouth. "Has this happened to you before?"

"Yeah," he remarked casually. "Couple times in the hospital."

"When was the last time?" Mari picked up her light from the floor and shined it into his mouth.

Javier smiled when she finished inspecting him and allowed him to close his lips. "Right before all my memories of you came back, *mijita*."

Mari sucked in a breath, eyes widening with a glance

up at us before looking at her father again. "Do you remember anything new now?"

He thought for a moment, frowning. "I don't know."

"Mom?" Mari asked hopefully.

Javier's frown deepened. "Not…really. I'm sorry."

Mari was quick to cover up her disappointment with a tight smile. "Don't be sorry, Dad. You can't force these things."

"What about…" Gunner's eyes flicked to her in a silent request for permission. When she nodded, he continued. "New Ireland? Your time there?"

"New Ireland?" Javier rubbed his jaw. "You mean the fortress? That's what everyone called it."

Everyone froze in temporary shock, then me and Gunner were scrambling to pull up chairs and sit facing him.

"The fortress?" I repeated. "You mean the place you were deployed from?"

"Yes, I think so." Javier sounded unsure at first, then he nodded more confidently. "Yes, it used to be New Mexico."

"Do you remember the inside of the fortress?" Gunner gripped the edge of the table, as if holding himself back.

"Yes, of course. I never left before we were sent out to attack."

"Javier." I put my palms together as if in prayer. "We need to know the layout of that fortress. It could be our only chance to get Reaper and Shadow back." I looked at Mari, knowing she wouldn't disagree, but her dad's recovery was important too. Trying too hard to remember things gave him intense headaches and fatigue.

"Jandro's right, Dad," she said quietly, taking one of his hands. "They're my family, and we need you."

"I'll tell you everything I can remember." He squeezed his daughter's hand and looked once more at me and Gunner. "Because you're my family now too."

ELEVEN

SHADOW

"Shadow, I love you." Warm hands drifted over my face, rousing me gently.

"Mari?" I reached for her before my eyes opened, my fingers finding purchase on the slender, curving waist I'd held so many times before. "Mari!" My eyes snapped open to find that I wasn't dreaming. Her beautiful face was in front of me in the sharpest detail, from the curve of her lips to the freckles on her nose. She was here! Oh thank fucking everything, she found us.

"Mari, check on Reaper. He's in bad shape." I took her hands from my face, trying to look around the dungeon to see if she came alone or with the others, but I couldn't seem to see beyond where she sat in front of me.

"He's fine." She returned a palm to my cheek, her skin so soft and warm, I wanted to rest my whole, weary head in her hand. "I missed you so much, Shadow."

"I missed you too." I blinked, waiting for the rest of the room to come into focus. I was fully awake now, but why was it so dark? Did she sneak in late at night? Even with my night vision, I couldn't make out anything in the blackness beyond her. My stomach clenched with an instinct of warning, and I looked at Mari again. "Are you sure Reaper's okay?"

"Yes," she replied quickly. "Shadow, do you love me?"

My stomach clamped harder. "Yes," I said with a note of caution.

"You would do anything for me?"

I grabbed her wrist and removed her hand from my face again. "What are you asking me to do?"

Mari's face flickered for a split second, a quick distortion, like an image on paper being folded. I would have missed it if I wasn't watching so carefully. Despair crushed my relief like a cruel fist and I scrambled to get away from this illusion using my wife's face and voice. Maybe this wasn't a dream but it sure as fuck wasn't *real*.

"Let the Sha inside your mind, Shadow." Mari's voice had deepened, distorting into the Sha's strange cadence. "Take the leash off of the monster you're holding back. You'll feel so much better when you're free."

"No!" I scooted away as far as my chains would allow me. I kicked something metallic-sounding, probably a metal water bowl. Empty blackness still surrounded me, so I had no sense of place or proximity.

"You can't fight it forever," the Sha taunted me through Mari's mouth. "All you know is dungeons, blood, and violence. No woman or brotherhood can change what you really are."

"That's not who I am!" I hated how desperate and in denial I sounded.

"My brother tried to fix you but you are *perfect*, Shadow. You would make the perfect instrument for me."

"I am no one's instrument!" I roared back. "Especially not one who uses my wife to manipulate me."

"Oh but you will be, Shadow." The Sha sounded more than confident, like his victory was inevitable. "And if I must, I will sway you to me through Mariposa's visage. She is the one weak spot in your defenses."

"I *know* her," I bit back. "You won't fool me using her face again. She would never—"

The illusion of Mari zipped forward at an impossible speed. I flinched, trying to back away again, but I had reached the ends of my chains. She—it—sat down, straddling my waist. I bit the inside of my cheek and shut my eyes, stifling my groan. It felt just like her—the slight weight of her on my lower stomach and the squeeze of her thighs around my body. The physical memory of her was so sweet. I almost unclenched my hands with the need to touch her.

It's not her. It's not her. Don't you ever fucking forget that this is not *her.*

"Get off me!" I would have shoved the Sha's illusion away if I trusted myself to touch it again. But the fact of the matter was, I didn't.

And the Sha knew that. I saw it in the smug curve of Mari's lips as the illusion stood, lifting away from my body.

"You may know her, but you have not seen her for a

very long time. This face," the Sha traced a hand along the illusion's jaw—Mari's jaw. The gesture was odd, even jarring, because I knew Mari would never touch her own face like that. "I could feel your relief, your utter joy when you saw this face. When you heard this voice say, *I love you, Shadow.*" The Sha's voice morphed back to Mari's for those last four words and I flinched as if they physically pained me.

It's not her. It's not her.

"You're wasting your time," I said. "I won't fall for this."

"Maybe not today, but soon." Mari's image flicked her hair back over her shoulder, and that was hard to see because she *did* often do that. "You'll start missing your wife so much, you'll do anything to see her again." The illusion traced a finger around Mari's mouth." You'll do anything these lips will tell you to."

"I won't," I insisted, but even I was becoming less convinced of that with each passing minute.

That became evident with the Sha's knowing, parting smile as the illusion of Mari disappeared. What I felt next wasn't the cramping hunger in my stomach, the weakness in my limbs, or the dryness in my throat.

It was the constant, gnawing ache of not seeing her face anymore.

I WOKE WITH A START, gasping like my lungs could never get enough air. A cough wracked through my chest. Unlike Reaper's wet, hacking cough, my lungs and throat felt dryer than the desert. I knew I was dehydrated—I'd been giving him most of my water. It had been nearly a decade since I had to, but I knew how to ration water so that I could survive on very little.

I looked around for my bowl, eager for just a little water to soothe my cough, then spotted it turned over across the dungeon near the door.

Oh fuck, the Sha.

My legs drew up toward my stomach at the memory, the dream, hallucination, or whatever it was. The Sha might not have been able to break in and control me yet, but he *knew* how much I loved Mari. He knew she was my one exploitable weakness, and pulled no punches in letting my guard down. And fuck me, I almost did.

I couldn't even process how violating that encounter felt. That it kept making me touch the illusion of my wife, that it knew exactly what she felt and looked like, all from information in my own head. Information that it had no right to see.

What I hated most of all was how right the Sha had been. I had been so happy to see her, to hear her voice, and feel her skin exactly how I remembered her. It scared me how much I wanted that, what I was willing to give just to see Mari's face again.

"No," I said aloud to myself. "It's not her. She would never want me to do this. I'm not an instrument. I won't be used."

This is how they will break us, I realized. For Reaper, they intended to break him down physically. They knew I wouldn't respond to pain, so for me, the torture would be all mental.

"Oh fuck. Reaper!"

He was still lying in the same position as the guards left him in. Shit, how long had that been, hours? A full day? Coagulated blood surrounded his body and I couldn't tell if he was breathing.

"Reaper!" I called to him, my panic rising to an all-time high. "Reaper, wake up. Do something to show me you're still there."

He remained silent and eerily still.

"Reaper!" I shouted again, pulling at my chains to get closer. "Wake up, president. I need you." When there was still no change, I tried his given name. "Rory! Rory Daley, wake up now! Get up and punch me in the face for calling you that. You know you want to."

I yelled and shouted his name until I was hoarse, his name a desperate whisper of disbelief as I slumped back against my wall. No, it couldn't be. He was my president, for fuck's sake. I was supposed to die before him.

I couldn't tear my eyes away from his body, dumbfounded by the utter lack of movement. He couldn't be dead. It wasn't *right*. My own breathing, an erratic sawing of air in and out of my chest, grew painful while I just stared at him. Like even my lungs knew how unfair it was for me to be alive if he was dead.

Only the metal clanking of a key through our cell door drew my eyes away. The door creaked noisily open and a familiar, black-clad figure slipped inside.

"You," I rasped at the Sha's female guard, the one who gave Reaper water and washed his face before.

"Shhh," she hissed at me, making her way to where Reaper lay. Her eyes looked like they were narrowed in annoyance above her mask. "I would have come sooner if you'd have stopped screaming his name," she whispered.

I didn't give a shit about blowing her cover right then. He needed help hours ago. "Is he…"

She carefully rolled Reaper to his back. The limp flopping of his hands at his sides made me feel sick. I held my breath as she brought her ear down next to his mouth.

"He's alive," she reported, and the air left me in a big whoosh. "But barely," she added with a finger on the pulse at his neck. "He won't survive another beating."

"Is there anything you can do?" My voice was heavy with desperation. I didn't know who this woman was. She could have been just another player in a game set up by the Sha, giving us false hope to break us even more. But I didn't care. Maybe I was already losing mentally because I was ready to cling on to anything.

"The others won't touch him," she said. "Not until he becomes conscious again or dies first."

"Can you get him out of here?" I asked. "Get him to a medic, anyone who will stabilize him? *Please.*"

"No. I'm sorry." The woman shook her head. "I'll be discovered if I try anything. I shouldn't even be in here."

I stared at her, helpless and confused. "Who *are* you? How are you getting by undetected at all?"

Because of me.

A voice brushed against my mind, sparking up the musty air in the dungeon. That was a familiar sensation now, but the last thing I expected to hear in this hellhole was a new god speaking.

Fear and awe mingled together in my chest. "Who's here?"

The woman's robe moved at the shoulder. She extended one arm toward the ground while the movement slowly made its way down toward her wrist, the loose fabric rippling from what hid underneath.

"What the…fuck!"

I stumbled back toward the wall when a fucking rattlesnake slithered out from under her robe to the floor. Its forked tongue darted out, tasting the air, while its unblinking eyes regarded me curiously.

Don't be afraid, my son. I will not harm you or your friend.

"This is Quetzalcoatl," the woman said. At my blank expression, she added, "I call him Q."

"You have a companion god," I said, watching the snake glide across the floor to Reaper. "Like…us."

The woman nodded, both of us watching now as Q's long body moved over Reaper's chest and abdomen. "He's a god of wisdom and knowledge. I think it's because of my bond with him that the Sha doesn't detect my disloyalty."

Q's head inched toward Reaper's face, tongue flicking out mere inches away from his mouth and nose. *I can hold him back from the underworld temporarily, but he needs more healing than I can provide.* The snake swung his head toward me. *You have not harnessed the bonds between your companion gods and your fellow humans. Why?*

"I don't understand," I admitted. "Harnessed them how?"

Ah. You don't know. Then I suppose neither do they. The snake slithered off of Reaper's chest and paused next to the robed woman. *I will return, daughter.*

"Return?" the woman repeated in a panic. "Where are you going?"

These bonded humans lack the knowledge of the potential they wield. With harnessed bonds, they may be able to rescue these two, and put an end to the Sha.

"Will the Sha detect me if you go?" the woman asked.

No. The bond between us protects you. Be patient and trust in us. Trust in the humans that will come. Q slithered toward the barred door. *When I return, you will know.*

The serpent god then left the cell and disappeared.

TWELVE

GUNNER

I didn't tell anybody I went scouting alone, and as my bike's shocks groaned and protested over the rocky terrain, I realized that was probably a mistake.

Mari or Jandro would have wanted to come with me, but we couldn't risk losing any more of us to the Sha's black swarm. General Bray was trying his best to keep it together, but he was clearly distraught at potentially losing another son. And truthfully, army escorts with me would have drawn attention or slowed me down, neither of which I wanted.

We kept bashing our heads against the wall, circling back to square one, then getting pissed off at the lack of options again. The longer we sat around coming up with bad ideas, the longer Reaper and Shadow suffered. Everyone knew we were running out of time and getting no closer, which only angered and worried us more.

Every time I brought up checking out the New Ireland compound with Horus, Mari or Jandro shut it down immediately. It was too dangerous. I could end up taken too.

But I had Horus' eyes, a rough sketch of the compound's interior pieced together by what Mari's dad could remember, and we had no other options.

Still, it probably would have been smart to have left a note.

I left hours ago, so they had to know something was up by now. I just hoped they weren't following me out this way, for their own safety.

Horus was silent, a dark speck in the sky as I rode across the desert terrain below. He almost never spoke to me in the way he did with Mari or Shadow. It didn't bother me as much as I thought it would. The falcon god and I were always in sync somehow, without spoken language between us. Even when he wasn't on my shoulder or in my line of sight, I always seemed to know instinctively where he was. When I needed him, he was there, ready to take flight. Like early this morning when I snuck my bike out of the garage, he was waiting for me on a fence post like he already knew where we were going.

As I approached the compound, I started looking for a spot to camp out, several miles away from New Ireland. It wasn't like I needed to see anything with my own eyes. Getting too close risked being caught anyway —seeing them meant they had a chance of seeing me.

Roughly five miles out from the border, I spotted a large cluster of boulders that would do nicely for cover. Horus was already flying ahead of me by the time I stopped and got to work camouflaging myself and my bike.

"Thanks for the tip, Blakeworth," I muttered, rubbing some dirt on my forehead and cheekbones before covering my mouth, nose, and hair with a hood and mask. I'd brought a few different options and picked the ones that blended best with the landscape surrounding me.

Hiding my bike proved to be a bit more difficult, as there wasn't a lot of vegetation out here for me to cover it. Finally I was able to wedge it mostly out of sight between two boulders, which would have to do.

Once it was in place, I turned around to sit on the front tire and lean back against the headlight. When I found a position that ensured I wouldn't fall and crack my head open on a rock, I let my consciousness slip into Horus.

Seeing through him always felt like a massive breath of fresh air. I was lighter, freer, not held down by anything like gravity or the limits of a human body. The sense of freedom was short-lived, however, when I saw the massive compound looming up ahead.

Easy, I warned Horus with a thought. *They might be looking for you.*

The Sha is absolutely looking for me, he said back. The response startled me so much that I nearly came back to my own body. *But for the Sha, his wish to end me is personal,* Horus went on.

Why's that?

Set and I are brothers who have warred with each other since our stories were first told. We cannot coexist in harmony, it's simply impossible. One must always defeat the other.

It would have been nice to know that before we set out on this trip, you know.

Would you have done anything differently? The question sounded like a challenge.

Probably not, I admitted.

Horus was silent for a long few seconds before speaking again. *You may use my sight to learn all that you can. But know you may return alone and with only your own sight and mind to guide you.*

I'm not leaving you behind! I retorted.

You may not have a choice, my son.

Well, just don't do any stupid bird shit.

Horus didn't laugh but a feeling of amusement passed over me. The compound loomed closer and it was clear that talking time was over. I needed to observe and not miss any detail. Any bit of information could be crucial to getting Reaper and Shadow back.

The falcon banked left, taking us around the fortress in a wide loop. I noted the tall, stone walls wrapped around the perimeter—similar to what we had at Sheol, but at least twice as high. Spaced out along the top were small platforms, each with an armed soldier keeping watch. Thankfully they paid no special attention to Horus or any of the other fauna in the general area.

I counted twenty guard platforms as we circled the fortress. Fucking hell, the Sha really wasn't messing around. It turned my stomach knowing that Reaper, Shadow, and Andrea were in there. Mari's dad had been in there and had only gotten out by sheer, crazy luck.

Let's go higher and straight over the top, I suggested to Horus.

That's not wise, I have been sensed, the sky god said in reply.

Shit! By the Sha?

No. By…another.

Another? I repeated. *A god? Who?*

I'm unsure. The presence is unfamiliar to me.

Should we leave?

Horus completed one more wide loop around the fortress without saying a word, and while waiting for his answer, I tried to memorize the structures I could see within the walls.

This presence does not appear to be a threat, Horus finally reported. *It wants to meet us.*

I'm not sure that's wise, I said, parroting back what he just told me. *What if it's a trap?*

It may be, the falcon admitted.

Let's just fly overhead and see what we see, I suggested.

He said nothing in response but angled his body like a fighter jet toward the fortress. Swells of hot air carried us closer, though we were still high enough not to be identified by any human eyes.

Thousands of feet in the air, I could clearly see faces, though many were covered by hoods and masks so that only their eyes were visible. Some soldiers milled about, their faces clear and out in the open, but they were few and far between. I wondered at what point they became part of the black-masked swarm, if there were some kind of trials or tests to go through.

A coldness ran through me at the thought of

everyone in the hospital back at home—people like Mari's dad whose memory came back in bits and pieces. Or the worst ones who remained catatonic. I didn't have to be a medic to know there was no one home behind those dead, blank eyes.

Run, I wanted to say to the soldiers who were still in control of their own minds. *Get away while you still can.*

Horus seemed to sense my thoughts. *They chose this.* His mental voice bristled. *The ones who do not have control are the ones who resisted. The ones who remain free needed no coercion to join the Sha's cause. They are free as long as they're loyal.*

Who would choose this? I didn't bother to hide my disgust. *To contribute to the destruction of all people?*

Who would choose to follow Hitler? Or Mussolini? Horus answered. *Perhaps they have been bribed with lofty rewards in exchange for their service, but these people made their choices.*

It was a morbid thought, but I felt a weird sense of gratitude that there were so few of them. If the majority of the black swarm was controlled, that meant they fought back. They were given a choice and said no, they would not follow the Sha in wiping out humanity, and accepted the terrible consequences.

Mari's dad had been one of those, and it made me respect him even more.

We are drawing attention, Horus warned. *We should leave.*

He was right. The scouts along the wall had started following our movement with their binoculars and more people on the ground had begun to peer up at the dark speck flying overhead. It was creepy how people turned and looked at the exact same time, their heads tilted at the same angle. Fuck, they had to be some sort of hive-mind. Like the Sha was a queen bee with the ability to control thousands of drones with a single thought.

Yeah, let's go, I agreed. *Don't make it look obvious, though.*

Horus flew in one more leisurely circle over the fortress. I prayed we'd be written off as just a normal, desert raptor scoping the place out for food. He started heading away from the compound and I almost let myself feel relieved.

Until the shots rang out.

Shit!

Horus dove hard, the ground racing up to meet us at terrifying speed. Right when I thought we would splat on the ground, he shot straight up into the air again. It was then that I realized he was zigzagging to avoid the onslaught of bullets aimed at us. He shot up and dove down, banking hard from left to right. If I'd been in a human body, it would have felt like the most sickness-inducing rollercoaster in existence.

We were almost out of range of the fortress' snipers when Horus changed direction hard *again*, this time doubling back toward the compound, and kept going that way.

Horus, what are you doing? I cried in a mental panic. *We were almost in the clear! Why are you going back?*

He is that way. I have no other chance to retrieve him.

Who?!

The other presence I felt.

The one that might be a fucking trap?

The sky god was silent as he made another pass over the top of the fortress, flying lower this time, which gave the snipers much clearer shots.

Horus, we can't! You're going to get killed.

I warned you I might, he said lightly. *If I do, then it's your responsibility to communicate with this presence.*

How am I supposed to—

A close shot cut me off, grazing just the edge of Horus' wing tip, but it was enough to knock us off-course. Horus went spinning through the air, dropping altitude fast, but was able to right himself after a few terrifying seconds.

Fuck this other presence Horus, we have to go!

We cannot.

Somehow we cleared flying over the compound again, but the snipers on this wall were ready. They coordinated their fire so that not even zigzagging could protect us. Horus dove toward the brush just beyond the wall when the shot hit.

Pain exploded up my right limb like I got shot in the arm. Horus screeched in agony as we tumbled down toward earth. I could feel the urge to withdraw from the pain, to get back into my own body to escape it, but I wasn't leaving Horus alone. To my complete shock, he was still flapping it and keeping us hovering in the air, though I couldn't begin to understand why. We were an even easier target now.

Take cover in the brush, friends. I will meet you halfway. Another voice spoke to us—low, ancient and calming.

What?! Who are you? I demanded.

I got no answer, but Horus stretched his talons out toward the cluster of bushes. The pain was blinding as he braced his wings out, preparing to catch…

A rattlesnake?

It was indeed a snake's head looming out of the top of a bush, but that was all I saw before Horus' talons snagged the reptile's midsection and continued flying on.

I didn't bother asking what was going on anymore because they weren't talking, and I thought I'd pass out from pain any minute. Footsteps now hurried after us on the ground and the panic from that overshadowed everything. Horus was slowing down, hovering so low over the ground that the snake's rattle nearly brushed the earth. In seconds, they'd be able to catch us easily.

Now, friend, the snake, who I assumed was the presence, instructed.

Horus dropped the snake, and we went tumbling. The falcon hit the ground rolling and I heard a snap that made my whole right side feel like it was on fire.

Fuck, Horus! I'm getting my bike and coming to get you.

No, stay. The command from the sky god felt unshakable. Only the slightest strain in his voice indicated he felt pain in the falcon's form. *Do not alert them to your human body. Have faith in our new friend.*

The snake was roughly twenty yards behind where we crash-landed. Its lower half coiled on the ground, head and upper body erect as it shook the rattle on its tail. The approaching soldiers could see us clearly, their faces hard and determined. This unit wasn't mind-controlled and that worried me even more. They only slowed when they noticed the rattlesnake in their way.

While most of the soldiers came to a stop in a straight line, a couple dared to take a few steps closer. The snake arched higher, shaking its rattle more insistently. The sound became a constant low hum, like static or white noise. It grew louder, making my head feel like it was stuffed with cotton.

One by one, the soldier's faces slackened into blank expressions. Their hands loosened on their weapons, arms flopping loosely to their sides. The rattling continued until all of them appeared to have been lulled into some kind of hypnotic state.

Now go, the snake said. *I cannot keep them in such a state permanently.*

Horus rolled painstakingly to his feet. He was forced to hop and flap awkwardly with his good wing, which was slow and cumbersome.

Let me go back, I said. *Then I'll carry you.*

Yes. The sky god sounded exhausted.

The last thing I saw through Horus' eyes before slingshotting back to my human body was the rattlesnake striking as he bit one of the soldiers in the leg.

———

THE MOMENT I WAS BACK, the weight of my own body had me sliding off my tire to the ground. It took a moment for the vertigo to pass, then I shot to my feet and pulled my bike out from its hiding place. With the noise it'd make, riding probably wasn't the best idea, but Horus' wing had been bleeding badly. And it fucking scared me how worn out and exhausted he'd sounded in my mind. As a god, I figured he wouldn't be dead-dead, but I still wasn't ready to lose my falcon buddy.

I kicked the bike to life and headed off toward the fortress to find my companion god.

Well *gods* now, I guess.

Horus and the snake had covered a good amount of distance before I reached them. I only rode about three and half miles before I spotted the falcon hobbling along the ground with the rattlesnake at its side.

If he hadn't been injured so badly, I would have scooped them both up without stopping and headed straight home. But I didn't want Horus bleeding out or being injured worse on the ride, so I stopped and lifted him gingerly off the ground.

"Hey buddy. You're lucky a coyote didn't find you first."

Horus clicked his beak like he wasn't amused.

"Shit man, you're still bleeding." His wing looked like a giant mess of bloody feathers that I couldn't make heads or tails of. What I would give for a fraction of Mari's medical knowledge right now. The best I could tell was that he was shot near his shoulder joint. "I'm gonna wrap your bullet wound," I told him. "I don't know what I'm doing though, so I'm sorry in advance."

While I tore off a strip of my T-shirt, the rattlesnake slithered up next to my rear tire. His head stretched up toward the seat, tongue flicking out.

You've chosen an interesting human, sky god, the snake observed.

They are all interesting. Horus vocalized through small chirps and screeches while I tried my best to wrap his wing.

"So who might you be, snake god?" It was

unnerving having a damn rattlesnake so close to me, but remembering he was more than a simple animal helped.

I am Quetzalcoatl.

I paused in my wing-wrapping. "No disrespect, but would you mind repeating that?"

Something like an exasperated sigh passed through my mind. *You may call me Q, if you wish.*

"Thanks, I probably will." I began to tie off the wrapping on Horus' wing. "So…you're a snake god, huh?"

I am known as the feathered serpent to the Mexica, yes.

"Mexica?"

You may know them as the Aztecs.

"Oh, right. So wait, who are you bonded to?"

I will explain everything, but you must take me to your other companion gods. The snake's rattle shook a little, it seemed not with warning but with eagerness. *The Sha will soon be aware of your fly-by and will act accordingly.*

"No offense, Q, but why should I trust you?" I cradled Horus carefully against my chest. I'd hold onto him for the whole ride if I needed to.

Aside from the fact that I just gave venomous bites to five loyalists of the Sha and saved you from them? Q's rattle shook a little more insistently. *I am the primary force keeping your president alive.*

"My president?" I repeated, dumbfounded. "Reaper? He's alive?"

Barely, the snake clipped.

Let's go, Horus insisted.

"Alright then." I still wasn't sure about this snake god, but he had a point about saving our asses. And

Horus seemed to trust him enough. "Make yourself comfortable in one of the saddlebags, Q."

With a final, quick rattle of its tail, the reptile slithered up and coiled itself into one of my compartments. I closed it, made sure it was secure, then settled back in the seat with Horus still against my chest.

"Hang on for me, buddy." My free hand went to the handlebars and we were tearing across the landscape in seconds. I just hoped Mari wouldn't be too pissed at me for going off alone and that she could work her magic to nurse Horus back to health.

THIRTEEN

MARIPOSA

"Where the everloving fuck have you been?"

Gunner, who had been gone all day, at least had the decency to *look* guilty as he hopped off his bike and left it running as he jogged up the driveway toward me. He was dressed in desert camouflage and had dirt smeared on his face. But what alarmed me most of all was the bundle of feathers clutched to his chest and his shirt stained with blood.

"Baby girl—"

"What happened?! Is that Horus?"

"He got shot and I think broke a wing," Gunner explained in a rush of breath as he came to a stop in front of me. "Can you help him?"

"Ohh, Horus..." The poor bird was barely conscious, eyelids closing. The shock must have worn off hours ago. "I'm not a vet, but I can do my best."

"Please! You have to." Gunner held the limp bird out to me. "I'm sorry to put this on you, baby girl, but please help him. I'll explain everything."

"You better," I muttered, accepting the bird carefully into my arms. "Jandro!"

"Mariposita!" He answered me through the open sliding door to the backyard, where he and my dad tended to the chickens.

"You remember Erica, the medic who rotates shifts with me?"

"Um, yeah. I think so."

"Can you bring her over from the hospital? Tell her we've got a bird with a gunshot and a broken wing."

"Okay." Jandro looked puzzled but still set aside his rake and came inside.

"She used to be a vet tech," I explained. "She's the best person to help."

"You got it!"

Jandro hurried to the garage, then stopped in his tracks when Gunner yelled, "Take my bike! It's faster."

Jandro was out the front door and settled into Gunner's seat within moments, then promptly screamed and jumped off. "Gun, there's a fucking rattlesnake coming out of your saddlebag!"

"What the fuck?!" I cried.

"Yeah, that's the other thing." Gunner rubbed his forehead, not sounding alarmed or surprised, just weary. "Ran into another god who hitched a ride."

I couldn't have heard him correctly. "*Another* god?"

I'm Quetzalcoatl, and I will not harm you, a warm, ancient voice soothed me.

Sure enough, a six-foot long rattlesnake moved with fluid grace up my driveway, porch, and into my house.

Despite its assurance of no harm, I found myself backing away from the reptile.

Heal the sky god first, Quetzalcoatl said. *Then we will have much to discuss.*

He was right. I had a barrage of questions, but taking care of Horus was the first priority. Jandro had gotten over his freak-out and had already taken off for the hospital. I went into the kitchen so that I could lay Horus down on a flat, clean surface.

"Freyja?"

I am here, daughter. The black cat jumped gracefully onto the table, making her way toward Horus.

"How bad is it?" I watched her sniff him delicately.

Very, but he lives, she reported.

"What do you need?" Gunner was already scrubbing his hands in the kitchen sink.

"A bright light, forceps, alcohol, gauze," I rattled off. "Something to use for a splint, like a wooden dowel or something."

"I'm on it." He raced off to grab my supplies while I examined the injured bird as carefully as I could.

"I'm so sorry if this hurts you, Horus," I muttered, saddened by every one of his soft chirps of pain.

I wasn't sure how to go about setting the broken bone in his wing, so I decided I'd wait for Erica to handle that. In the meantime, I was an expert at treating gunshot wounds at this point.

I had just extracted the slug and was wrapping up the wound with gauze when I heard Jandro's motorcycle rumble up the driveway. Perfect timing!

"Erica, thank you so much for coming," I said when

the two of them walked in. "I'll explain later, but can you set a broken wing?"

She blinked once, taking in the sight of animals all around us. Hades and the rattlesnake were also nearby, looking at her hopefully. With a short laugh, she then pushed her sleeves up and headed for the sink to wash up. "Believe it or not, this isn't the craziest house call I've ever gotten."

"You're an angel," I breathed with relief.

Erica quickly figured out how best to set the bone, and it was my job to hold Horus still. After the most tense count to three of my life and a firm *snap*, I fought against every instinct in my body to let the bird go. His screech rattled my eardrums, his good wing beating against the table in an effort to get away.

"I'm sorry, I'm so sorry," I whispered to him.

"We need more hands to hold this splint in place while I wrap the wing," Erica said.

The guys sprang into action, all four of us lending a hand to keep Horus still. Moments later, it was over. His wing was wrapped in two places, the thick bandages making one side comically bigger than the other.

"No flying for eight weeks," Erica instructed as she went to wash her hands again. "You can give him pain relief, just microdose in comparison to humans."

"Thank you," I breathed, pulling her into a weary hug. "Really, we can't thank you enough."

"You don't know how much this means to us," Gunner added, lifting the bird carefully to hold him against his chest.

"My pleasure." Erica grinned. "Animals are just special in a different way than humans."

"Can we repay you in any way?" Jandro asked. Her eyes only had to slide toward the backyard for him to say, "Eggs? All yours. A lifetime supply."

"Don't mind if I do," Erica laughed.

She and Jandro immediately went to collect some while I hunted for pain relief for Horus. I had almost forgotten about Quetzalcoatl until I returned with a syringe of analgesic to find the rattlesnake curled up on the living room floor, mere inches away from Gunner's feet.

"So what happened today?" I settled on the couch next to Gunner, who was still holding Horus in his arms like a baby.

"Jandro just took Erica back to the hospital, let's wait til he's back." Gunner watched while I gave Horus the painkiller through a shot in the leg. "This is big. It affects…everything."

The rattlesnake lifted up, its head and upper third of its body leaning toward me as it tasted the air with its tongue.

A shame I did not find you before Freyja did, Quetzalcoatl remarked. *It probably wouldn't have worked, but things may have turned out very differently.*

"What do you mean?"

I am of your heritage, daughter. Your blood. The unblinking, reptilian eyes focused on me. *But you already had your companion gods, so I chose to bond with your next of kin.*

"Next of kin?" I repeated. "You mean my dad?"

Sadly, no. The Sha had already taken advantage of your

father's fragile mind. I was too late to protect him, but I could guard the one closest to him.

"Closest to him?" I hardly dared to believe it, but who else could it be? "My mom?"

Yes, daughter. Your mother lives, truly *lives. Her mind is safe under my protection. She is not controlled.*

I probably should have asked more questions, namely how and what proof did he have, but the only information I could process was that *my mother was alive and safe.*

"She's okay?" I squeaked out, barely aware of the tears already rolling down my cheeks. "Really okay?" Dad's memory of her still wasn't quite there, but he would be overjoyed to hear this news.

Yes, dear daughter.

Gunner pressed a kiss to my cheek. I didn't know whether he heard the entire conversation or just one side, but his smile against my skin indicated that he got the gist of it. "We'll get her back too, baby girl."

"Hey—whoa!" Jandro came through the front door right then, immediately backing up a step at the snake reared up and hovering right in front of my face. "I don't like snakes as it is, but snakes that make you cry are the fucking worst of them."

"My mom's alive!" I blurted out. "Quetzal…um, is her companion god."

You can call me Q, if you wish, the snake's mental voice sighed.

"For real?" Jandro stared in disbelief.

"Now that we're all here," Gunner motioned him

toward a seat on the couch, "I'll come straight out with it—I went to the fortress with Horus."

"Fuckin' knew it," Jandro grumbled.

"Alone?" My mood shifted from elated to anger on a hairpin turn. "How could you? Without even telling us?"

"Because I knew I'd get a reaction like this," Gunner sighed. "Look, it turned out okay—"

"*Okay?* You almost lost Horus!"

"It was weird." Gunner looked down at the bundle of feathers in his arms. "I decided I had to go, and it was like he was just waiting for me to make that decision. He even seemed to expect that he wouldn't make it back."

"*What?!*"

"I can't explain it, baby girl, other than it was a feeling."

The other piece of information clicked for me and I turned back to the snake. "Wait, my mom is at the fortress? The Sha's fortress?"

She is, Q chimed in. *And she's watching over your captured men.*

I nearly slid off the couch onto the floor. "My mom is with Reaper and Shadow? How are they?"

Q took a moment to answer. *Not well. They may perish if we don't act quickly, which is why I've come to you.*

All my caution went out the window with that information. This snake could tell me to walk into a volcano to save them and I'd do it without hesitation.

"Please." The word came from Jandro now, who also

seemed to throw away his dislike of snakes over what this one just said. "What can we do? We're listening."

You have not harnessed your bonds. Why?

The three of us looked at each other with blank expressions. "What do you mean?"

Your bonds! Q repeated with an air of exasperation. His tail began to rattle slightly. *Between each other, fortified by your companion gods.*

Again, we exchanged glances like kids in a classroom being reprimanded by a teacher. "I'm sorry, I don't understand," I told the snake, watching his tail.

You are lovers, yes? His tongue flicked the air in front of me. *You love both of these men?*

"Yes, of course I do."

The feeling is mutual?

"*Yes,*" Jandro and Gunner answered solemnly together.

And you are aware that that creates a bond? The god's tone dripped with condescension, like talking down to a child. *One that is intangible but you can feel it. You know it's there as sure as you can see me with your own eyes.*

"Okay, and?" I prompted.

The bonds with your companion gods are similar. Harnessing all of these bonds is like threading strings together to make a length of rope. With this, your strengths become even stronger, more durable. You are capable of more, and can use these bonds to sense each other without touching or speaking.

"How do we do this?" Gunner leaned forward eagerly in his seat.

Q's rattling calmed as he swung his head toward

Gunner. *You simply reach out for your partners as you would your companion god.*

"Question." Jandro lifted a hand.

Yes? The snake's agitated rattling picked up again.

Jandro rested his forearms on his knees. "Unless Foghorn counts, I don't have a companion god."

Human, of course you do. The snake sounded like he'd had it up to here with our stupidity. *You have two.*

"I do?"

You have been touched by both Gods of Death who watch over your whole family. I see their marks on you.

"I...have?" Jandro paled.

"The drone attack back in Sheol," I blurted out as the awful memory hit me. "When you were almost gone and I had to resuscitate you."

Clarity dawned on Jandro's face. "That's right," he said softly. "I skirted the edge of death and met Hades and Freyja. They spoke to me."

And you, daughter of my blood. The snake god swung his head back toward me. *You are bonded to all three companion gods, which is remarkable. I have never seen such a thing before.*

"All three?" I repeated.

You have the touch of love and healing. You have flown on wings and seen the world from the sky. The snake paused before continuing. *And it seems you have had your own brush with death.*

His observations—particularly the last one—were chilling, leaving me completely open and exposed. What Shadow had done was a terrible accident, one I was happy to move on from and leave in the past. I never realized Hades might have been involved in my near death experience, but it seemed obvious now.

"How do you know?"

I can see the hands of the gods on you, daughter, Q said. *I am also a god of wisdom and knowledge. The connections between the tangible and intangible are where I specialize.*

My men slid in closer to me on either side as the god spoke, subtly forming a protective shield.

What else is remarkable, Q went on, *is how perfectly balanced your three gods are. Covering the spectrum of human experience while powered by devotion from three very different civilizations. The underworld, the sky, and everything in between. Simply fascinating.*

"What does this mean for Mari?" Gunner asked. "That she has three?"

The snake god seemed pleased that we finally stopped asking the stupid questions. *A balance of harnessed bonds between three people is a rarity in itself.* His ancient voice brimmed with excitement. *But three bonds, perfectly balanced, across multiple pantheons, within one human? It has never been done, and the strength from you is powerful and focused. It may be the only way to defeat the Sha and his army.*

"How?" I demanded.

You must draw on the bonds with your gods and your fellow bonded humans. Like pulling on a rope, you can send and receive feedback through the senses. The gods are the source, and you are the conduit, Mariposa.

"I'm still not following," Jandro admitted.

"When I reach for Horus to see through him, it is like mentally pulling on a string to see if he's there," Gunner explained, then looked at me.

"Similar with Freyja," I agreed. "Although, I've never tried reaching for the other two."

Try it now, Q suggested. *Reach for your men, Mariposa. They will feel the bonds of the gods through you.*

Jandro and Gunner each grabbed one of my hands, anchoring and supporting me between them. I took a deep, steadying breath and reached for Jandro with my mind, much like I did with Freyja when I needed her.

The result was subtle, a small shift in perception, like when you blink one eye and then the other. First I was in the middle, then I shifted slightly to the left where Jandro sat next to me. He jerked in surprise, bringing me back right away.

"Was that—" He slapped a hand to his chest, breath quickening.

I squeezed his hand. "How was that? Are you okay?"

"I felt you." Jandro stared at me in awe and disbelief. "I felt you pulling me that way, like we switched places for a second."

"Yes, that's exactly it!"

"Now imagine using this in a battle," Gunner said, his brow already furrowed in concentration. "We can watch each other's backs, basically seeing in all directions."

"But what about Horus?" I looked down at the bird, which now seemed to be sleeping against Gunner's chest.

You do not need the gods' animal forms with you. In fact, it's better if they're not present. If their animal bodies are killed, the bond will be severed, Q said. *We are outside of time and physical space. Your bonded gods are always with you. You only need to reach for them.*

"And how do we prevent the Sha from breaking into our heads?" Jandro asked. "I doubt this mission will be very successful if we're writhing in pain and bleeding from the ears."

Your companion gods will continue to shield your minds from afar, Q said. *The harnessed bonds between the three of you is an additional shield. I can also provide defense, as I do with Mariposa's mother.*

"What I want to know is," my gaze shifted across the room to where Freyja and Hades looked on, "how did we never hear about harnessed bonds before?" If they had told me about this when I came pleading to them for help, we would have been ten steps ahead by now.

I am just as surprised as you, daughter. Freyja took a few tentative steps toward the snake, her dark pupils wide. *I'm well-versed in the power of love, certainly. But no bonded human of mine throughout history has ever loved another person with a companion god. You are the first I've seen.*

My experience is the same, Hades said. *Had we known of these harnessed bonds, we certainly would have shared that with you.*

Old gods can learn new tricks after all, the snake mused, tail rattling gently.

Hades only responded with a soft growl before silence fell over the room. My men and I just sat for a few moments with the weight of this information. We had our answer now. Finally, something to act on.

Gunner broke the silence first. "We need to tell

Finn." He looked at Jandro and I solemnly. "If the three of us going in is the only way, he has to know."

"My dad too," I said, my gaze shifting toward the bedroom where Dad rested. "If we don't come back, they both need to know why."

"If we don't come back," Jandro pulled my hand into his lap, "the Sha will come for all of them soon enough."

"Not happening," Gunner said with a low growl. "They've taken enough from us. We're getting everyone out—Reaper, Shadow, and Mari's mom."

"Don't forget Andrea," I said.

"Andrea too," Gunner agreed. With that, he stood up, then turned around to place Horus carefully in a small nest of blankets on the couch. "Time to start making a plan. A real one," he said before heading upstairs to gather his maps.

GUNNER

Mari's dad reacted better than we could have imagined. Maybe he didn't remember it all entirely, but somewhere in his head he knew about gods, including the one who had controlled him.

"Yes, the snake!" Javier's eyes brightened once we finished telling him everything. "The snake kept your mom safe, *mija*. I remember now."

Mari, Jandro, and I were all gathered in her father's room, suited up for riding to meet with Finn at City Hall once we told Javier the news.

And once we told Finn, we'd be riding out to New Ireland. Depending on what the general decided, we'd either go alone or with the support of the Four Corners army. No matter what, we were getting everyone back. Tonight.

Mari reached across the bed and squeezed her dad's forearm. Her lip wobbled for a moment before she steeled her features. "We're getting Mom back. I promise."

Javier, too, had to compose himself before smiling at his daughter. "If anyone can, I know it's you, *mijita*."

Mari scooted closer, bringing her arms around her father in a hug. "I love you, Dad."

"Silly girl," he chuckled, but hugged her back fiercely. "You got this, it's a walk in the park. You'll be back before you know it." He held onto her tightly for an extra long second. "And I love you too."

When they separated, Javier's eyes were hard on Jandro and me. "You guys watch over my girl."

"We will," I said, my voice just as hard.

Jandro said something in Spanish, his tone hard-edged and determined. Javier nodded just as Mari came to stand between us.

"We'll see you soon, *viejito*," she said before the three of us turned and left the room.

Normally Mari would ride with one of us, but three separate bikes awaited us in the garage. Jandro and I had our most trusted steeds ready, while Mari borrowed a lightweight Harley from Noelle. We all had to anticipate carrying at least one extra person if we made it back alive.

Hades and Freyja also waited for us in the garage. The black cat, unsurprisingly, jumped onto Mari's bike and snuggled her way inside the front of Mari's jacket.

Hades sat like a regal statue next to my bike, which *was* surprising.

We will join you for the meeting with the general and see you off to the fortress. The death god's voice rumbled with authority in my head.

"What about Horus?" I asked, throwing a leg over my seat.

Quetzalcoatl will guard the falcon here. But I must tell you all... the dog cocked his head while Mari and Jandro paused to listen. *We may not be occupying these forms when you return.*

"What do you mean?" Jandro leaned forward over his handlebars. "You'll be just a dog?"

If you succeed, then I, Hades, will exist as I always have since my inception. But yes, the creature you're looking at now will only be a dog.

"Why?" Mari unzipped the top of her jacket to allow Freyja's ears and head to poke out.

Because you will have fulfilled your purpose and no longer need our guidance in these forms, the cat goddess said.

"Shit," I blurted out, thinking back to when Horus and I last spoke. He told me he might not make it through that mission but when he did, I had no idea it might be the last time we spoke. The last time we would fly together.

We will not be gone, son, Freyja said, as if sensing my regret. *We watched over as you were born and will stand guard when your children are born. As long as humanity persists, we will always be here.*

I nodded, more to myself than anyone else. Horus had been in my life as a falcon for under two years. We'd grown so close in that time, to the point where I never imagined *not* having him. It was jarring to think about, but less so if I considered the fact that he had always watched over me.

I would have to sit with that idea later though. We needed to get moving now.

"You ready, VP?" I called to Jandro over my shoulder. Without Reaper here, it fell on Jandro to lead us out.

"Aye-aye, captain," he cracked, just like old times.

He eased out of the garage, then took off with a roar once he hit the driveway. I nodded at Mari to follow him, then drove out behind her with Hades loping at my side.

If Jandro took Reaper's place, I had to take Shadow's. It was strangely fitting with him leading our pack and me bringing up the rear to protect the rider between us.

Bonded to three gods and four men, I was convinced Mari was the key to everything. But even without the god stuff, she was everything to us. To me.

And I would be my woman's shield until my dying breath.

———

"YOU KIDS CAN'T BE serious about this," General Bray groaned, looking to Mari with hope in his eyes that she would be a voice of reason. "Sweetheart, tell me you're not actually doing this."

"We are," she told him firmly. "It has to be the three of us, Finn. That's the only way this has even the slimmest chance of working."

The general looked more put-together today, his uniform crisp and buttoned correctly. But he still looked weary, and his hair had begun sticking out in all directions from constantly running his hands through it. A habit that Reaper also picked up when he was stressed.

"Listen, I don't doubt these bonds with the gods you all have. I've seen the remarkable things you can do. But..." His eyes scanned over us. "Is it enough to end *all* of this?"

"We don't know," I admitted. "But it's the only shot we have, General. And we *have* to do it now. Any longer and we can pretty much expect to never see Reaper or Shadow again."

"Or Andrea, or my mom," Mari added.

"Worst case, we do see them, but it's as one of those fucking zombies coming after us," Jandro chimed in.

Finn sighed heavily, dropping his head into his hands. "There's nothing I can do to keep you from going, is there?"

"Nope. Sorry, General," I said. "And since we're protected by a fourth god now, you don't have the excuse of saying our minds are compromised."

Mari shot me a scathing look that was completely justified. I was a little salty that we got detained by the army before the last attack, even though Finn had made the best possible decision with the knowledge he had.

"I don't like this one fucking bit." Finn shook his head. "You're not my blood but you guys are my kids, and you're just heading off to be slaughtered."

"Will you support us or not?" Mari asked, cutting to the chase. "We'd rather not do this completely alone, but if you disapprove of us rescuing *your* sons, my husbands, so much, we will do it ourselves."

Her words hung in the air, a challenge demanding an answer. The silence was brief as Finn dipped his chin slightly.

"What do you need from me?"

"Armored Jeeps, rifle units," I said. "Hanging back, maybe a mile or so. We mainly need cover for when we're leaving the fortress with injured people in tow."

"Also medical staff," Mari added. "But I can't lead them since I'll be busting inside with these guys."

"I'll have Dr. Brooks send me a handful of his best," the general promised. "Anything else?"

Our side of the table was silent once again. "That's really it." I shrugged. "We need cover and support for getting everyone back home. Other than that," my fingers tangled with Mari's at my side, "it's up to us and the gods."

FIFTEEN

SHADOW

The female guard stopped by daily to check on Reaper and sneak me small, extra rations of food and water. She did what she could to keep Reaper hydrated but short of him waking up or her hooking him up to an IV, we had no way of making him drink.

It was the same routine. She showed up, checked his pulse, washed his face, and dribbled some water into his mouth. She'd let me know he was still alive, and then she left.

"He doesn't have much longer," she informed me on the third visit since Quetzalcoatl left. Her finger pressed to Reaper's neck while her ear rested on his chest. "Maybe a day, if that."

"How long has it been?" I asked after taking a careful, small, measured mouthful of water.

"Just over two days." Her brows pinched in sympathy above her mask. "I'm sorry."

"We still have a day." The words felt hollow as they left my body. I didn't really have any optimism left. I had a terrible feeling instead that if Reaper were to die, that would be it for me too.

The Sha wouldn't even need to use Mari's image to weaken me enough for control. The grief over losing my friend and president, my guilt over being unable to save him, would be enough.

Usually the woman was quick to leave but today, she hesitated. She even sat cross-legged on the floor as though she planned to stay.

"How long have you known him?" she asked.

"Around ten years, but we haven't really been close until recently." I was surprised at how easily the words came out. Who knew someone like me would be so eager to talk to another person? And a woman at that.

The guard's head cocked to the side, her eyes wide and inquisitive. "Close like...?"

"Not like that," I said. "He was, *is*, my president. The leader of our club. We never interacted much besides him giving me orders. But more recently, I guess you can say we've become friends."

"What prompted the change?" The woman glanced over at Reaper and reached over to touch the back of her fingers to his cheek. "No fever at least," she muttered to herself.

"It's a lot to explain." I shifted to a more comfortable sitting position myself, the clinking of my chains echoing softly throughout the dungeon. "But the core of it is, we share a wife."

The woman's head snapped back toward me, eyes narrowing with suspicion or confusion, I couldn't tell. "What do you mean, 'share a wife'?"

"Our wife has four husbands. He was her first," I nodded at Reaper, "I was her last."

The woman's hand drifted over her loose clothing as if searching for a weapon. "Did you buy her from one of those human auctions? Split the cost up between the four of you?" Her words carried venom now, and I bet she wished that the snake had attacked us rather than helped us.

"No, no. It's not like that," I rushed to tell her. "We don't own her, it's quite the opposite really." I huffed out a bitter laugh, recalling the longing and the heartbreak from the Sha's trick. I was fucking doomed if I stayed here another day. "She's with us willingly, and she has so much power over us. She's our whole world. We love and cherish her. She *chose* me, when I never thought in a million years she would."

The guard's tense position relaxed a little, her hand returning to her lap. "What's your wife's name?"

"Mariposa." The taste of her name in my mouth was as sweet as the water I drank.

The guard stiffened again, her eyes wide and burning into mine. "What did you say?"

"Mariposa," I repeated. "It means butterfly."

"I know what it means!" the guard snapped, her apparent vitriol coming out of nowhere. "What's her last name?"

"Why?" My own defenses rose up, confused by this woman's reaction to the mere mention of my wife's name. "Do you know her?"

"Is it Wilder?" she demanded. "Is your wife Mariposa Wilder?"

"What's it to you?" I probably already said too much since Mari's given name was unique enough, but if this woman meant her harm, I wouldn't give her another inch.

"She's my fucking daughter, that's what she is to me!"

I froze, at first in disbelief, then all the clarity dawned on me. The snake god, being hidden in plain sight. *Of course.*

"Will you take off your mask and hood?" I asked.

I didn't think she would, but the woman shoved away the loose fabrics covering head and face as though they were suffocating her.

The resemblance was uncanny. Her hair was a lighter shade of brown than Mari's and her eyes were blue instead of that shifting green-to-brown. But her nose, lips, and cheekbones were identical to my wife's. If it weren't for the deep lines around her eyes and mouth, they could have been sisters.

"I'm Emma," the guard said softly. "Emma Wilder."

"I wish we could have met under better circumstances, Emma." A sudden realization jolted me. "Your husband! Mari's father."

All of the suspicion and distrust drained out of Emma right then. She let out a soft gasp and scooted toward me across the floor until she crouched directly in front of me. If my hands were free, I could have touched her.

"Javier? Have you seen him?" she asked rapidly. "Is he...is he himself?"

My eyes dropped toward the floor, wishing I had

better news to tell her. "Last I saw, he was being treated for injuries at our field hospital. When Mari saw him, he didn't recognize her."

I wasn't there for it, but Jandro had let me know what happened. By the time I'd been able to see her, we were all rounded up and held at the hospital because of the Sha trying to break into our minds.

Emma clapped a hand to her mouth, her fingers shaking.

"I'm sorry," I offered her. "His condition was improving, from what I understand. But then the Sha's forces swarmed over Four Corners. We evacuated the field hospital, but that's when we got captured."

Emma rocked backward until she sat on the floor again, her mind somewhere far outside of this prison cell. She was silent for a long time and I was too exhausted, thirsty, and hungry to get a sense of her mood.

"You love my daughter?" she asked to break the silence.

"Yes." My eyes were half-closed and Mari was all I could see. Imagining her was my only escape from this hellhole. "She taught me what love means. She's the most incredible person I've ever met. If we die in here," I let my head rest against the wall, "it'll be worth it, knowing she loved me back."

"The Sha won't let you die." Emma's voice was clipped as she replaced the hood over her hair and covered her mouth and nose again with the mask. "Him, maybe." She jerked her head toward Reaper. "But I think the Sha has a special interest in breaking and controlling you."

"Story of my life," I muttered.

Emma reached into her robes and pulled out something that made my breath shorten and my heart accelerate--a dagger with a slender but wickedly sharp blade. Just as quickly as she showed it to me, she hid it underneath her clothing again.

"It will be your choice," she whispered. "Just say the word, and I'll give you one final mercy. But you have one day, maybe less, to decide."

The gravity of what she was saying settled heavily over me. I didn't *want* to die but I wanted to be controlled like a zombie even less. However, her method of choice just might tip me in the opposite direction.

"Is there another way?" My chest felt tight as old, bygone fears began rising to the surface. "Other than a blade?"

Emma blinked, her stare curious now in a different way. Blue eyes shifted over me as if taking in my scarred exterior for the first time.

"Taking a gun could blow my cover." She stood from the floor, heading toward the cell door. "I've already been here too long as it is." Her keys jangled as she unlocked it, metal hinges creaking as she let herself out. "The next time you see me, I need to know your decision."

———

"OH, my son. Have you missed me?"

The voice jolted me awake. Fuck. No. I couldn't be awake. Not if *she* was here.

My mother's gaunt face hovered in front of me, only empty blackness surrounded her. Blood dripped from her mouth and her hairline. Whether that blood belonged to me or her, as a result of the village getting massacred, I didn't know.

"You're not real." I tried to close my eyes and turn my face away, but there was no escaping her. There never was. "You're dead. You don't haunt me anymore."

"I'll always haunt you, you worthless stain. Where do you think you'll go when that woman, my earthly sister, finally ends your pathetic life?" She grinned, her teeth stained dark with blood. "And with a blade, no less. Isn't that poetic?"

"She's not like you!" I roared back. "She didn't lock her child in a cage!"

I should have done my deep breathing, should have thought of Mari to calm myself. But I was so tired, so weak and desperate. My mother's ghost showed up at the perfect time to get under my skin and dredge up everything I fought so hard to keep at bay.

"Because she had a daughter!" my mother cackled. "A beautiful, perfect daughter. Too bad the girl wasn't raised right. She was stupid enough to love you, even to almost get killed by you. You see? Men are *horrible.*"

"*You* made me that way! Because you're an abusive, psychotic bitch!"

I should have saved the last of my strength rather than spend it yelling my lungs out at this ghost, hallucination, whatever she was. But I was too deep in my rage, completely lost to the storming sea of anger and hatred that used to rule me. Hatred at myself for what I was, anger at her, at everything, for never allowing me to have a normal life.

"No, you're just proof that the Elder was right. Our goddess was right! Men do nothing but destroy everything they touch. You almost killed a woman you supposedly love! She could have died just like *so* many others."

The echo of a thought whispered through my mind, *She's right...*

"You're wrong," I said in an attempt to squash the voice, but my doubt began to bleed through. I was good at killing, and little else. What if I wasn't a good man? I did hurt Mari, the one who mattered to me the most...

No, no. You've been here before. Don't go down this path again. Come back, Shadow.

I managed to find my breathing somehow, focusing my attention on a memory of Mari's face and the shallow expanding of my lungs.

My mother's image was still there, but it flickered like it was fading.

"I accept responsibility for what I did to her," I said, calmer than moments ago. "And I know you died never feeling an ounce of responsibility for what you did to me." I lifted my head, looking my mother square in the eye. "That alone makes me a better person than you ever were."

She flickered even more rapidly, like the flame of a candle under a gust of wind. "I have been a victim of *men* my whole life, including you!" She stuck a bony, trembling finger in my face. "You almost killed me too when you were born, you know."

"I wish I did."

There was no reasoning with her, no way to make her see that it had been me who was a victim of hers. The only difference between now and back then was the knowledge that she no longer had power over me. "Fuck, I wish I could've watched you bleed to death when that militia rolled in and killed everyone."

"You're a sick, evil *man!*" she spat.

"I hope you're in some kind of Hell right now," I went on. "And all the men you killed for bullshit sacrifices for your fake fucking goddess are treating you exactly like how you treated me."

"I should have killed you when you first drew breath outside of my womb!"

"I hope you feel every bit of pain I stopped feeling years ago." My life likely would be ending soon, so now seemed like the best time to unload everything I wished for the monster who birthed me into the world. "The pain isn't even the worst part. I hope you feel so utterly lonely that abuse becomes attention you're grateful for. I hope that every time you feel a shred of happiness, it's ripped away from you in the most cruel and unbearable way."

I shut my eyes against her visage, which held on stubbornly despite its flickering and fading. "If I live beyond one more day, I'll never speak of you or waste another thought on you again. Your power over me is gone, and you don't deserve to live another miserable second in my head."

A sensation washed over me, like I had been paralyzed before but now I could move. She was gone when I opened my eyes, but I didn't know if that was a victory or defeat.

Reaper continued to lie motionless on the other side of the dingey cell. I was still chained to a wall and growing weaker by the hour, mentally and physically. I had said what I'd wanted to say to my mother for years, but the closure was overshadowed by the fact that I was still in a dungeon. I would probably watch my friend die and follow him soon after. I might never see Mari again.

I needed to give Emma an answer when she returned in a day. What scared me the most was, I didn't know if I had the courage to tell her yes.

SIXTEEN

JANDRO

I paced in front of the bikes, unable to sit still. I was both eager and filled with dread at this ride out to the fortress. It could be my last ride on this earth.

Only Hades and Freyja were with me, watching me wear a hole into the pavement like it was a spectator sport. Gunner was off with the general, finalizing the number of troops we'd need. And Mari said she wanted a moment alone while they did that. Unusual for her, but I tried not to worry. Everything depended on the success of this mission. The weight of it on all of our shoulders was no small thing.

I reached out to Mari with the god-infused, harnessed leash-bond or whatever it was. Here I thought I was the most basic dude of our group, but it turned out I had some special abilities too.

My perception overlapped with Mari's as I focused on our bond. She was out on one of the balconies, watching the tail end of the sunset fade into dusk. I felt the smooth glass of her butterfly pendant as she stroked a finger over it, heard the soft click of metal as her ring touched the necklace too. A gust of wind blew, and I could *feel* her dagger earrings swing like tiny windchimes along the sides of her face. And when she placed a hand on her left hip, I knew she was thinking of the man who tattooed her there.

She tugged back on our bond, the sensation like a string in my chest. It startled me, and I stopped reaching with a gasp and an elevated heart rate.

A few seconds passed and Mari reached for me again, amusement bleeding through our connection. I realized I could sense her proximity too. She no longer stood at the balcony now and was on her way toward me.

"Spying on me?" Mari asked with a smirk when she entered the garage, her voice echoing through the space.

"Just checking on you," I said, reaching for her with my arms now. "And trying this bond thing out since I only learned about it like an hour ago."

Mari accepted my embrace with ease, leaning into my chest. "How does it feel?"

"Honestly? I love it." I leaned against my bike, pulling her with me. "Even if we don't have the gods after all this, I hope *this* stays."

"Really?" Mari's hands wound around the back of my neck, her expression curious.

"Yeah." I folded my hands on her lower back. "I mean, I knew we always had something between us. It's just nice to feel *it*, the connection we have, physically."

"It is. And it feels so natural, like it was always there and we knew it. We just didn't see it." She smiled, tipping her head back. "Gunner's on his way back. He'll be here soon."

I swallowed, finding the question on my mind too unbearable to keep to myself. "Can you feel them? Reap and Shadow?"

Mari's smile fell with a small shake of her head. "No. I tried reaching on our way over here and there's no response, no feedback. I'm…scared of what that might mean."

"Hey." I lowered my forehead to hers. "Don't let your mind go there." But she already was. I could feel her frazzled emotions through our bond.

"What if we're already too late, Jandro?" Her fingers on my neck started to shake and I reached up to hold them.

"We don't know that," I said, trying to push steadiness and calm through my connection with her. "I don't want to have false hope either, babe. But we can't start thinking of the worst yet."

"I never got to tell Reaper I'm sorry." She brought her forehead to my chest and I immediately tucked her head under my chin, bringing a hand to the back of her head to hold her there.

"You have nothing to be sorry for, *Mariposita*. He understands."

"I don't know how that's possible because *I* didn't even understand! I pushed him away for no fucking reason."

"You had a reason, even if you didn't understand it. If it didn't feel right, it didn't feel right." I pulled away to cup her face and look in her eyes. "And you had no way of knowing this would've happened."

Mari closed her eyes and took a few shuddering breaths. When her face started to relax and I felt less tension through our bond, I pulled her back into my chest again. Whether from bullets, fire, or her own fears, I would protect her from it all.

"Do you really think we can do this, Jandro?" she whispered against my shirt.

My chest lifted with the deep breath I took before releasing it with a sigh. "You want to know my honest answer?"

She hesitated before answering quietly, "Yes."

"I do. I really fuckin' do. You want to know why?" I nuzzled the side of her face until my mouth touched her ear. "'Cause they may be gods, but we're fucking Demons."

Mari's lips twitched into a smile as she squirmed in my arms. "*That's* your reason?"

"Yeah, I mean it." I held tight and grabbed her chin to make her look at me. "They fucked with our family and tried to run away. So we're bringing Hell to them. I don't know what we'll find when we arrive, but we'll make the Sha regret ever taking form here."

She nodded, lips still wobbling slightly but the fire in her gaze had returned. "You're right."

"That's it. Get mad, girl. They took *your* men from you." I swore I felt the heat of her anger simmering in our connection too. Sex with these bonds had to be on a whole other level. Hopefully we still had them and would still be alive after tonight.

"You guys ready?" Gunner's voice echoed as he hollered across the concrete garage.

Mari pulled away from me to embrace him, but she didn't melt into his chest like she did with me. She grabbed the back of Gunner's neck and pulled him down for a rough, biting kiss. It was so fast that he even stumbled from the momentum but found purchase on her waist and kissed her back with same ferocity.

I was grinning when they both came up for air—Gunner a little breathless with a dopey smile on his face, but Mari…

Mari strode over to her bike, looking ready to not only go to war, but to burn cities down that stood in her way. She cast one last look at Hades and Freyja, who stood off to the side of our exit in silent observation.

We are with you even when you cannot see us, Hades said. *Remember that you three are not battling alone.*

Horus and Quetzalcoatl are with you as well, Freyja added. *We carry you on our wings and in our hearts, bonded humans.*

With that, Gunner and I mounted up, flanking Mari on either side. No words were needed as we rode out of the garage, we all knew none of us would come back the same.

If at all.

SEVENTEEN

MARIPOSA

Outside of our bike engines, the ride to New Ireland was silent. Externally, anyway. Gunner, Jandro, and I didn't speak, but our bonds to each other, tethered and strengthened by the gods, were full of activity.

The best I could describe it would be like having a conversation without words. Like when two partners or best friends know exactly what the other is thinking just with a look, a subtle hand gesture, or a facial expression.

It was like that between the three of us, only amplified and solidified into an invisible thread that connected all of us. Without words, touch, or even looking at each other, we expressed worries and fears at what we would find. We also reassured each other and validated each other's strength and determination. We were completely in sync, my two men and I. And when that first glimpse of the fortress broke the line on the horizon, I felt the cold, steel-like focus straighten all of our spines.

Jandro and I picked up speed, maneuvering to let

Gunner hang back slightly in the middle. I didn't need to look to know Gunner was pulling his first rifle from the holster on his back. We were still thousands of yards away, and his rifle didn't have a sniper scope, but he didn't need one.

Gunner's shots broke the low, constant hum of our bikes. He took out the guards atop the front perimeter wall cleanly, despite them looking like specks in the distance.

In my head, I could see the layout of the interior, thanks to the map Gunner drew with help from my dad's memory. I wanted to veer left, to start sneaking around the back of the compound and send the Sha's zombie army on a wild goose chase. But Jandro and Gunner urged me back into the middle of our formation with our mental bond. They wanted me between them, shielded at all costs.

I gave in to their tugging, veering back to the center while Gunner drove out to take my place. He was reloading his rifle one-handed when the enemy returned fire.

The bonds made me aware of the returned fire from all angles, like I was in multiple places at once. More soldiers spread out on top of the perimeter wall. I sent Jandro a tug of warning about a cluster of soldiers aiming straight for him, and he zigzagged to avoid their shots.

I pulled out my rifle and aimed straight ahead when my shots were clear enough. My shots were true from the first trigger pull. I returned fire with no fear of the bullets whizzing past me and plinking off my bike. I hit soldiers in the chest, even the head, while keeping the balance of my bike rock-steady with my left hand. If I had a moment to think, I'd wonder if I borrowed Gunner's marksmanship and Jandro's natural ease on the bike, thanks to our bonds.

But my mind was calm and blissfully blank. Like the glassy surface of a lake, so still and tranquil. My whole body was the weapon, and my mind, the clean, efficient mechanism.

Jandro took out the ground soldiers guarding the gate to the inside of the fortress. Like me, he also had better accuracy than normal. When the men fell, he shot at the heavy chain and lock system holding the doors together. But those on the inside did our work for us.

The tall doors burst open, and an endless stream of black poured out to greet us, like ink spilling on a page.

We were ready.

The three of us pulled the pins on our grenades and tossed them. Mine bounced toward the front of the swarm, Jandro's landed in the middle, and Gunner's sailed the farthest. Three simultaneous explosions rocked our eardrums and the earth beneath our tires, but we stayed upright and drove straight through the carnage.

Did you hear that, Reaper? Shadow? Mom? We're coming for you. Another thought followed on the heels of that one. *Can your earthly body hear us, Set? We're coming for you too.*

The explosion cleared enough space for us to drive into the first courtyard and form a circle with our bikes.

With the swarm quickly recuperating to close in on us again, it was time to bring out the big guns.

Our motions were fluid, well-practiced and confident as we readied our assault rifles. The spray of fire we rained down was merciless. All the panicked shouts and rapid spraying of bullets was just background noise to the cold, rigid focus in my mind. I didn't even care in that moment that these were people being puppeted and forced to attack us. They stood between me and my loved ones and would kill me first if I let them.

The swarm's assault was never-ending, but thankfully so was our gunfire. These weapons had come from Gunner's prized stash and had been altered to fit long, winding bandoliers of ammo rather than magazines. Too destructive for typical warfare, Gunner had originally procured these as collector's items. Now the three of us were draped in yards and yards of ammunition, firing endlessly into the crush of bodies closing in on us and barely making a dent.

I ground my teeth against my gun becoming so hot that it burned the palms of my hands. My whole body was numb from the constant rattle and vibration of my firing. But I couldn't stop to rest, not even for a moment. They just kept coming.

My bonds to Gunner and Jandro were wide open, keeping me aware of everything from their perspectives as well as mine. Gunner was in a precarious spot, having to swing his weapon in a wide arc to keep the enemy at bay. Every time he swung in one direction, they creeped in closer from the opposite side. Back and forth he had to do this, never missing a single shot, just to keep us covered. I felt his worry, his realization that he couldn't continue like this forever.

Really, none of us could. We had just entered the compound and how long had we been sitting here already? Minutes? Hours? We still had the Sha to deal with, and then getting our people out. Spending all our energy and firepower here would kill this mission before it ever began.

I pushed all my determination and support to my men and just kept firing. What else could I do? The bodies piled up all around us, but it did no good. Soldiers walked or jumped over them. Some started dragging or shoving the bodies away to clear more paths to us. They never, *ever* stopped, so how could we?

My arms ached all the way up to my shoulders. The gun was heavy, and while I was pumped full of adrenaline, my physical strength could only carry me so far, and I was reaching the end of my limit. My hands were surely burned and blistered from gripping the hot metal by now. As my strength faded, my shots went lower and lower, hitting at waist and leg height. I pulled up on my barrel as soon as I realized it, but my arms screamed in protest.

My guys weren't faring much better. I could feel the fatigue in Gunner's arms, taste the blood in Jandro's mouth from biting his cheek so hard. The longer we carried on, the more we began to slow down. And our enemies took every single opening they saw.

"Gunner, your left!" I cried out, still without taking my eyes off of the onslaught in front of me.

Gunner swung wide with his weapon, his weariness

making him overshoot the arc and allow a pocket of mind-controlled drones to creep in closer on the other side. Jandro took them out moments before they could touch Gunner, but then that left Jandro vulnerable and I swung to protect his open side.

"Mari, watch out!"

I ducked just in time to avoid Jandro's spray of bullets over my head. Blood rained down on me, the remains of my would-be attackers.

What began as such a strong attack quickly turned into us backing into a corner. We were all defensive now, our ammunition and stamina dangerously low. Our bonds were stronger and more connected than ever— really they were the only reason we covered each other so effectively, but now they were overridden with panic.

And the enemy never stopped coming.

They crept closer with every beat, every half-second we lowered our guns and paused our shooting because our hands burned and we were so damn weary.

We're not going to make it. The thought bubbled to the surface, breaking through my confidence, calm, and razor-sharp focus. I tried to shove it back down, to override it before the guys sensed it through our connection, but the damage had already been done.

Their minds latched onto that thought and fed into it, giving it more power that threatened to shatter our resolve, to make us lose sight of the whole reason we risked everything to come here.

Get Mari out of here. I didn't so much hear my guys' thoughts as much as felt them.

"No!"

I screamed the word at the top of my lungs, a final battle cry as I used my last well of strength to lift my weapon and fire at the swarm of black.

They were so close now, mere inches away. I could see their blank, empty eyes under their hoods and many had been able to touch my bike before I shot them dead. It wouldn't be long now, just moments until one of them grabbed my leg or snatched my gun out of my hand.

Calmness returned to my mind, the panic and fear subsiding. Only instead of focus and determination, I was filled with resigned acceptance. We tried our best. I would kill as many of them as I could and see this through to the end. The end which was moments away.

I'm so sorry, Reaper. Shadow. Mom. Andrea. But especially you, Reaper. Our last moments together are my only regret.

As soon as I finished the thought, I fired my last round and my gun clicked empty.

EIGHTEEN

JANDRO

My thousands upon thousands of bullets ran out. And when my gun clicked empty, I still couldn't hesitate. Still couldn't give them a fucking inch.

On that last click, I swung my gun around and crashed the butt against the nearest zombie's face. His jaw broke, but he kept coming at me with dead, empty eyes. It was like the blow never registered. Even Shadow flinched when he took a hit, but this swarm felt *nothing*.

I hit him again and again and again, until I could see brain matter peeking through the bloody mess of his skull and his body finally gave out.

Killing that one took way too long. It allowed ample time for the rest of them to close the short distance and attack me from all directions. The swarm climbed over my bike, grabbing at my legs, arms, and torso.

I twisted and swung, throwing my elbows out and using my assault rifle like a police baton, trying to beat away everything that touched me. The feeling of the swarm closing in on me was amplified by knowing that

Mari and Gunner were going through the same thing. If I focused on the bond, I could feel their desperation, the sensation of overwhelm and being crushed under the weight of *so* many. The mind-controlled soldiers never fucking stopped, never let up.

I was somehow still straddling my bike, squeezing the machine with my legs so hard just to maintain some higher ground. If one of these fuckers got an arm around my neck, I knew I'd be done for. It was how they got Reaper.

"Mari!"

I felt Mari's fear and panic hit a new spike through our bond just as Gunner frantically shouted her name. She had been dragged off of her bike and was now desperately kicking and swinging her gun from the ground.

Sensing her cost me a precious second of focus, and my air was abruptly cut off by an arm around my throat.

I couldn't yell, couldn't even feel the ground as I got dragged off my bike. Desperately, I pulled at the arm choking me. It didn't even feel like it belonged to an especially strong person, I should have been able to pull out of the hold with no problem, but it wouldn't even budge.

I started seeing black dots, felt my extremities going numb as I struggled for the tiniest sip of air. *It wasn't supposed to be like this. How could we fail so badly to protect Mari?*

If suffocating wouldn't end me here, the punches and kicks would surely do it. I barely felt the blows raining down on me, trying to disassociate so that Mari and Gunner wouldn't feel them and suffer even more than they already were.

Giving up so soon, my son?

I would have choked out a, "What?" if I could fucking breathe.

We told Mari this was out of the question, Hades mused inside my head. *But you are quickly declining, and we can't allow that to happen. As a last resort, I can make your body my vessel. I only need your permission.*

Do it! Do it! I screamed inside my head as I could feel the life draining from me. Who knew what the consequences of this would be, but they certainly couldn't be any worse than the fast-track toward death I was on now.

Hades went silent and for a moment, nothing was different. My vision was mostly black and my lungs had all but lost their desperate battle for air. Then a single pulse of energy thumped from my chest, like a heartbeat but different. It spread throughout my body and then everything was still.

And I mean, *everything*.

No more hits came down to assault me, and the arm around my neck was gone. Instead of the chaos of a swarm piling on to attack me, there was only eerie, death-like stillness.

I rolled to my side, then onto my knees to look around.

Death surrounded me, the swarm of soldiers was lifeless and scattered around everywhere. Mari was just rolling upright from where she had been dragged to the ground.

"Shit! Jandro, your eyes!" Mari cried out, stumbling to her feet and hurrying toward me.

"What? What's up with *your* eyes?" I retorted, scrambling backward on my butt at the sight of them. The pupils, irises, and whites of her eyes were gone, replaced by a single shade of bright, glowing green.

"Your eyes are all black." Mari fell to her knees in front of me, reaching for my face.

"Yours are green." It was so fucking creepy and weird, but honestly the least of my concerns the moment she touched me. "You're not hurt?" Creepy eyes aside, she looked fine, only dirty and disheveled from the ground.

"I was getting the shit kicked out of me but, no. I'm fine." Her fingers trailed from my face over my neck. "How about you? You don't look hurt."

"I was fucking seconds away from dying, I couldn't breathe," I confessed. "But...I feel okay too."

"Gunner!" Mari pulled away from me to look at carnage all around us. "Where's Gunner?"

"Here, baby girl."

We both looked in the direction of his voice to see Gunner standing, turning in a slow circle as he observed our surroundings. When he faced us, his eyes were replaced by a single shade of bright, sky blue.

"The gods are within us," Gunner said in a low, reverent tone. "Can you feel them?"

"Yes," Mari and I answered in unison, then looked at each other. "Hades?" she asked.

"Yes," my mouth replied, but it wasn't *me* that spoke. "Freyja." Hades inclined my head in Mari's direction first and then in Gunner's. "Horus."

"Wait, stop." I slapped my hand over my own mouth, then dropped the hand to my side. "You can control our bodies?"

I trusted these gods, I really did. And in a moment of desperation, I allowed Hades to take me as a vessel. But the fact that he used my mouth and voice to speak hit too close to home, considering we were dealing with a massive army of mind-controlled soldiers.

"Your control has not been removed." The tone of Mari's voice made it clear that Freyja was the one speaking. "Just as you can reach for your bonds between each other, you can remove us from your earthly vessels."

"No," Gunner said. "We're still alive because you've possessed us."

"You're alive because Hades is within Jandro and gave him power over death," Freyja said. She held up a hand, Mari's hand, and rotated her palm from front to back. "Your injuries are gone because I am within Mari and have given her my power to heal."

"And Gunner?" My gaze shifted toward him.

"I'm the sky," Gunner said in an awed whisper. "I can see everything. I know exactly where the Sha is. Our loved ones are in different areas of the fortress, but I can see them all."

"Well shit. What are we waiting for?"

"Wait." Freyja held up Mari's hand again. "There is a reason we do not take human vessels unless absolutely necessary. Your mind will start to deteriorate within hours. We don't want that for any of you, so our possession of you is temporary. Once we leave, you'll no longer have our abilities."

"Fine by me," I huffed. "Let's go."

Wait. Now Hades was speaking to me privately. *With your permission, I must do something before we move on.*

"What now?" I demanded of myself like a crazy person.

Look closely at the departed. Do you see them?

It took me a moment, but after some squinting, I did. Hovering over the dead bodies was some light, ethereal substance like smoke. It hovered a few feet in the air above the deceased, moving and shifting in space, like a person who couldn't get comfortable.

Their humanity was stripped away, their bodies driven like vehicles, and now they have been ejected from life altogether. I must put them to rest.

I understood right away. These people, people that *I* killed, needed peace.

Okay, I agreed.

Do not feel guilty, son, Hades told me as we approached the shimmery, smoke-like substance. *They will understand that we have set them free. I'm only shepherding them to their final state of rest.*

It was over quickly. The death god waved my hand through the smoke, which felt cool to the touch but charged, like static electricity, and used my mouth to utter one word.

"Rest."

The twisting, writhing movements of the cloud gradually stilled and then faded away into nothing. The tension in the air that I hadn't noticed before was gone. The eerie silence of the courtyard now felt peaceful, if even tranquil. No ghosts would haunt this place. With any luck, we would leave no remnants of the Sha at all.

"What now?" I turned back to Mari and Gunner.

"Now we go to the Sha and end this." Gunner's lip curled, and I wasn't certain if it was really him or Horus speaking. That could have been the sky god himself, seeking retribution against his brother, or his bonded human wanting it for him. "He already knows what happened in this courtyard and is sending double the amount of troops in hopes of overwhelming us. We'll cut through them easily and head directly for him."

"And if we can't kill him?" Mari's weird, glowing eyes shifted between me and Gunner. Now that I was getting used to it, they looked cool on her, like she was some kind of comic book superhero.

"Then we'll find and kill his council members, as we discussed," Hades said.

"The last time Set took form as the Sha," Horus used Gunner's pretty-boy lips to smirk, "he was torn apart by a pack of jackals. Some say he was trying to raise an army from the dead, and the jackals were sent by Anubis to protect their graves."

"So hopefully guns will be enough?" Mari asked, already loading up on the rest of her weapons from her toppled bike.

"They should," Horus answered. "He can certainly be killed by earthly means, but the jackal incident has made him cautious. I imagine that's why he's never revealed himself publicly. We should expect him to be heavily guarded."

Mari's gaze focused on me, but I knew it was Hades she spoke to. "Can you do the same thing to him that you did to this swarm? Kill him with a single pulse of power?"

"Sadly, no, daughter," Hades replied.

I wish you wouldn't call her that. It feels really weird coming out of my mouth, I informed him.

Hades ignored me. "With a few exceptions, gods' abilities are for humanity, not for each other." He directed my eyes toward Gunner. "I suppose that's why Anubis chose to use jackals the first time around."

"You're correct," the sky god confirmed.

Mari accepted that answer, nodding curtly as she holstered a handgun and filled her remaining pockets with loaded magazines. "Then I'll be happy to fill him up with holes and watch him fade away."

NINETEEN

MARIPOSA

W e hurried across the fortress, making our way easily through any swarm that tried to surround us. A single pulse of power radiated out from Jandro and everyone was dead in the blink of an eye. Hades put the souls to rest, and Horus directed us closer to the Sha's inner chamber.

It all started to make sense to me as we got closer. The Sha was never seen out in public. Even his own soldiers within the compound knew him as General Tash, and only the General Council members that Andrea told us about, had a direct line to the mysterious general.

The Sha was afraid. I'd even go as far as to say that he was a fucking coward.

He knew a gun could kill him, knew his earthly body was just as vulnerable as any other body. The mysterious general persona, all the mind-controlled soldiers he threw into battle like they were nothing, it was all just to protect his slimy, cowardly hide.

The deeper we marched into the fortress, the hotter my anger burned. The Sha threw my father out into battle and stole my husbands, probably to use them as more armor to hide behind.

To my surprise, Freyja seemed pleased at my budding anger. I felt her within me and sort of outside of me, like a friend walking so closely behind me that I could sense her just over my shoulder.

Don't forget that I am also a goddess of death, she reminded me. *Death is the greatest sacrifice for love. This anger you feel now is a result of your love, dear daughter. Your passion and devotion to the men who were taken from you. Let it fuel you and guide your hand.*

Am I right, though? I asked in response. *Or am I way off base about the Sha being so afraid?*

I have never had the pleasure of meeting Set in any of his forms. Freyja's mental voice bristled. *In any case, it does not matter. You have found a source of strength. Now use it.*

Before long, we approached a set of massive wooden doors carved intricately with hieroglyphics. At any other time I would have liked to study the symbols, run my fingers through the deep grooves of the wood. It'd be even better if Shadow was with me, book in hand as we tried to decipher the ancient language together. But the thing that took him from me likely resided on the other side of those doors. I'd blast those intricate carvings to splinters without a second thought if it got me any closer to my men.

Gunner, or Horus rather, looked back to face me, those blue eyes like slivers of sky. "The Sha is in there,"

Horus confirmed with a jerk of Gunner's head toward the doors.

Jandro turned to me next, focusing those endlessly black eyes on me while extending a palm in my direction. "Stay back. Let us go through first."

I wasn't sure if it was Jandro or Hades speaking but I nodded regardless, tightening my grip on my handgun. We'd used all of our big guns on the initial swarm, and I prayed to the gods inhabiting us that 9mm and .40 caliber rounds would be enough to kill the Sha.

Gunner and Jandro approached the doors, flattening their palms against the wood as they began to shove. The doors gave only a centimeter with a heavy groan of wood before it halted them from pushing any further.

"It's braced from the other side," Gunner remarked. He only gave a nod to Jandro, who returned the gesture, before they began pushing again.

"Guys, what—"

I ate my words the moment I heard a massive crack, like a tree branch breaking off from the trunk. The doors moved inward, the seam between them widening as Gunner and Jandro pushed harder, arms straight out in front of them and muscles taut with effort.

No, not Gunner and Jandro. Horus and Hades.

Because no human man had the brute strength to push open twenty-foot tall, solid wood doors that were barricaded from the other side. That cracking sound must have been the bracer, snapping like a toothpick once the gods decided to give my men a huge boost of strength.

"Shit, man, can I keep this?" That was definitely Jandro.

I didn't know if Hades answered. Once the doors were all the way open, ten figures awaited us on the other side. These people wore loose-fitting pants and tunics, their heads and mouths covered, and gold pins of the Sha affixed to their shoulders.

Each person also held an assault rifle pointed directly at us.

"The General's Council, I presume," Horus said with a sneer on Gunner's beautiful face.

These were the Sha's most loyal followers, his mouthpieces and representatives for dealing with humans. The pulse of death could not come soon enough for these traitors to humanity.

"Smoke 'em, Hades." Jandro's expression morphed just as the words left his mouth, and I knew something was wrong the moment Hades took over.

"I can't." Hades sounded dumbfounded through Jandro's mouth. "The Sha has—"

They opened fire before he could answer.

Pain burned through my body before I realized what was happening. I looked down to see holes through my stomach and chest, blood spreading quickly from the open wounds. I opened my mouth to scream but couldn't breathe. Blood erupted from my mouth in a wet, hacking cough as I fell to the ground.

Freyja, heal me! Heal them! I cried out in my terrified, pain-stricken mind.

Shoot them, daughter. Use your weapons. Use that strength that was just fueling you moments ago.

But I'm shot! I'm dying!

I will not let you die, daughter. But my abilities are limited, and they will only shoot you again if I heal you completely. Shoot them while they think you're not a threat.

The goddess went silent in my mind, but I knew she was still present and protecting me. It was that knowledge that drove me to reach my shaking, blood-soaked hand to my holster. The pain was excruciating as I wrapped my fingers around the pistol's grip and used all of my strength to pull it out.

Fuck, everything hurt. Everything was burning, even my lungs. I was still coughing up blood as I tried to take in gulps of air. How I wasn't suffocating to death, I had no idea, but could only attribute it to Freyja keeping me alive.

I rolled to my stomach, every bullet wound feeling like a knife sinking deeper into my body as the ground pressed into those areas. I needed to brace my forearm on the ground to push up, but I didn't even feel strong enough to lift my head. The ground beneath me was soaked with my blood, the sight of it spreading out around me cementing how close to death I really was.

Can't do this. I can't…

You can. Freyja's voice returned with a ferocity in my head. *You will. I did not choose a weak human. You can do this, Mariposa.*

You need to do it for me. I can't even raise my arm to shoot.

The more I manipulate your body, the less healing I will be able to do. Remember why you came here. Remember the reason you're filled with bullet holes right now.

I didn't know. I couldn't remember. All I wanted was

for the pain to stop, to close my eyes to the pool of blood surrounding me and be happy at home with my men.

My men. Mine.

My eyes snapped open to look ahead of me. Gunner and Jandro were also on the ground, blood soaking their clothes and darkening the earth surrounding them. It seemed they'd been able to shoot a few of the General's Council before taking hits themselves—only seven of the black-clad figures were standing, the remaining three fallen and lifeless.

So they weren't completely invincible, just somehow immune to Hades' instant death ability.

My men, they need my help. I raised my shooting arm but could only get the gun a few inches off the ground. My hand shook, slippery with blood.

Movement drew my eye to Gunner. He released one weapon with a clatter and drew a new one holstered at his lower back. Despite being prone and bleeding, and likely in an enormous amount of pain, his shots were swift and his arm steady. Years of practice made him incredibly effective with firearms, and he took out two more of the armed council members. Their bodies dropped like stones but that left five remaining, all of whom pointed their barrels at Gunner.

"No!" I cried out, mouth pouring blood as they rained fire down on him. Not him. I couldn't lose anyone else.

Two of the council swung to fire at Jandro, who had started crawling in my and Gunner's direction. He covered his head and curled up to protect his chest and stomach, but the onslaught of bullets still struck across his broad back.

Not my men.

A swell of fury lifted my chest from the ground. My left forearm pressed into the ground to lift myself higher, my shooting arm raised and extended. I fired, unleashing hell on those who dared to hurt my family. Not just my husbands, but my parents. All the medics and soldiers we lost. The countless families torn apart because this chaos god needed slaves to spread his destruction far and wide.

I didn't aim, and truly didn't know if my hits were landing. All I saw was Gunner and Jandro, clinging to life when these beautiful, loving men should have been vibrant and full of life. All five of us still had lives to live —parties, laughter, and quiet moments. Adventures across the country on motorcycles and milestones with our future children. My men had so much taken from them already. None of them would be taken from *me* again.

My shooting was only halted by a pulse of energy radiating from my chest. It knocked the wind out of me like I'd been kicked, sending me sprawling flat on the ground again as I took huge gulps of air.

Air! I could breathe!

I pressed up to my knees, still shaky, but not as weak as I was moments ago. My clothes were tattered with holes and I was still drenched in my own blood, but the bullet wounds were gone.

"Mari, get down!"

I flattened myself to the ground just as rapid fire sailed over my head. More shooting filled the air for the next few seconds, then silence. Peeking up carefully, I saw Jandro and Gunner sitting up, looking exhausted but very much alive. The same couldn't be said for the General's Council, whose dead bodies littered the massive foyer we opened the doors to.

"We got 'em all," Jandro said with a weary breath. "Fuck, I thought that was it."

"Felt a bullet actually touch my brain. That was wild." Gunner tried for his signature easy smile, but I could see how the shootout had rattled him too. His expression changed, looking oddly serious as Horus took over. "Thank you, Freyja. You were wise to wait on the healing."

"The three of them were very near death." The goddess used my mouth to inform everyone. "I can't do much more in Mari's vessel before I must leave her. If the humans are badly injured again, I may not be able to heal them sufficiently."

Horus narrowed those endlessly blue eyes. "I don't believe there is anyone else between us and the Sha. He is expecting us."

The three of us—six of us?—got up from the floor and looked down the long corridor where another set of doors awaited. These were also carved with hieroglyphics and stretched to the tall, vaulted ceiling of the building we'd just entered.

Gunner and Jandro moved in closer to me, their presence calming and supportive. I reached out until our hands touched, just a light sweep of my fingers across their palms so I knew they were still with me.

"Let's not keep the Sha waiting," I said.

TWENTY

REAPER

"What's happening?"

I'd been having a fine, dandy visit with Hades and the other god in this dreamlike state for some time, with only the occasional pull toward the door of my childhood home. But the longer I stayed here, the worse I felt.

I was sweating, shivering, nauseous, and weak. Every glance toward the cabin's door, and every inch I moved in that direction, provided a small amount of relief that was never quite enough.

"Your body is failing." Hades stared at me, narrow-eyed, his mouth in a hard line. "You're inching closer to death."

"Fuck." I closed my fists at my side and turned my back toward the cabin. Each step I took away from that structure was pure agony, like fire stripping away the flesh from my legs. But I was no stranger to pain. *It's not real,* I reminded myself through gritted teeth. *This isn't my real body. I'm lying unconscious in a dungeon with Shadow, and I have to stay alive.*

It sure as fuck felt real though. I doubled over, my stomach roiling in protest. *Just one look. It'll take the edge off.*

The glance over my shoulder only made me feel worse, like my body was punishing me for putting more distance between me and that cabin.

"Quetzalcoatl," Hades snapped at the other god.

Pretzel-what?

"Can't you stabilize him any more? He's fading."

"I'm sorry. I've reached the limit of my healing abilities." The other god's hands stretched out in front of him, palms facing each other and fingers extended like he was playing one of those kid games with a piece of string. He was still standing on the front porch of the cabin, blocking the door, his face a mask of concentration, focused on his hands. Whatever he was doing may have been fascinating to watch, but all I could think about was him being in my fucking way.

"Move." I had doubled over so far, I was now on my hands and knees, crawling toward the only place that would give me relief. "Get out of my way."

"Don't, Reaper," Hades pleaded. "You must hold on."

"Then fucking stop me!"

The death god looked truly conflicted. "I can't interfere with your free will."

"You want to hold on, Reaper," the other god added, his fingers moving like he was weaving an invisible piece of string between them. "Your wife is on her way to you."

I halted my crawling, fingers curling into the dirt beneath my palms. "Mari? She's coming?"

"Yes."

He didn't elaborate. The unspoken words felt like an additional form of torture, bringing my agony to a new level. But it gave me something to fight the pull of death that so seductively promised me sweet relief.

I rocked back on my heels, bringing my chest up despite the motion feeling like barbed wire being wrapped around my heart. "Is she going to make it? How much longer?"

"I'm sorry. I know many things, but I don't know the answers to your questions."

My palms slapped back to the ground, frustration and defeat riding me hard. "Is she okay? Does she have a chance or should I just give in now?"

"Don't give in," Hades growled, sounding more like my dog than the man currently at my side. "I will take you to the underworld if I must but now is not your time to die, Reaper."

"How about…ugh…two minutes from now?" I wasn't even certain I could last that long.

"Mariposa and her men are currently alive." The god on my porch now had a small frown on his face, his brows knitting together.

"That's all you can fucking tell me?" Sweat poured off my face, hitting the dirt in front of me, the dark spots like rain. I inched closer to the cabin and it felt *so* good, but not enough. My pain level went down from ten to 9.8. *Maybe if I just stayed close enough without actually going inside…*

"I must go." Hades clapped a solid hand down on my shoulder, and I swore the motion drew me a few inches back. "Don't go into that cabin under any circumstances, Reaper."

"Wait, what?" I took a long, agonized look up at him, too consumed with pain to figure out what he was saying. "Where are you going?"

"We'll see each other again," he said ominously. "But I must focus my energy somewhere else at the moment. Hopefully, it will also help ease your suffering."

"What the fuck are you talking about?"

But he was gone in the next moment, and I was talking to an empty space. Looking ahead of me, the strange god was still frowning, his fingers moving more rapidly than before.

"Who are you again?" I asked, desperate to focus on anything but the agony riding me.

"Quetzalcoatl," he answered. "God of wisdom for the Mexica."

"And you're here, why?"

"To keep you alive," he answered with a mild scoff.

"Yes, I know, but—"

His head jerked up suddenly, dark eyes focused on some distant point while his moving hands abruptly froze.

"I must go too."

"What?" For a brief moment, my shock and panic overrode the pain. "No, you can't leave."

"I'm sorry, I can only focus my energy in so many places at once." His eyes met mine, looking genuinely apologetic. "I cannot keep you stable and provide mental shields against the Sha at the same time. You must do as Hades says."

"You are the only thing keeping me from going through that door," I protested. "If I'm here alone, then…"

"If I stay, Mariposa has no chance of saving you," he shot back. "And all your suffering will be in vain."

"Fuck…I don't think I can do it."

"You must. Everything that matters to you rides on your survival. Your wife, your family. They need you to live."

"Fuck!" I lowered my head to clasp it in my hands, tugging at the roots of my hair to alleviate the burning ache through my skull, but it was just more pain. And I didn't dare look up, knowing that if I saw no one there, I wouldn't be strong enough to stay.

I realized in that moment what my biggest fear was —dying alone.

Even if I wasn't really by myself, if Shadow was still next to my lifeless body yelling at me to wake up and drink water, I felt so fucking alone here.

My eyes squeezed shut, fighting the need to just look at the door, now that it had no obstacles in the way. It would be so easy to just walk through, to make all of this go away…

"Damn, Reap. Lookin' strung out."

The voice was like cool water on a burn. My heart jumped but I still wasn't prepared to uncurl from my fetal position and risk seeing that door.

"I haven't seen you look this shitty since that bad mushroom trip in Mexico. Remember that?"

My head lifted an inch, but my eyes remained pressed shut.

"Daren?"

"Yeah, it's me, bro. I got you."

I unfurled myself slowly, eyes peeking open to take in the young man sitting cross-legged in front me, blocking my view of the cabin. Daren had one elbow propped on his knee, cheek resting on his fist with a lazy smile.

It took a few minutes, but I slowly drew myself up to his level. His familiar face, those green eyes we share from our mother, hardened with determination once I sat up.

"I'm not letting you go, Reap," Daren said. "I went when it was my time. It's not yours yet." He leaned forward and thumped my tired, aching chest. "I told you you were gonna die an old fucking man, right? Remember that?"

"Yeah…" I forced a smile. Seeing him genuinely made me happy, even if everything hurt like a bitch. "Crazy thing is, I actually want to live to old age now."

"I know." Daren nodded solemnly. "So your ass is sitting right here 'til you wake up. I don't care what the gods say, I'll fuck with your free will if it means keeping you alive. Shit, I'll tie you up and find a tree to hang you in, if I have to."

I swallowed, the sensation like lava pouring down my throat. I still wanted to give in more than anything, to ease this pain and be free from it all. But Daren made it just a tiny bit easier, and I was no longer alone.

"Thanks for being here." I kept my gaze focused on

my brother's face, not the cabin behind him. "I miss you, kid. I think about you all the fucking time."

He flashed me that boyish grin, the one that made all the girls swoon. "I'm always around, Reap. Can't reach the world of the living anymore, but dream states are a nice little loophole."

"Can you see anything?" I knew Daren's premonitions had continued after his death. It was his warning after all that had stopped Shadow from killing Mari. "Do you know what's gonna happen?"

Daren shook his head, his expression apologetic. "It's all blank from here on. Not even the gods know. This is the turning point."

My gaze flicked up to the cabin door, rooted to that focal point until Daren grabbed the sides of my face and forcibly turned my head away.

"Don't even think about it," he growled. "You're staying put."

Dragging my eyes away from the sight felt like they were being pepper-sprayed. A fresh sweat broke out on my skin and I felt absolutely terrible. But I had my little brother with me, and I'd never pass up the opportunity to talk to him again.

"So this is all I can do, huh?" I said, refocusing on him. "Just wait?"

"Yeah," he sighed. "We wait."

TWENTY-ONE

MARIPOSA

The second set of doors opened easily, revealing a mostly-empty room, save for the high-backed, throne-like chair at the far end.

And the creature sitting in it.

Most of the Sha's body was covered by a shroud. Long swaths of black fabric draped over its head and most of its legs and torso. But the parts I did see made my breath choke.

Large hands with gray skin and curving black claws gripped the chair's armrests. Instead of feet on the floor, there appeared to be paws underneath the Sha's body. While his body was still, movement drew my eye to the lower left side of the chair. A tail covered in short, dark fur flicked forward. It was forked down the middle, the two ends twitching playfully, if even excitedly.

The Sha stood from his throne once we came to a stop in the center of the room. Tension crackled between me and the guys, lighting up our bonds with the desire to strike at this thing. But the Sha appeared carefree, even relaxed, as he walked on those two, pawed feet toward us. He didn't seem to notice or mind how we tracked every single one of his movements. A long snout, like the muzzle of a dog, peeked out from under his hood. His lips pulled back as if smiling, revealing long rows of sharp, predatory teeth.

"You eliminated my council, despite my infusing them with my god-resistant abilities." The Sha's voice was ancient and heavy like our gods, but carried a strange cadence. Not exactly an accent, but more like his mouth wasn't built for speaking human languages.

Regardless, he didn't sound upset that his council members were dead. If anything, he seemed amused by it.

"They were just flesh and blood in the end," I said, raising my handgun to point it directly at the shroud covering his chest. "As are you."

The Sha lowered his head, pointing his snout to the floor as a low chuckle rumbled from his throat. The sound gradually grew louder, transforming into a wild, maniacal laugh as it echoed off the walls and ceiling.

My temples immediately throbbed with pain, and I forced myself to keep my gun pointed and steady. That was the same laugh we all heard in our heads, the sound that tried to break us open from the inside.

"Oh, little Mariposa," the Sha sighed once his laughter ceased. "After all this time, and everything you've seen me accomplish, you still believe that?"

"If I'm wrong, this gun will clear it up real quick."

"Are you *sure* you want to use that on me?" Bright,

round eyes scanned across all three of us from under the Sha's hood. "I don't think any of you want to shoot me."

I started to lower my gun. He was right, I didn't want to shoot him. But wait, why? I was going to shoot him a moment ago, but I just changed my mind.

"Fuck!" The exclamation came from Jandro, who clasped his hands against his head. "He's in our heads right now."

Cold dread filled me. My temples continued to pulse with pain, although it was manageable. I was aware and in control of myself, but I kept looking at my gun and thinking shooting the Sha was a bad idea.

"Your bonds between each other and your pet gods are impressive," the Sha mused, his toothy grin growing wider. "But I can still slip through the cracks."

"How?" Gunner's voice was so infused with bitterness and rage, I knew it was Horus speaking.

"Easily, brother," the Sha answered jovially. "The fall of the United States was the catalyst, as you know. This ripple through the human consciousness awakened me unlike any other time before. But where your lot sought to fix it, this Collapse gave me brand new life."

The Sha curled one clawed hand into a fist and re-opened it. "So much power from so many humans falling into violence, chaos, and unrest. I'd never seen anything so beautiful." His eyes scanned over the three of us. "All of you have fed into my power in ways you can't even imagine, simply by being alive at this point in time." The Sha's eyes settled on me. "But none more so than you, Mariposa."

"Me?" My voice went high with surprise. "What are

you talking about? Ever since the Collapse, I've only ever wanted to heal the damage that's been done."

The Sha tilted his head as if considering my words. "Not you specifically, but your blood. Even with all my power building and becoming concentrated, I still needed to bond to a human to take physical form." He stepped closer, to the point of looming over me. "I needed someone with a mind that was broken and weak to be the first of my many drone soldiers. Do you know who that was, Mariposa?"

There was a long beat of silence as I gazed up at the Sha's roughly-canine face under the hood, that smug toothy grin that I hated so fucking much.

"Fuck you," I spat. "My father was never weak. *You* broke him and discarded him like a toy."

"He served his usefulness," the Sha said dismissively. "But oh, that post-traumatic stress disorder," he clicked his tongue, "provided so many delightful nooks and crannies for me to settle into." The Sha perked up as if excitedly remembering something. "Your man Shadow has many of the same."

"No." I wanted to scream the word but it came out as a defeated whisper. "You did not get inside Shadow, or Reaper. They're too strong, too *good*."

"Conquering them was a most thrilling challenge," the Sha continued to goad me. "But I must award the title of my favorite conquest to either your little spy, Andrea, or," he grinned wider than ever, "your mother."

"You piece of *shit!* I'll kill you!" I finally found my voice, but my shooting hand remained stubbornly at my side. The fucker was still influencing that part of my mind that wanted to fill him up with bullet holes. I was aware, pissed beyond all reason, and could easily raise my gun to shoot a hole in the ceiling. But he had pinched down on that desire to kill or injure *him.*

And judging by how the guys at my sides struggled and grimaced, they were dealing with the same issue.

A bitter laugh erupted from my throat. "You're such a fucking coward."

"Mari." Horus barked out my name in a gruff warning, but I was already seeing red.

"*You're* weak, Set," I went on. "I'm not addressing your earthly form, I'm talking to you, the god. What kind of god needs to control thousands of people to be considered powerful?"

The Sha tilted his head, another throaty chuckle emerging.

"Mari, don't." The warning came from Hades this time.

"What kind of god," I stepped forward until I was directly under the Sha's hood, "hides behind an army of thousands? Behind barricaded doors and armed guards infused with godlike power themselves?" I tilted my face up until my nose was just inches away from that long snout. "One who's afraid of a little gunshot wound?"

The Sha growled and a burning pain sliced through my forehead, forcing me to clutch my head with a hiss and stumble backward.

"I've held back this long because your human antics have been most amusing," the Sha rumbled. "But it seems the obvious has escaped you, Mariposa. I cannot die. Look at me."

The Sha threw back his hood to reveal a roughly dog-shaped head with triangular ears. His neck was longer than a human's, but his arms, shoulders, and torso were humanoid, covered in dark gray skin and a layer of fur-like hair.

"What am I?" the Sha taunted, spreading his arms to the sides. He took another step forward, knees bending backward like the legs of a bird. "I am neither human nor animal, unlike your pets. Something like me was never meant to live." He brought a clawed hand to his chest, that toothy grin maniacal. "Therefore, I cannot be killed."

"Let's test that theory," I shot back. "Let us go. No matter how nonsensical you are, you're still made of flesh and blood."

"I think not," the Sha purred. "As amusing as you have been, I'm tired of your thorns in my hide. Chaos must spread like the beautiful sickness it is, until all humans have fallen to it."

"Coward!" I yelled in his face. "You think you're so fucking powerful, but you're afraid of us!"

"Mari!"

Whoever yelled my name was too late, the pain felt like my head was being split apart by a crowbar. My knees hit the floor, but that was nothing compared to the agony driving through my skull.

He's overpowered the bonds! I could barely hear Freyja's frantic voice in my head over the scorching hot poker driving into my ears. *I can't shield you from him, daughter!*

Buried underneath the pain splitting my head apart, my desire to kill the Sha returned with a vengeance. He had finally released his hold, but now my brain was being literally scrambled and beaten within my skull. I couldn't even tell if I was holding a gun anymore.

I'm gonna die. Oh fuck, it hurts so bad...

"You're not dying that quickly, human." The Sha's voice cut through everything—my head, my skin. It stabbed through every organ in my body, twisting and plunging deeper. "You still doubt my power? I am not flesh and blood, but a *god*."

"Stop...please..."

I hated that I was begging, but I also didn't care anymore. The pain went so deep, was so constant, that I would have given up everything to make it stop. My breaking point was miles behind me. I had been dragged across it, over jagged glass shards and with burning hot hooks embedded in my flesh. The only reason I was still alive was because the Sha wanted me to experience this agony.

"I'm just getting started with you," the Sha purred pleasantly. "I hope you enjoy these scenes as I have."

The open throne room melted away, replaced by a room much smaller, darker, and dingier, like a basement. The shift in room size was so sudden, I was taken aback by how the brick walls seemed to close in on me.

"Reaper!" I whimpered when the figure slumped against the wall came into focus.

He was filthy and bleeding, arms and legs shackled to the wall while his head hung low and defeated.

My pain never let up for a moment but at least I had something to focus on now, the whole reason I came here.

"Reaper, I'm here. Can you hear me?" I tried to approach him but couldn't sense my hands or legs. I might as well have been floating in space.

A wide, swinging movement came down too quickly for me to follow. It collided with Reaper's head, forcing him to slump lower to the floor and curl up to protect himself.

"No, stop!" I screamed, full of my own agony and sympathy on his behalf.

Robed, hooded figures crowded around him, blocking my view while they connected kicks and punches to my husband's body. I screamed loud enough for the whole territory to hear, full of pain and rage at not being able to do anything.

"Stop! Stop! You'll kill him!"

I tried to rush forward, to tear and pull at Reaper's attackers, but my hands went straight through them. I tried to get in front of them, to act as a shield, but remained in place no matter how hard I pumped my arms and legs. It was like I'd become a ghost.

"I have enjoyed taking him to the brink of death, only to heal him and start the fun all over again." The Sha spoke with a pleased purr, but his voice was like thousands of knives dragging over my skin. "Would you like to see all the ways I tortured him?"

"No…no, please! Please stop." I shook all over— pain, grief, and horror shocking my system. I could *feel* myself breaking down beyond repair.

"The big one thought he could fool me by pretending to be affected by pain. But the best torture was making him watch my guards have fun with poor little Reaper."

Something about the Sha's taunts broke off pieces of me, but not the parts I expected. He wanted me to cower, to feel terrified, weak, helpless, and I did. But seeing what he did to my men awoke something else. Instead of pleading for my own life, for mercy from the pain at any cost, the part of me that cared for my own survival broke away.

We had our gods, harnessed our bonds, and had gotten so close. Here I was, close enough to Reaper to touch and help him, and I could do nothing but watch. Pieces of me were crumbling away to dust, but that feeling of utter helplessness did something else.

Like the core of a planet, it compacted and solidified all that was left of me, which wasn't much anymore. But what remained was hardened and dense, a final shield that no more pieces could be broken off of.

If I had to die—if my men had to die—then I wanted the Sha to remember me as the bitch who gave him hell long after I was gone.

TWENTY-TWO

MARIPOSA

"You're weaker than I thought." I couldn't determine the volume of my own voice, so I made sure to say and think it as loud as I could. "For a god, you're fucking pathetic, Set."

His energetic presence shifted around me without a response. The pain sensations switched up too--now it felt like hot oil rained down on me in a relentless downpour. But I was too far gone to react to the pain anymore. All that mattered was getting under this cruel god's skin, to remain that thorn in his side and live inside his head, rent-free.

"You can't even beat up one weakened, shackled mortal man yourself?" I continued. "You have to make your minions do it? Your followers should be embarrassed."

"Do you wish for eternal suffering so badly, human? Because I will happily grant that to you."

Ah, so Set had just as fragile of an ego as I suspected.

"Sure you can. You have two men chained up in your dungeon and you can't break into either of their minds to control them. You know what?" I plastered a grin on my face, despite feeling dead and lifeless to my core. "You couldn't keep my father under your control either."

"You're speaking nonsense, girl. Seems I've scrambled you well."

"Oh no, I'm still all here." I was shocked to still feel in control of my faculties, but I wasn't about to question it. "And my dad remembers me. I saw the damage you did, but it seems you underestimated his so-called 'weak and damaged' mind."

"What do you hope to accomplish with lies, fool?" The Sha was clearly agitated now, barking at me for running my mouth.

"You know I'm not lying, you idiot god." I kept pushing. "You're right in here with me. All my thoughts, fears, and desires are laid bare to you. You *could* be powerful if you really tried. But you can't do shit."

The Sha yelled something else at me, but he sounded far away and muffled like he was underwater. Pressure closed in around my head, softening and blurring the world around me until it all went out of focus. Then there was a popping sensation and...I was back.

I stared at the ceiling of the throne room. Reaper, his attackers, my pain—everything was gone.

Daughter, I can reach you again! Freyja cried victoriously before I felt her healing pulse of energy spread out from my chest to the room.

Harness the bonds now, another voice commanded.

Quetzalcoatl! *I'm shielding your minds, but you must end this now.*

"What..." I rolled over and grabbed for my gun that was a few feet away. On either side of me, Jandro and Gunner came to and reached for their weapons as well.

You three are an unbreakable chain, the snake god said. *The underworld, the sky, and the thread that binds them together. You are the natural order of existence, a trinity of which the pieces must always be interconnected to work.*

"It's us," I realized, coming slowly to my feet. "It's always been us."

"No death without life," Hades said softly, black eyes trained on the Sha.

"No sky without earth." Horus raised Gunner's weapon.

"No love without loss." Freyja said the words, but pointing the gun and squeezing the trigger was all me.

The three of us hit the Sha in the abdomen.

Time seemed to stand still for a single beat, a single moment of nothingness as we waited to find out if this truly was the end of chaos' reign.

Or if the Sha had been right all along.

The creature that was never supposed to exist touched a clawed hand to his chest. His palm came away stained dark with blood. The Sha's eyes widened in genuine disbelief as he slumped back into his throne.

"This can't be...I can't be..." Those dark claws closed into fists as he snarled at us like a cornered animal. "I *broke* the trinity! How can you three harness your bonds against me?"

"You shouldn't have stopped at Reaper and Shadow," I said, aiming right between those creepy eyes. "It never occurred to you that the gods would bond with my other men? And that *I* was the link you were missing?"

The Sha growled again, only it came out sounding more like a pained wheeze. The front of his robes were drenched in blood now, and instead of a dark gray, his complexion had paled to ash.

"I am *not* dying...I cannot find your mind now, but when I do, I will rip each of your brain cells apart and ensure you feel every single one."

"You are dying," I informed him. "Because this form is flesh and blood, Set. Just like I told you. And you can't find any of our minds because, aside from the natural order, there's something else your senseless violence can't detect."

"And what would that be?" the Sha wheezed.

"Wisdom," I answered. "Knowledge and learning. That was the final piece we needed to beat you."

"You haven't beaten me yet, human." The Sha curled his bloodstained hands over the armrests of his throne and leaned forward. "And you'll never be rid of me for good. I am as eternal as violence itself."

"I know, but you'll be nothing more than an idea. A concept floating in the ether. For as long as I can help it, you'll never take a physical form again." I curled my finger around the trigger. "And you sure as fuck will never touch my family again."

I squeezed that trigger and didn't stop until my gun was empty. Jandro and Gunner joined me in the beautiful chorus of gunfire, making the Sha's corpse jerk with each shot long after its life was gone. The silence that followed after the clicks of our empty weapons was something I didn't know how to comprehend.

"We did it."

Whispering out loud didn't make it feel any more real.

The Sha's body shifted, and the three of us immediately scrambled for fresh magazines to reload.

But there was no need. The lifeless, physical embodiment of Set slumped out of the throne to the floor. Before our eyes, the Sha broke down into a dark, dust-like substance which seemed to sink or fade into the floor until it was gone.

"Never meant to exist means no body left behind when it dies," Jandro observed quietly.

Reality hit me all at once then. I dropped my gun and threw my arms around his neck in an exhausted, sagging hug.

"It's over," I whispered into his throat, a sob choking off my voice. "We did it."

"*You* did it, *Mariposita*." Jandro squeezed around me quickly, smiling wearily as he pulled away. His eyes were back to normal, the beautiful hazel color shining brightly.

Just as he spun me around and pushed me into Gunner's arms, I heard Freyja's voice in my head.

I must leave your vessel, child, before my occupation does irreparable damage to you. I've healed you all that I can.

"Wait!" I barked out loud, quickly releasing Gunner to bring my hand to my aching temple. "I need you a little longer, Freyja. We have to heal Reaper and Shadow."

I will leave you with some in reserve, but I'm afraid it's not much. I must go, daughter.

Something about that final statement felt awfully permanent, and an odd pang wracked through my chest.

Will we ever speak again? I asked the goddess in my head.

Oh yes, daughter. Freyja sounded like she was smiling. *Perhaps not with language, but I am always with you. You can always speak to me and I will answer. You only need to listen. I am so very proud of you, dearest Mariposa.*

With that, I felt Freyja's presence simply leave my body. I turned to my guys, the question on the tip of my tongue, but they already knew.

"Horus has left." Gunner cupped my cheek and lowered his forehead to mine. "But I know where Reap and Shadow are."

"Hades is gone too," Jandro confirmed. "But we'll do a proper farewell party later. Let's get our boys back."

Gunner pointed to another set of doors at the right side of the room, and together we took off running toward them.

I prayed to all the gods that brought us this far that we weren't too late.

TWENTY-THREE

SHADOW

Dread consumed me like a sickness while I watched Emma hover over Reaper's still body. She pressed her ear to his chest for a long time, and checked his pulse in several places. When she finally looked up, her gaze hit me like a kick to the chest.

"I'm sorry," she said. "I can't detect anything."

"Can't you breathe into his mouth?" I pleaded weakly. "Do chest compressions to restart his heart. Do anything. Please."

Emma shook her head, pulling her mask down to reveal her downturned mouth. "I don't know CPR, I could cause further damage. I'm…I'm so sorry."

"The snake god," I tried next. "Have you heard anything from him?"

Another slow, apologetic shake of her head.

I was grasping at straws and she knew it. Reaper's chest hadn't moved for hours. I couldn't hear any breathing besides my own since yesterday.

My president was gone.

I slumped back against my wall with a clatter of chains.

These fucking chains.

A ball of anger and grief expanded in my chest, and I slammed the back of my head against the brick wall with the little remaining strength I had.

Pain, now. Please.

Anything to take the edge off these emotions consuming me from the inside. I didn't know what to do with any of this, couldn't hurt myself or the people who did this to Reaper.

Emma just stared at me quietly, listening to my weak, wheezing breaths now punctuated by wracking sobs of grief.

"Have you made a decision?" she asked during a quiet moment, referring to the last conversation we had.

"No," I admitted, fists tightening at the thought of her shining blade. She wanted it to wear my blood, but it would prevent me from being a mind-controlled puppet.

She gave me a hard, impatient look. "I can't help you after I leave. I have to report to the Sha that your friend is dead."

Dead. Such a normal, mundane word for the absence of such an extraordinary man from this world.

"I have a problem with blades." Who knew why I was telling her this. Whatever I chose, my own death was near either way. "I was…abused from childhood to adulthood with knives, as you can probably tell." I gestured down at myself. "If there was another way, I would tell you yes in a heartbeat."

Emma's expression softened in sympathy. "I'll do it as quickly as possible. You won't feel any pain."

"It's not about that, I can't feel pain anyway. It's… just a mental thing."

"Oh, right."

Several beats of silence passed while I tried to gather up the courage to tell her yes. *Step into your fear,* Freyja once told me. Once upon a time, that had to do with talking to Mari, but couldn't the same advice be applied here? I would be doing this for her, for my friends and everyone in Four Corners. If I died now, my body wouldn't be used as a weapon against them. If I did this, they would have a chance.

All I had to do was say yes to a blade through my heart. From a woman. My wife's mother, no less.

"If you see Mari again," I began, taking a heavy swallow. "Will you tell her that I love her?"

Emma softened even more, the black robe of her uniform pooling around her. "Yes, of course."

"And can you tell her that…" I swallowed again, my final words made even more difficult by severe dehydration. "Tell her I'm sorry I couldn't save Reaper."

"There is nothing you could have done—"

"Please," I begged. "She'll know it's really me if I say that. That I never fell under the Sha's control."

With a heavy sigh, Emma nodded reluctantly. Large blue eyes rested on me, patiently waiting for me to say anything else.

"Tell Jandro and Gunner that I'm grateful to them,"

I went on. "They helped me become someone who deserved her."

Emma nodded again slowly, her expression becoming more conflicted as I talked.

"That's all," I decided with the deepest breath I could manage. "Go ahead."

The woman shrouded in black stood from her kneeling position at Reaper's side. I cast one more look at him as she approached me. At least the others would never know how much he suffered. I would take that burden with me.

"You may want to close your eyes if the sight of a blade bothers you," she offered gently.

"Just get on with it," I huffed. My fists clenched, gaze fixed on Reaper. Maybe I'd see him again soon. Maybe closing my eyes was a good idea, I didn't know. I didn't want to die like a coward, but most of all, I wished she'd hurry up so I wouldn't have to think about this anymore.

"You're being very brave." I heard the metallic hiss of Emma's dagger being unsheathed. "My daughter is lucky to have had you. I wish we could have met under different circumstances."

"That's kind of you to say." I shifted my gaze to her and immediately regretted it. Her blade was out, sharp and glinting, and it was going to cut my fucking skin. "Please don't stall anymore. If you're going to do this, do it."

Emma's breath was shaky as I went back to looking at Reaper's body. Her fingers trembled as they prodded the left side of my chest, finding the best place to stab me in the heart. It turned out to be right in the forehead of the skull in my Steel Demons tattoo.

Some loud commotion in the corridor outside the cell startled us both. It sounded like doors slamming against walls and running footsteps coming for us quickly.

"The other guards!" Emma whispered in a panic, turning toward the door. "I've been found out."

I grabbed her forearm before she could get away and pulled her back to me, bringing her dagger tip to indent the skin on my chest.

"Do what you came here to do," I growled at her. "Do it now!"

Emma's focus and resolve were gone, her attention torn between me and the cell door. Fuck. I started wrestling the knife out of her hand, determined to finish the job myself if she couldn't.

The stampede of footsteps halted right outside. "Get the fuck away from him!" A single shot fired through the bars, causing sparks to fly as the bullet ricocheted off the walls.

Emma and I both instinctively ducked, covering our heads while I tried to process the familiar female voice that had just yelled at us.

"Oh fuck, oh no. Is that Reaper? Reaper!"

I glanced up, certain that I was hallucinating, to see Mari, Gunner, and Jandro at the door. The guys struggled with the lock while Mari pointed her gun into the cell.

"I said, get the fuck away from him!" Mari's expression was feral, if even downright bloodthirsty as she angled her weapon toward her mother's back. My wife's face was streaked with dirt, sweat, and dried blood. More blood stained the front of her clothing in a reddish-brown tint, like she'd been lying in a pool of it.

This was no illusion from the Sha, no carbon copy of my wife with her gorgeous face and sweet voice trying to undo me. Nothing was polished or perfected about this image of her, covered in filth, pointing a gun, and yelling obscenities through the door.

This was...real?

"Mari?" I croaked in disbelief.

Her eyes jerked to me, the fury in them dimming slightly. "It's us," she said, her voice softer. "We're here. It's all over, love. It's going to be okay."

I couldn't afford to feel relief, joy, or anything yet. There was still the matter of getting them inside. My leg kicked out, nudging Emma who had moved away from me as ordered, still covering her head.

"Unlock the door," I told her. Then to Mari, "Don't shoot her."

"*Her?*" Mari's puzzled frown turned wide-eyed as her mother carefully glanced up, still with her hands above her head as she moved to the door. "Mom?" she squeaked out.

"Hey, sweet pea." Emma was already fumbling for the keys on her keyring. "Haven't heard you yell like that since you were a teenager."

The door opened and Mari sidestepped her mother's arms, spread in open invitation for a hug. My wife went straight to Reaper's body, falling to her knees as she placed her hands on his chest.

I felt a pulse of…something the moment she did that, like a refreshing gust of air. Right away, I noticed a slight change in my body. I could breathe a little easier and didn't feel as weak, although I was still nowhere near full strength. Mari started performing CPR on Reaper and that was when it hit me. She was here. We were getting out.

"Hey dude." Jandro and Gunner approached me, their faces trying to mask whatever they saw at the condition I was in. "Let's get you out of these, alright? Unless you're really committed to this new fashion trend."

I coughed out a weak laugh. Leave it to Jandro to make a joke right now, but it also felt so fucking good to hear him say dumb shit again. "Yeah. Get me out of these."

Gunner had to shoot the shackles binding my ankles and wrists. Good thing I trusted his accuracy. Then together they had to shoot the end of the thick chain attached to the wall that was wrapped around my neck. When it finally fell away, I could breathe even easier.

"Don't touch that," Gunner warned as I started to bring a hand up to my throat. "Your skin's all rubbed raw, man. It could get infected."

I moved that hand to the wall instead, using it for support as I painstakingly rose to my full height.

"Here, dude. I got you." Jandro nudged his shoulder under my armpit to give me further support, wrapping an arm around my waist to help hoist me up. "Can you walk?"

"I think so." My upper body wavered unsteadily on

my feet, dizziness hitting me hard, and I threw my arm over his shoulders for added support. The lack of chains on my body made me feel strangely weightless. Stiff muscles in my back cramped and protested from being unused in a week.

Mari looked at me from where she knelt over Reaper. "How long has he been unconscious?"

"About three days," I told her, allowing my weight to lean on Jandro. "Is he…?"

"He's got a weak pulse. He needs medical attention *now.*"

My legs buckled and I almost sank back to the floor. We didn't lose him! Not yet, at least. That pulse of energy from her must have done something. I wasn't about to question it and knew she'd tell me about it at some point. Right now, we still had to make our way out.

Gunner pulled a small radio from his cut and spoke into it, the words too mumbled and coded for me to catch. I wanted to sleep for another week, I was so fucking tired.

"I told Four Corners' army that the fortress is clear," Gunner reported to the room. "They're on their way in with medics at the front line."

"Good. Gun, can you shoot off these restraints and help me carry him?"

He fired off four quick shots, then Mari slid an arm under Reaper's shoulders and pushed his torso up. Together, she and Gunner managed to get him slung over Gunner's shoulders. "Get him and Shadow to the medics," Mari ordered, huffing for breath as she stood. "I'll be right behind you."

"Hold up," Jandro said. "What are you gonna do?"

Mari's gaze slid over to her mother, really acknowledging the other woman for the first time. "We still have to find Andrea."

MARIPOSA

I couldn't fully process the fact that *my mother* was in the cell with Reaper and Shadow, nor that she was dressed like one of the Sha's guards and had a knife pointed at Shadow's chest when we showed up. No, she was not the priority. Nor was Shadow, honestly, once we got her away from him. He was still breathing.

My only priority had been Reaper, lying still and pale against the far wall. I used the last pulse of Freyja's healing power on him, which was far weaker than the previous ones. I didn't know if it would be enough, he looked like a corpse already. So I started up CPR immediately.

That soft pulse under his skin was the most beautiful sign of life I'd ever felt. I wanted to throw myself over his body and kiss him. *You're still here, my love. We haven't lost you yet.*

But we had no time to waste. CPR could only do so much when he needed oxygen, fluids, X-rays, and most likely several surgeries. My relief was short-lived as I watched Gunner carry him out of the cell. Reaper still had many obstacles ahead of him, but for now, I could focus on the different matter at hand.

Once the guys left the cell and started down the corridor, I brandished my gun again and held it to the side of my body so my mother could see it clearly. "You have ten seconds to tell me why you were about to murder my husband."

She blinked at the sight of my weapon and a heavy breath left her chest. With the Sha gone, she wasn't under any kind of mind control and therefore owed me a fucking explanation before we could reunite as a happy family.

"It was going to be a mercy killing," she said quickly. "We heard nothing from Quetzalcoatl, so we didn't think you were coming. I gave him the choice. His only other option was to become the Sha's tool."

I relaxed my grip on my gun just a fraction. "The Sha is dead. We killed him."

A smile twitched onto my mother's lips. "I figured as much, since you made it here."

"Why are you dressed like a guard?" Q told me she'd been watching over them, but her black garb and the fact that she was about to *kill my husband* had me rattled. "Were you under his control?"

"No, sweet pea. I made the Sha believe that I was loyal to him," she answered. "Q shielded my mind from him, so he never saw my true thoughts. I found out your dad was here, Mari, and had to get close to him. I pretended to be a loyalist for two years so I could try to save your dad, *mija*." My mom's lip wobbled, tears filling her eyes. "I know he's still technically alive, Shadow told me. But he's been so badly damaged. I *failed* him."

Only then did I holster my gun, elation and sweet relief sweeping through me.

"He's okay," I told her, smiling through my own tears. "He remembers everything now. He's living at our house. Everything is…" I had to pause, barely believing the words I was about to say were true. "Everything is going to be okay, Mom."

"He is?" She stared at me, wide-eyed. "He remembers?"

"Yes!" Giddy laughter escaped me now. "He's still recovering, but he's going to be fine."

Unable to hold back any longer, the two of us collided in a tight, clasping hug. My mom was a little shorter than me, so I kissed her forehead like I used to when I teased her about her height. She laughed and swatted my backside, squeezing me tighter.

"I missed you so much, Mom," I whimpered into her shoulder.

"Oh my sweet girl, I missed you too. Not a day's passed that I haven't thought of you." She pulled away slightly, eyebrows raised. "And *four* husbands? You have a lot to tell me, young lady."

I wiped my cheeks with a laugh. "It's not that weird. Dad already loves both Jandro and Gunner."

"Can't imagine why." She smirked. "So." She let go of me reluctantly and stepped back. "There's someone else you need to break out of here?"

"Yes," I said, returning to seriousness. "A woman

named Andrea, though she probably didn't give that name here. She came here almost two months ago as an informant for us. Dark hair, blue eyes, mid-thirties, really pretty."

My mother's face went solemn, recognition lighting up her eyes. "I know exactly where she is. Come with me."

———

MOM LED me down another series of corridors, heading the opposite way me and the guys came from. It became clear she was leading me to an area purposely kept separate from the rest of the fortress.

"What's this area all about?" I tried to keep the worry out of my voice, but nothing stopped the bricks forming in my stomach.

"It's a…conditioning area," Mom told me hesitantly. "For the ones newly controlled by the Sha and that were still being conditioned into full obedience. Or those who were particularly difficult to control."

As disturbing as that was to hear, it gave me fresh hope. "Then they'll probably make a full recovery, if they aren't completely gone. How many are there?"

Rather than answer, Mom stuck a key in a door at the end of the corridor we reached. Once unlocked, she pulled a handle to slide it open. The room inside was massive, like a gymnasium, and it was packed with people. Men and women of every age, size, and ethnicity filled the room. It was a small comfort that there were no children, at least.

Hundreds of curious eyes turned and stared at us. Most were wide-eyed in fear, no doubt fearing some kind of torture or illusion like the Sha had bestowed upon me. I didn't see Andrea right away, but she had to be somewhere in this sea of faces.

"Hello, everyone." I raised my hand in greeting and put on my friendliest smile. "My name is Mariposa Wilder and I'm a medic from Four Corners. The Sha has been defeated. You're all free now. You have nothing to fear." I tried to make eye contact with everyone looking at me, hoping they realized that I was sincere. "This is not a trick, you have my word. Medical help is on the way for anyone who needs it. If you have family or loved ones, we'll do our best to put you back in touch with them."

Hushed murmurs and movement rippled through the crowd as people talked amongst each other. If they didn't believe me right away, that was fine. Their minds had been manipulated and abused to the point where suspicion was natural.

"Mari? Is that really you?"

My heart stopped at the voice calling out from the crowd. "Andrea?" I answered hopefully.

A section of people moved out of the way for someone pushing through to the front. I still couldn't see her and my heart drummed louder the closer she got. When she finally came into view, I wanted to burst into tears.

Andrea had lost so much weight. Her skin was covered in scratches and scabs, and her beautiful mane of black hair, which she once took so much pride in styling, had been shaved off. But it was her. She was alive and she recognized me.

"Drea," I choked out, finally losing it. "I'm so sorry. Oh my God, I'm so fucking sorry."

"Come here," she huffed, pulling me into a hug against her bony body. "It's not your fault, I signed up for this. And…it's over, right?"

"Yeah," I squeaked out, returning her hug as tightly as I could without crushing her. "It's over. We're gonna be okay." No matter how much I said the words, I still couldn't believe them yet.

"Tessa and the kids?"

"They're good." I nodded against her shoulder. "Good, just waiting for you to come home."

"And your men? The Demons?" She pulled away to look at my face.

"Um, they're okay." I pulled in a shaky breath. "A lot has happened. We'll fill you in."

She nodded, releasing me slowly as she turned back to face the crowd of people. "It's true, everyone! We can go home."

The hesitant murmurings rose excitedly, a buzz of hopeful energy filling the air. Mom and I stepped aside, pulling the door all the way open to let people through. My mother had discarded her black guard's tunic, revealing a simple outfit of linen pants and a shirt underneath.

"I'm proud of you, sweet pea." She knocked her shoulder into mine as we started walking alongside the crowd to guide them out.

"Thanks, Mom." My hand squeezed around hers, still hardly daring to believe she was really here. That she and my dad, my whole family, would be back together soon. "Let's go home."

TWENTY-FIVE

JANDRO

Word must have traveled fast in Four Corners once the army deployed. Once we got back, the whole town was rallying to help. And thank fuck, 'cause we needed it.

Mari and her mom had met us in front of the compound with two hundred people in tow, in addition to the Sha's former soldiers who were still alive and in various stages of mental breakdowns due to no longer being mind-controlled.

People with vehicles volunteered to drive out and pick up those we couldn't carry with the army's first wave. Even with the extra help, Finn's units had to take several trips back and forth to get everyone alive transported out.

Those with the most life-threatening conditions were rushed to the hospital first, and no one was in worse shape than Reaper. Shadow wasn't looking good either, but his condition at least wasn't critical. If I hadn't seen him as an emaciated shell of himself in prison all those years ago, I wouldn't have recognized him in that fucking dungeon.

The next few days passed by in a blur. We were still short on medics, so Mari worked herself to the bone to distract herself while Reaper was in surgery. And I swore he spent all those days in the operating room. Every update from Dr. Brooks was a horror show. Reaper had severe, probably permanent, nerve damage in his hands. Shattered bones in multiple places, including his face. Teams of medics had to spend hours reconstructing his bones like a jigsaw puzzle. He also had internal bleeding and organ damage. And on top of all of that was the coma, which meant likely brain damage and no estimate of when or if he would ever wake up.

But his heart kept beating. He *was* alive, which counted for something. We would cross all other bridges when we got to them.

There were some beautiful moments in those first few chaotic days, though. Seeing Mari's parents reunite with tearful embraces was a sight I'd never forget. It would be one of those stories we'd tell our kids one day, the happily ever after to all the shit their parents and grandparents went through.

Calmness finally seemed to settle over Four Corners the day Reaper was moved out of surgery and into one of the recovery rooms. Dr. Brooks said there was nothing left to do now except let him heal, rest, and wait for him to wake up. And no one was more eager for all of that than Mari.

She was already at his side when I entered the room,

chair pulled up next to his bed and hands clasped around his. Her gaze was locked onto his face, watching him like he could wake up any moment if it weren't for the sedative still wearing off.

"Hey," I greeted her softly as I walked in, my voice no louder than the beeps of the machines monitoring Reaper's vitals. "Finally quit working?" I squeezed her shoulder, standing behind her.

Mari grabbed my hand and looked up at me with a weary smile. "Rhonda kicked me out. Literally whacked me with her cane and said I'd done enough."

"She's right." My grip moved to the back of her neck, massaging her there. Mari's head immediately rolled back, eyelids fluttering, and her lips parted in a soft sigh, which I promptly leaned down to kiss. "You need to rest too."

"I asked Dr. B to bring a cot in here for me." She returned to looking straight ahead, at the man we were all desperate to have back. "I want to be here when he wakes up."

I bit back my argument that she should come home —soak in one of her baths, eat a home cooked meal, and sleep in an actual bed. Let us fucking pamper her for telling chaos itself to fuck off, essentially saving the entire fucking world.

I knew it would be fruitless, that she wouldn't leave Reaper's side if the whole hospital came crashing down.

"Okay," I said. "But let me know if you need anything from home, huh?"

Mari looked up at me again, guilt crossing her face. "How's Shadow?"

"Oh, big dude's fine," I told her, stroking over her hair. "I'm going to see him before I head home for stuff. They're gonna discharge him in the next day or two."

"Tell him I'm sorry I haven't—"

"Stop right there." I cut her off with another kiss. "You're not apologizing for shit."

Mari kept up her frown, so I kept kissing it away until she was finally laughing.

"We know," I whispered. "We're your husbands. We understand."

My eyes lifted to Reaper, stretched out and motionless except for the shallow breaths he took. Most of his body was casted or bandaged. It went without saying that the road ahead of him would be long and difficult. He'd be recovering from what happened to him for the rest of his life, and not only physically.

But Mari would be there. We all would be.

I bent to kiss her one more time. "Gonna check on the big dude, then I'll be back with some clothes and food, okay?"

"Thank you." She kept squeezing my hand as we separated, letting me go only at the last possible moment. It was a simple gesture, but one that warmed me up like a crushing, full-body hug. Even with all her attention focused on Reaper, she still needed me.

I left the room with my heart lifted at that sweet reminder.

———

"HOW'S REAPER?" It was the first thing Shadow asked me when I stepped into his room. He looked comically huge in his hospital bed, feet dangling off the far end and tucking his arms close to his sides if he didn't want them falling off the edges.

"Looking like a mummy, but fine. He got put in a recovery room and the anesthesia is wearing off. Now it's up to him to wake up."

Shadow shifted like he was trying to get comfortable in the too-small bed. "And Mari?"

"What you'd expect," I said with a small smile. "Had to be forced to stop working, now she's glued to his side."

Shadow returned my smile. "So she's fine."

"Given...everything, yeah."

He turned his head on the pillow to look at me more directly. "And how are you, Jandro?"

"I'm..." It took me a moment to answer. I didn't get asked that question a lot, as the guy who usually looked after everyone else. My needs were simple and few—laughs with the guys, some love from my girl, and getting my hands dirty in some machinery.

But *this*, everything that happened...it was over, but it was going to stick with us for a long time, if not forever. What Mari, Gunner, and I did in that fortress felt like a faraway dream. But also so real, like a gross film I couldn't scrape off my skin. Everything had changed, but I didn't *feel* all that different.

"I dunno," I admitted after a long silence. "I'm still processing, I guess. My muscle memory is telling me to prepare for meetings in the conference room, more fights, but I guess we don't have to do that anymore."

"Not for war, anyway," Shadow mused.

"How are you though, dude?" I directed the topic back to him.

"Fine, I'm getting discharged tomorrow morning. I got off way easier than Reaper." His jaw tightened at that. "Except for when it comes to these fucking hospital beds."

I gave a half-hearted chuckle at his attempt at a joke and decided to pry a little deeper. We had no secrets between us anymore.

"And mental health-wise?" I broached, trying not to sound like I was preparing for the worst.

But if there was ever going to be a setback to all his progress, a week of being tortured in a dungeon would probably do it.

"Oh, uh." Shadow looked surprised but not offended by the question. "I...think I'm okay." He frowned, thinking about it some more. "Not that anyone would be *okay* after that but it's like..." He paused, looking at me. "This might sound weird."

"Spill it, my man. You know I've heard it all from you."

He swallowed and continued, "It's almost like my early life prepared me for this."

I leaned back, sucking my breath through my teeth. "Okay, yeah, that is a weird thing to say."

"Physical torture," he lifted a shoulder in a nonchalant shrug, "it's nothing to me now. I knew how to ration my food and water, to conserve my energy in a cramped space. And I was able to..." He swallowed again. "Keep the brunt of the torture off of Reaper in the beginning."

"I get it. You're saying you knew how to survive because of what you'd been through. That you'd already been through worse. Fuck, you probably saved Reaper's life."

"No, that was the snake." Shadow shook his head. "Mentally...it wasn't like before, but I'm not sure how long I would have lasted. If Reaper had died, if you guys hadn't come when you did..."

"Mari told us about the choice her mom gave you," I said gently.

Shadow's fingers clenched in surprise. "She did?"

"For what it's worth, man," I crossed my arms in front of my chest, "I'm sure I would have done the same in your position. Shit, I bet any of us would."

Shadow's hand relaxed. "Thanks, Jandro. It really felt like there were no other options." He scrubbed a hand down his face with a dry laugh. "Fuck, maybe I'm not okay."

"And that is also okay." I stepped up to clap him on the shoulder. "We'll get through it, man. We're family."

"Yeah." The tension eased out of him slowly.

"You been sleeping?"

"Yeah, like the dead."

"Well that's a good sign, yeah?"

"Yeah," he repeated, nodding. "And I know what to do if that changes."

"Fuck yeah you do." I grinned at him. "And you've got people here to support you."

"I do," he whispered dreamily, like he still couldn't believe that *this* was his reality.

I thumped him on the shoulder again. "You want anything from the house?"

"Food," he said immediately. "The shit they feed us here is bullshit."

"Alright, you big baby. How many tacos you want?"

"Ten. Actually, no, better make it fifteen."

"Jesus, you trying to hibernate for the winter or what?"

"Those tortillas you use are really small."

"In your big mitts they are," I laughed, heading for the door.

"Scrambled eggs too, please," he called after me, grinning, but I knew he was serious. Eggs from my girls were gifts fit for gods.

"Sure," I mock-grumbled from the doorway. "Man, I can't wait 'til you're home so you can grab them your damn self."

"Me too," he sighed, waving at me from his bed. "Thanks, Jandro."

TWENTY-SIX

MARIPOSA

"Good morning, love." I took my seat at Reaper's bedside, throwing my wet hair up a careless bun before reaching for his hand. "You'll be happy to know that I did *not* doze off standing up in the shower today. I'll call that a win."

The soft, steady beeping of his heart monitor was my only reply. His fingers remained stiff and unresponsive to my touch. I took his thumb and rubbed over the stone of the ring he gave me, like he always did when our hands connected.

"I miss you," I said to my husband who looked peacefully asleep, despite all the wounds covering his body. "We all miss you. I thought for sure you'd wake up at the smell of Jandro's cooking, but you're being stubborn now too, huh?"

Dr. Brooks said talking to him might encourage him to come out of his coma. Attempting a joke seemed like it might lift my own spirits, but the silence that followed canceled that out completely. Even when my own jokes were lame, Reaper always validated them somehow. He'd laugh, groan, tease me, or just grab me and kiss me.

The past day of sitting next to him, finally being able to *see* him, brought all those little moments pouring back. I thought of the night he gave me the ring, how nervous he was when he asked me to be his wife. When I first told him I was going to spend the night with Jandro, how terrified I had been, wondering if I'd misunderstood everything.

All the regrets came pouring back too, like the night I took this same ring off and threw it at him. But nothing replayed on an endless loop like the day before he was captured.

How I had completely melted down after seeing my dad in that state, and Reaper was there through it all. How beautifully, painfully honest he was with me, and how I threw it all in his face.

I reached up to touch his face, taking in what would become new scars long after he healed. Even with all the injuries, he was still so beautiful. My touch ran over his eyebrows and forehead, wishing I could absorb all the suffering he went through for our family. For me.

"I need you to wake up, love," I whispered. "I need to tell you how sorry I am."

There was no movement beneath those eyelids, no sign that they would crack open and show me those green irises that always made my pulse race.

With a sigh, I moved back to sit down when I heard a soft knock at the doorway. The man filling the frame made my heart skip, and a sob choked my throat.

"Shadow," I whimpered.

"Lover," he answered, stoic face crumbling with emotion.

My body hit his before I realized I was moving. The solidness of his chest was the exact place I needed to land on, and the massive arms folding around my back was the shield I needed to stay strong.

He was thinner, his ribs more prominent as I hugged around him.

"I'm sorry, I should have been around to--"

"Stop," he grunted, cupping the back of my head. "No apologizing. Others needed you more than me."

"None of you damn men will let me apologize," I laughed, wiping my cheeks.

"Because no apology is needed," he told me matter-of-factly. "You can't be in more than one place at a time."

I pulled together after a few more moments of letting myself cry on him. "So you're okay? Discharged already?"

Shadow's thumbs swept the remaining moisture off my cheek. "Yes, lover. Want to sit down?"

I led him to my chair at Reaper's side, sat him down, and promptly curled into his lap. Shadow's content sigh against my body was the only thing that eased my stress level since we got back from the fortress.

"Pneumonia and dehydration were my biggest issues," he said. "Once they treated my infection, it was just a matter of me getting rest and fluids."

I rested my forehead in the crook of his neck, soaking up all the warmth and the familiar, cozy nearness of him that I could. "Good. I'm glad that's all it was."

Shadow's gaze lifted to Reaper's bed. "Any change since yesterday?"

"Not yet."

He rubbed my lower back, fingers moving in an idle, circular pattern, staring intently at Reaper.

I gave a light scratch to the beard on his jaw to get his attention. "Anything you want to talk about?"

Shadow's jaw clenched, a harsh huff of breath leaving his nostrils. "I wasn't able to protect him."

"Now you better not apologize," I warned. "He'd never want you to become a martyr for him, pain or no pain."

"I know. He told me as much." Shadow's rubbing at my back stopped. "It wasn't even so much the torture I wanted to protect him from but the aftermath." His hold tightened around me. "Dealing with what comes *after* torture, it can be so much worse."

"Oh, Shadow..." My arms draped around his neck, I was somehow still amazed at the massive heart and empathy of this man.

"He's going to deal with things like I did," Shadow continued. "Maybe not sleepwalking, but he'll have nightmares. There will be random sounds or words that will take his mind back there. I just wish I could have prevented that for him."

"He will heal." He had to wake up first, I refused to consider the possibility that that wouldn't happen. But once he did, we would rally around him. "We can take him to see Dr. Ellis if he needs it."

"You know how stubborn he is," Shadow muttered. "He'll have to swallow his pride and accept help."

"He will," I repeated. "He's already seen the results of it in you."

"I hope you're right. It was so—" Shadow stopped abruptly, squeezing around me tighter with a sharp breath. "It was awful, lover. What I went through in a year in my old life, they did to him in a week."

"I'm sorry you had to see that." I kissed his cheek just above his beard and felt the tension melt out of him.

"It was how the Sha tried to break me," he admitted. "To control my mind. He could tell I was mentally damaged—"

"You're not," I interrupted.

Shadow returned to looking at me. "He tried to use you," he admitted, like it was a shameful secret.

"What do you mean?" I rested a palm on his chest to calm him further, knowing that was where he felt most of his anxiety.

"He...conjured up an image of you and tried to make me believe you were there with me. Your face, your voice. I could even touch it and it *felt* like you."

"But you knew it wasn't."

"Yeah, I figured it out pretty quickly." His hand rested over mine on his chest, and our smiles connected in a long overdue kiss.

The familiar elation and joy he sparked so readily in me burst to life like a bonfire. My guys were home and alive, and this kiss was the thing that cemented it all into reality.

"I love you so much," I breathed. "I'm so glad you're okay. So glad you're back."

"I told you I'd never leave," he said before kissing me again.

I was still exhausted and sleep-deprived but that mouth locking over mine, those hands smoothing up my back reinvigorated me in a way sleep and food never could. I couldn't wait to feel all my men together, their unique touches and kisses piling on me until I was breathing nothing but them.

"Something else happened," Shadow murmured when we paused for a breath.

"I'm listening," I said, moving a kiss to his forehead.

He turned his head in a way that made my lips brush against the scar cutting through his eye. "I think...I confronted the ghost of my mother."

"Really?" I leaned back to look at his face.

"It felt like I was under Doc's hypnosis," he explained. "I was aware of myself but not fully lucid. But she..." Shadow met my eyes and shook his head slowly. "She wasn't a memory. And while it's possible, I don't think it was the Sha fucking with me."

"What did you say to her?"

"Told her to fuck all the way off, pretty much." A smile pulled at his lips. "I told her she didn't control me anymore. That despite all the odds, I found someone who loves me." His eyes flicked downward to our connected hands. "Who forgives me."

I pressed another kiss to his forehead. "I bet that pissed her off."

"It did." His fingers stroked the band of my ring.

"When she finally left, I felt...lighter. Like I'd been carrying her on my shoulders all this time and didn't even realize it."

I curled my fingers around his, nuzzling him for another kiss. "I'm proud of you."

His mouth ghosted over mine in a soft huff of breath. "I love you."

Our kiss connected to the sound of a fast knock at the door and then Gunner's voice. "What's shakin', lovebirds?"

"Gun!" I had barely seen him since the fortress too. As the unofficial diplomat of the family, he'd been running around letting my parents, Reaper's parents, the club, and all our other friends and acquaintances know what happened and where we were.

I started to get up but my golden man motioned for me to stay where I was. "You look comfy, baby girl." He leaned over and kissed me, lingering and sweet, with a hand on my cheek.

"How is everyone? And why do you have your sleeping bag?" I noticed the rolled up bundle slung over his shoulder when he resumed standing.

"Everyone's good. Sending their well-wishes."

"Except Slick, that guy's a turd," Jandro cut in as he entered the room, also with his sleeping bag slung over his shoulder.

"What—"

"Ah, fuck you, VP." Slick walked in next, thankfully *without* a sleeping bag, but with a folded table under his arm. "Hey Mari," he greeted cheerily as he began setting the table up against the far wall.

"Did you grab mine?" Shadow's breath ruffled my hair as he asked Jandro the question.

"It's on my bike, I'll get it in a sec."

I stared at Shadow accusingly. "You're in on something behind my back?"

"It's no big thing, baby girl." Gunner set his and Jandro's sleeping bags on my cot. "We just decided that if you were gonna stay with Reaper twenty-four-seven, we might as well too."

"Guys, no."

"*Si*," Jandro argued. "None of us are sleeping in separate rooms again, unless under dire circumstances."

"Don't worry, I'm not staying the night," Slick called over, although he still had a little conspiratorial smile that he tried to hide.

I narrowed my eyes at Jandro. "Okay, so what are you *not* telling me?"

"Hey, we're not late, are we?" Noelle strode into the room next, Larkan following closely behind her.

This time, I did get off Shadow's lap to hug the woman I loved as a sister. "Oh, Noelle..."

"Slick! I thought you were gonna bring booze." She didn't seem to notice my somber mood, patting me on the back distractedly.

"Oh shit." Jandro's apprentice blushed.

"We brought a thirty-pack, will that be enough?"

I looked to the doorway again to see Tessa, Andrea, and all of their children spill into the room, which was now becoming *very* crowded.

Shadow stood and handed his chair to the women who just walked in. "I don't know about the beer, but we definitely need more chairs." He went out into the hallway in an apparent search for more seating.

"Will someone tell me what the fuck is going on?" Laughter was pouring out of me joyously now as I hugged Tessa and the kids. Andrea must have been recently discharged, but she already looked like her old self. She was bright-eyed, alert, rocking her new buzz cut, and glued to Tessa's side.

"Nothing's going on, really." Larkan was already fishing a beer out of the cooler. "Gun told us what happened, so we figured we'd give old Pres something worth waking up to." He passed me a beer. "A good old Steel Demons party."

"That's…actually not an awful idea." I laughed, accepting the beer after a moment of hesitation. It was nine in the morning, but what else was I going to do besides wait by Reaper's bedside?

And it really was a perfect idea. Reaper loved his community, this camaraderie and sense of brotherhood, more than anything else.

I scanned the small room as people chatted and caught up with each other like it was any other day. Slick shuffled playing cards on the table and more people started pulling drinks out of the cooler. The only ones this party was missing were...

"Room for three more?" T-Bone's gruff voice cut through the noise as the three Sons of Odin maneuvered their way into the room.

"Sons!" I shrieked, tearing up again at the sight of them. Now it was a party.

The three of them came straight for me, T-Bone

reaching me first as he swept me up into a bone-crushing hug.

"Knew you could do it, little lady," he whispered before planting a kiss on my cheek.

"Hey, hands off my wife!" Gunner called from the corner.

"As long as I get to put 'em on you next, pretty boy." T-Bone laughed as he set me down and cut through the crowd, heading straight for Gunner.

After hugs from Dyno and Grudge, I went back to Reaper's bedside and took his hand.

"Come on, love," I whispered, bringing his fingers to my lips. "You're going to be so mad if you miss this."

Everyone else in the room became background noise as I rubbed his palm and kissed each of his fingertips. My eyes never left his face, searching for any sign of awakeness.

He remained still in his bed, and when one of my men came up to rub my back, I reluctantly let go of Reaper's hand to let it rest next to his side.

TWENTY-SEVEN

MARIPOSA

A nother day passed. Then two more. And then a week.

Reaper did not wake up.

His body continued to heal quickly, I wondered if it was due to lingering effects from the pulse of power Freyja left with me. I hadn't seen or felt the goddess since the fortress.

After nearly two weeks, Reaper looked mostly normal. Most of his stitches and casts had been removed, the injuries fading to scars. His beard started growing out in that time and I had shaved his face twice. But not once did I see those eyes crack open.

My other three continued to spend the nights in his room with me, going about their different duties throughout the day, but always having meals and spending the evening with Reaper and I.

Others checked in daily too, usually Reaper's parents and mine. Finn and Lis moved back to their house to give us some space. My mom and dad were falling back into their old banter again—teasing each other and being all cute and affectionate. I wish I could say I was happy for them, happy to have my family back together. But a key piece of my happiness was missing.

My emotional state was all over the place. I'd put on a cheery mood when someone came to visit, then collapse into tears at Reaper's bedside when they left. I went from hopeful to deeply depressed and back again so many times. I questioned if it was cruel to hold onto him like this.

Dr. Brooks, and every other doctor he consulted, simply did not have answers for me. Reaper wasn't on life support. He wasn't brain dead. The possibility of talking to my husband again was greater than zero, so I kept waiting.

And waiting.

It was only my mom with me today—Dad was off doing something with the guys. I wasn't in the mood to talk, which Mom thankfully understood. Dad knew how to listen to me, Mom knew how to keep the silence away.

"We had dinner with Finn and Lis last night," she was telling me. "They're lovely, I think Javi and I will be good friends with them. They told us stories about when Rory and his sister were young, and their youngest boy too."

"Daren," I said without looking at her.

"Yes, all three of them; bright, feisty kids from the sounds of it." Distantly, I felt Mom squeeze my hand. "I'm glad you had them around, sweet pea. Everyone we met here is so kind and supportive. Oh! We met the governor and his daughter too, did I tell you that?"

"No," I said flatly.

Mom continued to talk, making pleasant background noise while I studied Reaper's face. The strong column of his throat, his jaw, and his lips were just as beautiful as ever. His left cheekbone had been shattered and had to be carefully reconstructed over several hours. No one would be able to tell now, except for the new scar under his eye.

His hair was growing back from being shaved to address his head wounds. More new scars lined his scalp and forehead. Scans showed no lingering brain damage, but Dr. Brooks wanted to keep checking for several months, even after he woke up. We never really knew how the head trauma would affect him until we saw symptoms. It could be memory loss, balance issues, or even personality changes.

"Mari?"

I looked at my mom, realizing she was trying to get my attention. "Yeah?"

She gave me a pained, sympathetic smile. "I'm going to head home for the night. Do you need anything?"

"No." I gave her a brief, distracted hug. "No, Mom. Thanks for sitting with me."

She squeezed me tighter and kissed my hair. "Always. I'll bring you some lunch tomorrow."

"Thanks," I said again, turning my full attention back to Reaper.

Now that we were alone, I leaned my chest against the side of the bed with a sigh, taking his thumb and rubbing it over the stone on my ring for the thousandth time.

"I really need you to come back," I whispered, bringing his limp hand up to my lips. "Please, please, my love. We all need you. And I—" My throat closed up but I forced the words out anyway. "I don't know how to go on without you."

At some point, many tears and pleading sobs later, I must have dozed off leaning over his bed. Someone was shaking my shoulder gently.

"Baby girl." Gunner placed soft kisses in my hair. "Come to bed." We had ditched the cot and sleeping bags for a big inflatable mattress that took up nearly half the room. Somehow, Shadow still dangled off of it.

"No." I removed Gunner's hand from my shoulder, I felt particularly masochistic tonight. "I want to stay by him."

Gunner breathed out a sigh but didn't argue as he placed a final kiss on the crown of my head, then backed away.

I felt Jandro and Shadow looming over me, but they thankfully didn't try to pull me away either.

"Love you," they both said with an affectionate touch and a goodnight kiss.

Someone put a blanket over my shoulders, the weight of it settling me down over the side of Reaper's bed again where I fell asleep.

———

THE BACK PAIN woke me up first. I sat up with a groan, still mostly asleep as I rubbed my face. Why did I insist on sleeping over the side of the bed again?

My eyes remained shut as I stretched and twisted, trying to alleviate this aching stiffness from my sleeping position. When I opened them, two hooded, but also opened eyes stared back at me.

I froze, convinced I was dreaming. But the pounding in my chest was too loud, too real. So were those lips moving slowly to whisper, "Hey, sugar."

"...R-R-Reaper?" I went from frozen to trembling. Did I get so used to watching him in stillness that it was such a shock to see him moving?

"Mari." His whisper was barely audible but his lips did move, and his hand scooted toward mine on the sheet. "...s'it really you?"

"Yes!" I wanted to scream it but could barely speak. One hand came to my mouth while the other clasped his fingers. I went to lean over him, shaking in a ball of nerves and unspent tears. "You're really back?"

"Think so." Reaper's eyes followed my movement, lids still hooded, but he *tracked* movement! He was awake, aware. The EKG started beeping faster as his heart beat accelerated.

The machine's noise grounded me in reality for a moment. "Stay calm, you're not totally out of the woods yet. We...we still need to run tests."

A corner of his mouth lifted in a ghost of a smirk. "I'm...calm, sugar. Are you?"

That question made the dam burst. Tears spilled and a sob tore out of my throat. Calm was another universe as I released everything I'd been holding back. Every fear and speculation, every unknown, every stressful moment of wondering when and if I'd ever hear his voice again, it all leaked out of my eyes and rolled down my face.

Every regret too. Never again would I ever spend a single moment with this man treating him like he didn't matter.

"I'm so sorry," I forced out between chest-heaving sobs. "Never again, I...I love you so much. I'll never...fuck, if I lost you, I don't know how..."

Reaper listened quietly while I blubbered and poured everything out. He was able to bend his elbow and stroke my hair, green eyes watching me thoughtfully. I leaned down further so he could touch my face, holding his hand against my cheek.

I started breathing normally, then he rubbed the stone on my ring and I almost started bawling again.

"My wife," he whispered, index finger stroking my cheekbone. "My sugar."

"Yes," I breathed, feeling a smile pull at my face for the first time in weeks. "My husband." I touched his face in return, still marveling at those gorgeous eyes blinking and watching me.

Reaper made a sound like he was trying to clear his throat and I sprung into action, finding a glass of water with a straw.

"Take it easy," I told him, my nose still sniffling. "You haven't swallowed or used your voice in a while."

He accepted a small, tentative drink and then tried again. "How...long?"

"You've been in a coma for about two weeks," I said. "We got you out when you'd been out for about three days already."

"Shadow?" His eyes widened with the question.

"He's fine." I squeezed his hand in assurance. "Everyone is."

I looked behind me to find the room empty, our air mattress bed made and blankets folded neatly over it. It must have been late morning for the guys to all be gone already.

"The Sha?" Reaper asked next, brow furrowed with concern. His voice was sounding stronger already.

"Gone," I said with a broad grin. "We have a lot to tell you, but...it's over, love. We beat him, got everybody out, then we were just waiting for you to wake up—"

I clapped a hand over my mouth because I wanted to scream and yell with victory. With absolute joy. There was nothing, *nothing*, left to kill myself with worry about. Reaper was awake! I had my whole family with me, and the enemy haunting us was gone forever.

"Come here." Reaper nudged a hand against my side to beckon me closer.

"Fuck," I breathed, holding the side of his face as I leaned down. "It is so good to hear your voice, my love."

"Closer," he said.

I leaned down until I was hovering just a few inches above him. He made a frustrated sound, then impatiently said, "Lips, woman."

I laughed at the realization of what he was asking for, then continued down until my mouth slanted over his.

Reaper in top shape would have held me down, kissed me like he needed my air to breathe, and would fight for every sip with teeth and tongue.

But this kiss was full of longing and relief, a sigh that released the last of our worries. He still wore compression wraps for his broken ribs, so I kept the kisses light--soft sips that didn't impact his breathing, despite the yearning I felt from him to deepen them.

He panted softly after a few moments. It was the most exertion he'd had in weeks, after all. I rested my forehead on his, held his hand and his face, not wanting to lose a single moment of contact with his skin.

"Can I...go home?" he asked after catching his breath.

"Not yet, love. Sorry." I placed a fast peck on his lips. "We still have a lot of work to do. But now that you're awake," I kissed his forehead, "we can get started, then get you home as soon as we can."

Reaper was quiet for another long few minutes, and I almost thought he fell back asleep.

"You're not...not mad...anymore?" he asked softly.

The regret rose up in me again and threatened to choke me like a rope.

"No, love. I haven't been." My fingers ran over his scalp. "I wanted to talk to you the next day, to apologize and finally move forward. But then..." My lips shook. "I'm such a fucking idiot. Fuck, I was so awful to you. I'm so, so sorry."

"Me too, sugar."

"No, stop." I brought my forehead back to his.

"You've apologized enough. I shouldn't have let it keep festering."

Reaper brought a finger under my chin, tilting my face up for another kiss, which I happily gave to him.

"Love you," he whispered on my lips. "My wife, forever."

"I love you too." My hand curled around his. "My husband, forever."

He smiled through his next kiss. "Forgiven?"

"Forgiven."

TWENTY-EIGHT

REAPER

I t was another week before I was cleared to go home.

Mari and the doctor got me up and out of bed the same day I woke up. I had to use a walker to get around the first two days, like I didn't feel fucking old and feeble enough. Then I moved on to a cane, which wasn't as bad. As long as I had a wall or something for support, I could swat Mari on the ass with it.

By the time I was discharged, I could walk, eat, and do most basic tasks on my own. But there were some things, both tangible and not, that I knew were permanently changed.

The nerve damage in my left hand caused me to lose feeling in my pinky and ring fingers. I could still hold objects and grip the handlebars of a bike, but I would never be able to fully extend those fingers.

I had areas without feeling on my head too, which I didn't realize until Mari was scratching my scalp one day. We had a whole back-and-forth, much to the other guys' amusement, where I thought she'd stopped but she insisted she didn't.

Mari and the others remained sleeping in my room, staying with me through downtime and my rigorous physical therapy. The guys only went home to grab food, clothes, and to feed the animals, who I missed more than I thought I would. Even that fucking rooster.

I grumbled about never having time to myself, but I was glad for their company, for the normalcy of it. To see the guys acting like dipshits with each other and being affectionate with Mari, it was everything. They filled me in on what happened, and I formally met Mari's parents for the first time. Her dad strolled into my room, spent the first five minutes speaking exclusively Spanish, and everyone thought it was hilarious.

I was weeks behind everyone else, but the reality started sinking in for me as more time passed. It was really fucking over.

The life we wanted, the world we'd been fighting for, it was here. And it was real.

Still, it was a crushing disappointment when I was told I couldn't ride my bike out of the hospital when discharged.

"Mari, tell 'em." I flung my hand in exasperation at the medics who kept telling me no. "I can fucking walk, dress, and feed myself. I can definitely fucking ride."

"Nope, sorry, love." She looked a little too delighted to be saying no to me as well. "I'm with them. You're much better, but you still have strength and balance to rebuild."

"Shadow can give you a piggyback ride," Jandro chimed in helpfully.

The big guy stared at him. "Don't volunteer me for shit."

"Your dad's on his way with the car," Gunner said through barely-controlled laughter.

"Great," I grumbled. "Dad's picking me up. How old am I again?"

"You'll be riding again before you know it." Mari rubbed my back, the only one trying to genuinely be helpful.

My dad pulled up not long after in his black SUV, while Mari and the others would ride home and meet us there. When Dad stepped out to hug me, I was surprised to see him in his pressed general's uniform.

"Aren't you out of a job now, General?" I cracked, slapping his back. "Thought you'd be decked out for golf or whatever retired people do."

"Sadly, not yet." He opened the passenger door for me with a chuckle, then elaborated when he got into the driver's seat. "We have a lot of diplomatic threads to iron out with Blakeworth and other neighboring territories. And now that New Ireland is free for the taking, we want to make sure its new occupants can remain civil."

"Someone looking to move in already?"

"A few," he confirmed, driving out onto the road. "We have a unit at the fortress just to maintain the place and make a smooth transition once we've established some agreements."

The drive was mostly quiet after that. I wasn't thinking of anything besides getting to the house. Would it *feel* like coming home or would everything be different? I figured as long as Mari and the guys were there, I could deal with any changes the place had gone through.

It wasn't until we crossed the small bridge into our still-developing neighborhood that my dad asked, "How are you, son? I mean really."

The question pulled me out of my simple fantasy of sitting on the back patio with a cigar and some whiskey. "I'm alright, I guess. I'll be better once I have some-where soft to land."

"This is me you're talking to," he reminded me, pulling into our long, gravel driveway. "I've seen torture, son. I've seen what it does to people."

So have I. I thought of Shadow, how timid he used to be despite being the most skilled assassin I'd ever seen. I thought of how he made strides and then regressions. And how he offered up himself to protect me in that dungeon. Since waking up, there was kind of unspoken solidarity between us. I understood him better now, and he knew better than anyone else how that experience had changed me.

I'd had a few nightmares since waking up from the coma, mostly flashes of the Sha grinning and laughing. Some other patient or random medic in the hallway would look vaguely like one of the guards who beat me and I'd feel phantom pains or a rush of adrenaline.

Mari knew. I was certain Shadow knew. The other guys probably figured out I'd have some lingering effects. And obviously my dad caught on.

I didn't like anyone in my business. I hated being

perceived as weak. My first impulse was to snap at my dad that I was fine, to quit digging into me.

But I paused with the words on the tip of my tongue, still reconciling the Shadow I first met with the man I knew now.

He was no weaker now that he had gotten real help. If anything, he was much stronger now. I never saw him regress once in that dungeon. He'd only been concerned for me. A year ago, I wouldn't have trusted him in the same room as Mari. Now, he was among the only three I trusted with her.

Mari only ever wanted to help him, to ease the suffering caused by a life of trauma. In that dungeon, Shadow tried to spare me as much suffering as he could. And I knew without a doubt, the rest of my family only wanted to help me too.

"I'm okay right now, Dad," I said as he pulled to a stop in front of the house. "Some days are better than others. Some nights are hard but, shit."

The others had pulled up next to us on their bikes. Jandro was the first to hop off and open the garage door, releasing a very excited, stubby-tail-wagging Hades.

"As long as I got this," I nodded to the scene outside the window, "I'll be okay."

Dad smiled at me, relief etched into his features as he clapped me on the shoulder. "Good, son. Lean on them. They'll hold you above water when it feels like you can't breathe."

"I will." I made a decision in that moment to really

act on those words, not just say them. If Shadow could, then I could.

"Let me get your door." Dad took off his seatbelt and started to get out of his seat.

"Pfft. I got it, old man. I'm not your wife, you can put away your chivalry."

He laughed but got out of the car anyway so he could greet everybody.

I stepped out of the passenger side, keeping one hand on the car for balance as I made my way around the hood. I had just made it past the first headlight when Hades caught my scent and zoomed toward me with an excited bark.

"Whoa, whoa. Hey." I leaned against the car as the massive dog jumped up so that he wouldn't tackle me to the ground and put me right back in the hospital.

He was all puppylike excitement—jumping up to lick my face, stubby tail going crazy, and rubbing into my ear scratches like nothing else in the world mattered. It never occurred to me until right then how weird it was for him to act completely like a dog.

"Hey, Hades." I held both sides of his head, trying to get a closer look into those endlessly black eyes. "You in there?"

The dog blinked and tried to lick my chin, then wiggled out of my hold and tried to sniff my pockets for treats. I knew from just a glance there was no longer a god inside this animal. He was just a dog.

When I looked up at the others, Mari answered the question in my expression.

"Since we killed the Sha," she said softly. "After they possessed us, they just...left."

"All of them?" I asked.

Mari nodded and Gunner spoke up next. "They still act mostly the same, probably because they've been with us since they were born, but...they're just animals now."

"He's still Freyja's favorite," Mari said, nudging Shadow.

"It's just because I'm the tallest and she likes to climb," he huffed.

The others gave him skeptical looks while I was still trying to process the information. "Why would they leave?"

"They haven't left," Mari corrected. "They're just not guiding us through animals anymore. And from what they said," she shrugged, "because they accomplished what they came here to do."

She was probably right. The gods came to us with a very specific purpose, but I didn't expect them to just retreat back into the void. It would take me a while to adjust to no longer being an instrument of death.

But still, the thought was freeing.

My dad helped us bring some belongings into the house and then took his leave, likely sensing that the five of us wanted to be alone together. The first thing I did was crash in the nearest bedroom. I didn't care or know whose room it was, I just wanted to lay down on a real bed in my house.

Mari's soft laugh floated in from the doorway the moment my back hit the mattress. "Do you, uh—"

"Get in here." I beckoned her in with my eyes still closed in bliss. "All you fuckers get in here."

The mattress dipped as she climbed on, then movement was all around me as the guys joined her. Mari nestled against my chest while Jandro spooned me from the other side with an exaggerated, contented sigh. I couldn't be bothered telling him to fuck off, even as a joke. He reached across my waist to rest his fingertips on Mari's side and I was damn glad he was there. That she had him while she didn't have Shadow and me.

Gunner snuggled up against Mari's back, sandwiching her between us while Shadow took Jandro's usual spot, scooting lower down the bed to rest his head on Mari's legs.

Once settled into our cuddle pile, the five of us let out a breath collectively. I couldn't explain why but it felt like a final release. The last nail in the coffin of the nightmare that had been our lives. We were all here, alive and at home. If I had any doubts, I could just reach out and touch any one of them.

Mari started laughing at our collective sigh. "So now what do we do?"

"Take naps," Gunner murmured, already sounding half-asleep.

"I'm all for that." Jandro snuggled harder against my back, purposely trying to get a reaction out of me.

Joke's on you, buddy. You're actually pretty comfy back there.

"Whatever the fuck we want." I reached back to pat his face.

Shadow looked up at Mari, idly caressing her legs. "Is there something you want to do now, lover?"

Mari seemed thoughtful, chewing her lip.

"Tell us, sugar," I urged, running a light touch over her face. "Now that nothing is in your way, what would you like to do?"

Her gaze met mine. "I think...I might want to become a doctor."

"Overachiever," Gunner grunted. Shadow growled and swung to hit him somewhere, the blow landing with a soft thud. "Ow, dude! I was fucking joking."

"Uh-huh." Mari laughed and tugged at Gunner's hair before looking again at me. "Dr. B's been talking about starting a training program. We really need a bigger team of doctors, and while I already do a lot of those duties, it would add to my credibility if I went back to school and actually got an MD."

"That all makes perfect sense," I said, trailing a finger along her jaw. "But is it what *you* want to do?"

Jandro's hand on her waist closed to hold her there. "We support whatever you want to do, Mariposita."

"I like the *idea* of it," Mari mused. "But I'm still not sure yet. Anyway, it'll be a while before the training program actually gets put together, so I have time to decide."

"Perfect." Gunner nuzzled the back of her head. "More time for naps."

She looked over her shoulder to kiss him, which exposed a long, beautiful sliver of neck to me. I leaned in to kiss her there, pausing to savor the heat of her skin on my mouth. Being able to touch her intimately was not possible at the hospital, but now...now we were *home*.

Mari's body shifted as Gunner and I subtly pressed

in toward her. Just the shape of her against me, the friction of her movements, made my hands curl into fists in her clothes. It had been so, so long. I *needed* my wife. If I didn't have her, I would...

Mari faced me again, catching my mouth in a kiss that matched my own hunger. I pulled her flush to me, bringing her leg over my hip and not caring who else was around as long as I had *her*.

I rolled to my back with Mari straddling me, clumsily pulling at her clothes with my gimpy hands until a stabbing pain shot through my arm.

"Ah, fuck!" I clutched at my arm, more in annoyance than anything else. I hadn't felt any random pains in a while and it was damned inconvenient for it to be happening right now.

Mari took my arm in both hands and rubbed over the area with her thumbs. "You're okay, love. Better?"

"Yeah." It had already faded to a dull throbbing under her touch.

"It's your connective tissue back here. Maybe even your nerves too." She smirked down at me. "Maybe you're not ready for sex yet."

I huffed dismissively. "I will be the judge of that—ah!" I tried to reach for her again, only to feel my arm and shoulder vehemently protesting.

"Relax, love." Mari placed my arm back down at my side. "Don't force it, you'll make it worse."

I let out a frustrated groan, staring up at the ceiling. "We have all the time in the world after I'm better, I guess."

Mari laughed and when I looked at her again, she

was pulling her shirt off and tossing it to a far corner of the room. Four pairs of eyes were now locked on her, bared to us. And from the way her hips wriggled out of her pants, she loved every piece of the attention.

"I never said *everything* was off the table." She crawled over me, one hand pushing my shirt up my abdomen.

A moment of hesitation hit me like I'd never felt before. I didn't look the same. I was thinner, although I'd get back to my normal weight in time. More scars covered me now, from my injuries in the dungeon and multiple surgeries. I'd never been a guy who was self-conscious of my looks before, so that sudden moment of doubt was jarring to me now.

I realized it was all for nothing as Mari's touch ran over me, just as indulgent and exploratory as she'd always been. If anything, she was even more eager now, making off with the rest of my clothes in a hurry. A heady thrill chased away the last of my self-conscious-ness, seeing that my wife wanted me just as fucking badly as I wanted her.

"Come here."

Her kiss pressed me down into the mattress, dark hair falling all around us like a curtain. She met me with every lash of tongue, scrape of lips, and sinking of teeth. It was every kiss I fantasized about when I missed her, all the pent up passion and longing and aching for months. I poured it all into her mouth and she gave hers to me.

"I won't repeat the past," she told me in a hushed whisper against my lips. "I promise."

"Neither will I," I panted, dizzy with love and lack of breath.

She stole the air out of my mouth again and again and I kept giving it to her, knowing she deserved more. I lost track of the other guys until Mari started down my body, the curtain of her hair pulled back as she lingered kisses over my abdomen. Beyond her, I saw three vaguely amused expressions looking back at me.

"Should we go?" Jandro asked, his grin widening.

"Fuck no," I barked. "The doctor says I'm not ready for the main event." I touched Mari's arm, the furthest I could reach without pain, as she headed lower. "So you fuckers better do what I can't."

"Y'all heard him." Jandro stood up, shucked off his shirt, and pulled apart his belt buckle. "Sounds like a direct order from the pres to me."

Gunner and Shadow quickly got up and started stripping as well, while Mari took an indulgent peek over her shoulder to watch.

Me? I grabbed a pillow for my head for a better angle to watch and relax.

Per the medic's orders.

TWENTY-NINE

MARIPOSA

Reaper's cock pulsed with an insistent need against my belly, but I didn't want to direct my attention there just yet. I wanted to learn my husband's body again, taste his skin and reacquaint myself with the man I had pushed away for so long.

I started at his collarbones, following the path to his throat with my fingertips and then my lips. He was missing his signature smell of cloves and whiskey, but I knew that would return as our life went back to normal. Regardless, he smelled delicious and masculine as I dragged my mouth indulgently down his chest.

He had some injuries here, healing scars creating blank spots in the large tattoo covering his torso. Shadow would fill them in, no doubt, so I kissed them lightly while they were visible. Reaper had endured so much. From me, from his time in captivity, and still now, from his painful recovery. He deserved every moment of R&R that he was ordered to take.

But that didn't mean I had to deprive him.

"Come here, *Mariposita*." With a hand on my back, Jandro directed me to the side of Reaper's body while I continued to kiss him and explore lower. I wasn't sure what he and the others had planned. My focus was on a single person for the time being.

Or was it?

I paused, taking note of four other distinct sparks of excitement in my chest. They were separate from my own and easy to miss if I didn't pay attention, but still there all the same. I smiled against Reaper's skin, realizing it was the bonds between my men and I. It was *their* excitement I was feeling, an echo of the bonds harnessed by the gods. I couldn't see from their perspectives anymore, nor borrow their abilities, but I loved knowing that we still had this--a tangible connection we could feel.

A warm hand pressed between my legs as palms swept over my ass and my back. My face hovered just over Reaper's cock now, and I dragged my tongue down the length of it, unable to contain myself any longer.

"Oh fuck," he cursed, his cock practically jumping at the contact with my mouth.

The familiar heat of him pulsed beneath my lips in time with the heat blooming between my legs. Jandro rubbed and caressed me there, stoking my fire while the others threw kindling on by touching me everywhere else.

A palm slid up my back to hold the nape of my neck, then a mouth breathed harshly against my ear. "Can I have your ass, baby girl?"

"Yes." I couldn't answer Gunner fast enough, the

anticipation sending a thrill up my spine to where he gripped tightly on my neck.

He used that grip to haul me up for a kiss, surging his tongue deep with a promise of what was to come. As Gunner released me, running that possessive touch down my spine, Jandro's touch skimmed my inner thighs and I felt a kiss on the back of my leg.

"Sit on my face," Jandro rasped, his kisses inching closer to my core.

We shifted around on the bed to make room for him underneath me, to allow me to continue pleasing Reaper, and for Gunner to keep stroking and kissing my back as he made his way leisurely to my ass. There was only one person missing.

I looked up to find Shadow sitting on the edge of the bed a few feet away, pupils blown wide under his hooded eyelids. He was just as naked as the others, the muscles in his arm and chest flexing as he stroked himself with a loose, relaxed grip.

"Come here, love." My voice hitched on a higher note as Jandro's mouth pressed to my pussy in a long, shiver-inducing kiss.

"I will," Shadow promised, his adoring gaze meeting mine. "I want to watch you with them first."

I smiled at my voyeur husband, keeping his gaze as I lowered my mouth to Reaper's hip. I kissed my way to his cock again, dragging my tongue over the thick organ as Jandro's tongue lapped at me. Jandro's strong fingers kneaded my thighs, spreading me apart for him to consume. A few inches away, Gunner massaged my hips and lower back, slowly treading closer to his destination.

My eyes dropped from Shadow's as I took Reaper into my mouth, gliding my lips over his silky head to the sound of a deep moan leaving his chest. I answered him with one of my own, savoring his taste while my lower body found a rhythm riding on Jandro's tongue, who hummed with delight underneath me.

"Holy fuck." The muttered curse of awe came from Gunner, his hands now sweeping forward to knead my breasts and pinch my nipples into hard points. "That's our girl. So beautiful."

"God, how could I go so long without this perfect mouth sucking me?" Reaper's hand clasped with mine alongside his ribs. "Don't stop, sugar."

My body sparked everywhere from their touches, from the praise. I went down further on Reaper's cock, mapping his shape and thickness with my tongue so I could never forget how he filled my mouth. He hissed out his pleasure, fingers tightening around mine. Jandro lashed at my clit, forcing me to rock against the delicious friction of his lips and tongue devouring me.

"Yes, baby girl. That's it." Gunner's fingers, now leaving a trail of slippery wetness and heat, finally started their way down the cleft of my ass. "Ride his fucking face. Suffocate him if that's what it takes to make you come."

"Mmm!" Jandro made a loud noise of protest but remained steadfast as he devoured me. His hand dug even harder into my thighs, sucking at my flesh and lashing at my clit like he had zero qualms with Gunner's suggestion. I could *feel* their love of pleasing me through our bond, and it only heightened my own pleasure.

Gunner's slick fingers teased my ass while Jandro ate me even more vigorously. My orgasm was imminent, a steady climb as I sucked Reaper harder and moaned out every delicious strike of pleasure consuming me.

"I want to feel you come on my cock," Reaper rasped. "Your scream, sugar. I want to feel it in your voice when you get there."

My chest was tight, heart already hammering from the build-up of pleasure and breathing through my nose to suck him. But the peak was so close, I didn't dare pull my mouth away for a breath. Gunner's fingers eased into my ass and that got me closer but not quite there. I teetered on the peak, right *there*, but not over the threshold. I could barely breathe but my body chased that release above all else.

Jandro made one small change with his mouth, sealing his lips around my clit as he stroked two fingers inside my pussy. He and Gunner stroked and filled me, Reaper thrust toward my throat, and it was that, being filled by my men, that sent me hurtling over the edge.

I released my scream over Reaper's cock just as he wanted, and he swelled and pulsed in response. Sensitivity hit me like lightning, edging me away from all the sensations. I let go of Reaper's cock and took a huge, gasping, moaning breath. I pulled away from Jandro's mouth and started scooting my hips down his body. He held me to his chest once my legs straddled his waist, his cock gently nudging against my thigh.

"So fucking incredible," Jandro whispered, stroking my back and kissing my face. "Breathe, babe. Take a breather."

The aftershocks rolled through me, making me shiver and prompting more kisses and praise from my men. When my heartbeat finally slowed, I looked up at Reaper who was still panting, cock erect and pulsing stiffly.

"Shadow, get in here," he said to our quiet observer. "Take my place for a bit. I need to calm this thing down."

With a soft chuckle, Shadow moved closer until he kneeled on the other side of Jandro.

"Did you enjoy watching?" I smiled up at him, still catching my breath as I took in all his gorgeous masculinity.

"Yes, lover." Shadow reached to stroke my face tenderly. "Seeing your pleasure is my absolute favorite thing."

I took his hand and drew him closer until he was within easy reach while I straddled Jandro. Wrapping a fist around the base of Shadow's cock, I pressed a kiss next to his hip bone. He sucked in a breath, waiting for that slight sting of pain he liked so much. I smiled up at him, teasing him with soft, gentle kisses while I stroked up and down his heavy length.

"Mari…" My name in his throat was such a sexy, desperate plea. This massive, incredibly strong man was completely, utterly mine and wanted to be nothing else.

I closed my teeth on his lower belly and sealed my lips, sucking hard on his flesh.

"Oh fuck yes," Shadow groaned, his hands digging into my hair and curling into fists.

"Damn man," Gunner observed. "Didn't know you were into that."

"I can only feel pain from her." Shadow's breath was short as I unlatched from him, leaving behind a dark red bruise. "And I only like it from her."

"Right on." Gunner's tone was lighthearted and curious, not an ounce of judgment to be heard.

I left Shadow matching hickeys on each side of his hips before running my mouth down the length of his cock, seeking his wide, blunt head with my tongue.

"Does she bite you there?" Gunner asked with a soft laugh.

"No," Shadow and I said together. "But I wouldn't be opposed to trying it," he added.

I shook my head at him. "I don't want to hurt you here."

"Fair enough, lover." Shadow stroked my neck and shoulder. "You can bite and scratch me anywhere else you'd like." He spoke to me so tenderly that I wanted to melt into a puddle at his feet.

But I sucked his wide cock into my mouth instead, sitting up tall to take more of him down my throat.

"Fuck, just look at her," Jandro breathed. He had a perfect view from down below, watching me suck and lick the man he took under his wing years ago. "Our wife. So fucking perfect." His hands slid up my ribcage, palms rolling over my breasts before he captured my nipples between his fingers.

"We're the four luckiest bastards in the world," Reaper agreed, his hand kneading my thigh.

I wanted to preen and bask in their adoration, soak

in their loving touches and words until I needed it like air to live. These were *my* men, mine. All of them devoted to me before anyone or anything else. We'd had missteps, miscommunications, and sometimes had made flat-out wrong decisions that were hurtful with devastating consequences.

But *this*, all of us together, was so pure and meaningful. It was everything. This was what the war had been for. All the struggles and heartbreaking moments brought us to this, this unfathomable, unbreakable love we shared.

I lowered to kiss Jandro, still stroking Shadow with my hand as I licked inside the mouth that had just made me come so intensely.

"*Te amo*," I whispered to him. "I love you so much. I never would have made it through this world without you."

"*Te amo, mi esposa*," he answered, cupping my face. "I was ready to die with you every step of the way. Now I'm ready to *live* with you."

Our kiss connected again, passionate and ravenous while my legs clamped around his hips. I ground against his body, searching for the heat and solidness of his cock to fill the empty ache inside me. Jandro released me with one hand to wrap it around his base, never breaking a kiss as he rubbed the fat head against my pussy. He teased me with it for a few swipes before pausing it at my entrance so I could sink down.

The width of him spread me open and my mouth broke away to moan at the delicious pressure. My head rested on his chest for a moment while I just lowered and lifted up, relishing in the feel of him spearing through me. I sat up after getting my bearings, returning my mouth to Shadow's cock, which waited for me so patiently.

A familiar hand stroked down my back, pausing once again at the entrance to my ass.

"Yes, please," I begged Gunner before sucking Shadow between my lips again.

Jandro took control below me, holding my waist while his hips rolled up to fuck me. With my spare hand, I reached over to Reaper, figuring he'd had a long enough breather already. He had softened, but not by much.

"Yes, fuck. Touch me, sugar. Just like that." He grunted out praise as I stroked him back to full hardness.

I drew Shadow down my throat as far as he would go, then released him with a gasping breath. Leaning to the other side, I took Reaper into my mouth, still working both men with my hands.

"Holy...shit," I heard from behind me.

"You gonna take her ass or what, Gun?" Jandro slowed his thrusts below me, hands sliding around my hips.

"Yeah, yeah. She's just fucking stunning, that's all."

"Don't blame you," Reaper purred with a caress down my arm.

I sucked him as Gunner eased his way into my ass, pausing often to lube himself more as he stretched me open. Jandro was fully seated inside me, not thrusting, but flexing his cock as Gunner worked his way inside. I lifted up from Reaper, sitting back on the two other men as I leaned my head against Shadow's thigh.

Gunner and Jandro started moving and I cried out at the sheer fullness in my body.

Shadow flinched at the sound. "Don't hurt her," he warned.

"I'm okay, I'm good," I panted, rolling my gaze up to his. "It doesn't hurt, it's just a lot."

He cupped the base of my skull and I knew he was watching me for any discomfort, even though my eyes rolled back and my lids slammed shut.

Just below Shadow's hand, Gunner kissed my upper back. "Good, baby girl?"

"Yes," I answered, my face tipped skyward and back arched in a deep curve. "Oh fuck, yes."

Gunner dragged out of my ass as Jandro thrust in, their alternating movements leaving no reprieve in my body. They slid against each other through a thin wall inside me and the mere thought of that, nevermind the sensation, was so utterly erotic that I felt another orgasm building immediately.

"Oh fuck, she's getting there..."

"She's so close, I can feel her..."

I didn't know who was talking but my need for that release had me taking over the movement, riding them both as I sucked Shadow back into my mouth. This time I wanted to scream over him as I came.

My hand was still wrapped around Reaper's cock, solid and slick as I stroked him with the rising and falling of my whole body. Jandro and Gunner held me steady for balance, but the control of this ride was all mine.

Again, I was right there, teetering on the edge. My lungs burned as Shadow filled my mouth, but his moans and touches kept me going. I wanted him to feel me even if he wasn't inside me.

My thighs ached as I rode them, bouncing and grinding and taking all the cock I could. Even my arm stroking Reaper was beginning to shake from fatigue. How could I not just come instantly with four gorgeous men touching, praising, and pleasing me?

A hand to my clit did it. I didn't know whose it was, but it was like pressing on a button that detonated a bomb. The release was explosive, my scream not only reverberating around Shadow's cock but filling the whole room.

And then I felt free and weightless, like smoke drifting back to earth.

GUNNER

I'd never seen such a beautiful display of multitasking in my life. Mari had Jandro and me inside her, then Shadow and Reaper in each hand. Her mouth went back and forth between the two of them until her orgasm rocked her to another dimension.

As Mari screamed through a mouthful of Shadow's cock, her ass clamped down around me so hard I thought for sure my dick would snap off. That *would* be the best and most epic way to lose it, but her convulsions thankfully ebbed after that first one.

Jandro stilled inside her, but I kept rolling my hips until she collapsed panting onto his chest. A light sheen of sweat coated her back, her skin tasting lightly of salt when I leaned over to kiss her shoulder blade.

"Did you guys break her?" Reaper ran a hand down her arm that still held his cock with a slack grip.

"She's fine, just gotta come back to earth." Jandro stroked a hair away from her face and kissed her forehead.

"Are you sure?" Shadow knelt next to the bed to get a closer look at her face.

"I'm fine, love." Mari laughed breathlessly, reaching out to scratch his beard. "I just need a second to recover."

"Kiss me and I'll be the judge of that." He was smiling now, quickly assured that our girl was nothing less than thoroughly pleased.

Mari's hips lifted as she reached to kiss Shadow, the movement causing Jandro and I to moan in unison.

"God, I wish I could fuck her," Reaper huffed. "I'm so fucking jealous."

"You should be." My voice strained with effort to concentrate. "It's so fucking good."

Every drag of her along my cock was on another level of pleasure. Just the slightest shifts and movements gripped and squeezed me like she was meant to fit me, even with another man inside her.

Especially with another man inside her, I realized. Mari was *ours*, and I had the privilege of sharing her with the three best men I knew. There were no words for how good it felt, all of us being together this way. Our gods were gone but I swore I felt the shockwaves of Mari's orgasm in me, like we still had a bond tethering us.

Shadow resumed standing and Mari sat up, her hands pressed to Jandro's chest. She looked over her shoulder at me, her side profile so beautifully breathtaking.

"Gunner?"

"Yes, baby girl?" I leaned into her, my chest brushing

her back as I reached for a kiss. "What do you need? Tell me. Anything."

Mari's lips skimmed mine in a sweet smile. "Kiss me and tell me what *you* need."

"I need nothing." My arms wrapped around her middle, pulling her back more firmly against my chest for this small moment of just me and her. "I have everything right here."

"You're sure?" Her smile grew, the kisses she peppered on me so sweet and reassuring.

"Positive." I dragged a kiss from her shoulder to her ear, trailing along the sensitive skin of her neck for the journey. "But I might like to try something."

Mari perked up immediately. "Such as?"

I tapped Jandro's leg to get his attention. "Switch spots with me."

"Um." His eyes flicked from me to Mari. "On the bed or in her?"

"The bed, dude!" I laughed and took a possessive grab of Mari's ass cheeks. "I ain't leaving this sweet ass for nothing."

"Alright, let's see if I can do this without slippin' out."

"Bet you a shot you can't," Reaper piped up.

"I'll take that bet," Shadow chimed in.

"Thanks for the faith, bro." Jandro fist-bumped the big dude before he started moving, sitting up in the bed. He and I looked around each other to figure out the best way to move while the other two looked on.

"You're not allowed to help him." Reaper smirked at Mari, stroking himself lazily.

"What do you mean?"

As soon as she asked the question, I felt it—a contraction of muscles squeezing around my dick that made me want to stop everything and thrust into her sweet, sexy ass until I filled her up.

"That!" Reaper pointed accusingly. "You just did it, I can see it in their faces."

Shadow chuckled under his breath. "She has to help them a little."

"Nah, Jandro's a gifted mechanic. I want to see if he's got the same dexterity in his dick. His dick-sterity."

"If you want to see me do tricks with it, you just have to ask," Jandro informed him.

"Guys, I think I figured it out," Mari declared. She leaned the back of her head on my shoulder and looked up at me. "You want to lie back on the bed, right?"

"Yeah." Completely unable to help myself, I slid a hand up her ribs to grab a breast.

"So just sit down and lean all the way back. Jandro can just come forward."

"You're making it too easy for them," Reaper complained.

"You're just mad you're not one of them." Shadow was truly laughing now, enjoying our antics.

"Fuck yeah I am," Reaper huffed. But there was no bite to the words. He was just giving us shit.

"You have a lot of faith in *my* dexterity, baby girl." I checked to make sure there was enough room behind me. "I don't know if I bend that way."

"Hurry up, I'm getting soft!" Jandro yelled.

I started leaning back, holding Mari to my chest

and Jandro followed us, leaning forward to stay inside her. She clenched around us again and it took work to stifle back my moan. We had to do some maneuvering with our legs, while Shadow and Reaper provided helpful commentary, but in the end, we were successful.

"Take a shot when we leave the bedroom, buddy." Jandro grinned victoriously at Reaper, who turned around and scooted toward the opposite end of the bed to lie next to Mari again.

"Whatever, I don't plan on leaving the bedroom." He slid closer to me and Mari, already seeking out her touch.

"I'll pour it down your throat, then," Shadow said as he moved closer to the other side of us.

"Damn," Reaper mused. "Didn't take you for that kind of guy."

"A deal's a deal."

"Anyway," I said loudly, running my hands over the gorgeous woman lying on top of me. "You comfortable, baby girl?"

"Very." Mari turned her head to kiss me. "Are you?"

"Couldn't be better." I grabbed her waist and rolled my hips up to press deeper into her ass, pulling a soft gasp from her mouth. "More?" My mouth scraped against her ear.

"Yes," she breathed, her voice going higher. "Please, both of you."

Her legs wrapped around Jandro's waist and the room filled with moans, creaks, and sighs as we started up again. Jandro and I alternated thrusts again, his hands planted on either side of Mari and me as his chest hovered over hers.

This was a great idea, I thought. Even while she kissed him, I could touch her and tease her. She loved it when we all touched her, it must have been some kind pleasure-sensory overload. And with some of the bond still there, I could feel some of what she felt. Her hands reached out to the sides for Reaper and Shadow as Jandro and I found a steady pace.

"Such a good girl," I whispered into her ear, punctuating each word with a thrust into her ass. "You take our cocks so well."

She answered with a moaning mouthful of Reaper, who kneeled next to us to give her better access. Her opposite hand was vigorously jerking Shadow, who stood stiffly with his hands clenched like he was trying to hold back from popping off too soon.

Yeah. Me too, dude.

Mari pulled her mouth off of Reaper, prompting Jandro to lean down and kiss her again.

"Fuck," he growled against her lips. "Too fucking good."

I could see the effort in his chest and arms as he held himself up. I could feel his thrusts fucking her harder, losing his resolve to how well she took him. Took both of us.

I was getting close too. My movement was more limited from our position but, God, her ass. Her beautiful, perfect ass that she let *me* have first. I loved fucking her here and cherished the fact that she trusted me with her body this much.

Not to mention that she was so tight and hot and felt fucking amazing back here. The harder Jandro fucked her, the tighter and more intense she felt on me.

"Fuck," I growled out through my teeth, fingers digging into her waist as I felt her tensing up, all her muscles coiling for another explosive release. If this was anywhere near as strong as her last one, I wouldn't last through it.

"Gonna come for us, *Mariposita?*" Jandro felt it too and brought a hand to her throat. It was a firm hold without squeezing, but she locked eyes with him and let out a whimpering, wordless plea. Barely a second passed before Mari wrapped her hand around his to tighten the hold.

"Oh, fuck." Jandro leaned his forehead on hers, gaze reverent as he squeezed her throat and crashed into her harder. "Oh, you want it hard. You're gonna come so hard."

Mari barely made a sound, just a tiny squeak as the orgasm rippled through her body. Her ass closed around my dick and I was done for. My release spilled out of me in a heady rush and I kept driving into her ass, trying to extend her orgasm, as well as mine, for as long as possible. A throbbing sensation that didn't match up with her convulsions made me realize that I felt Jandro's release too. He must have felt that overload of pleasure through the bond too, there was no way he couldn't.

The three of us all came down slowly in a sweaty, panting pile. Jandro sat back and sprawled on the opposite end of the bed, his chest heaving as he took great gulps of air. Mari slid off my body to the side, and I scooted away to give her more room.

"Well fuck," Reaper said, looking at a very spent Mari, now sandwiched between us. "That was hot."

"Thanks. Be here all week," Jandro panted from the far end of the bed.

"You two look wrung out," Shadow observed.

"Power of the pussy," Jandro moaned, throwing an arm over his eyes.

"And the ass," I agreed, scooting up to recline next to him. "You gotta take her ass, man," I said to Shadow. "It's incredible."

Shadow frowned in Mari's direction. "No, I'm too big."

"Well, shit. You don't gotta brag." I scooted up high to sit against the headboard. As relaxed and languid as I was now, I wanted to see what our girl had left in her.

Shadow took the spot I was just in, lying on his side as he skimmed a hand down Mari's back. "Had enough, lover?" he asked her gently.

She rolled toward him in answer, wrapped a leg around his hip, and brought his mouth to hers for a scorching kiss. Jandro and I watched them while catching our breath. I had never seen this side of Shadow before—a guy who kissed a woman with confidence and pulled her closer without hesitation. Who smiled at the private things she said to him and whispered things back that made her laugh and nuzzle into him.

"Proud of that guy," Jandro muttered, peeking under his arm.

"Me too, man." Mari rolled away from Shadow to make out with Reaper, sliding her body along his as she kissed him. "Proud of you too," I added with a nod in Jandro's direction.

"Me? What'd I do?"

"Gave him a place to go, for one." Shadow moved closer to Mari's back as she kissed Reaper, running a hand down her spine until his fingers dipped between her legs. "You also stood up to Reap and I when we were dumbasses."

Jandro sighed and propped his arm behind his head. "Someone had to question Reap to make sure he was making the right decisions. You, I knew you were just defaulting to him as president. I couldn't blame you in the same way because it wasn't your decision to make."

Mari slid lower down Reaper's body, taking his cock in her mouth while she wiggled her ass against Shadow's hand in invitation. The big guy groaned and nudged his cock where his hand had just been. His hips rolled against her ass, length sliding along her slick core to tease her for entry.

"I could have questioned him too," I said to Jandro. "But I guess I realized that too late."

"Nah." Jandro shook his head, his gaze never pulling away from the erotic scene in front of us. "If you backed me up, he would've just tossed your ass out too. I've just known him for so long, he was only okay with me telling him he was wrong." He nodded at the threesome a few feet away. "Me and her, really."

"For different reasons."

"Yeah." Jandro barked out a laugh. "You don't see *me* sucking his dick."

"Mmm, fuck...you know I can hear you."

Reaper finished the sentence just as Shadow pressed inside of Mari. Her muffled moans and the crash of his hips against her ass filled the room.

"Sorry, Reap. What was that?" Jandro placed his fingertips behind his ear. "Can't hear you."

Reaper just raised a middle finger in our direction. His face, eyes closed and blissed out, tipped up to the ceiling as Mari sucked more of him into her mouth. She rolled up to lean on hands and knees between his legs, and Shadow followed right after, kneeling behind her and never missing a thrust with the shift in position.

"It all worked out though," Jandro said, picking up our conversation from earlier.

"Yeah," I agreed. Reaper's cursing and moaning was getting louder, his fists clutching the sheets at his side. "But things are different now, aren't they?"

"They are." Jandro nodded. "None of us are the same people we used to be."

Shadow's breaths had turned to ragged groans, hips snapping with more force against Mari's perky ass. He reached around and underneath to play with her clit while he fucked her, turning her sexy moans into desperate whines as her release neared.

"But that's a good thing," I said to Jandro. "We're really a family now, not just club brothers."

A smile pulled at his face. "You got that right."

"Oh fuck, don't stop, sugar." Reaper was flushed and panting, hips driving up into the beautiful mouth wrapped around his cock. "That's perfect. Fuck, keep doing that."

Shadow bowed over Mari with his forehead on her shoulder blade, still rubbing her clit and fucking her with long, deep strokes. Our girl was getting red in the face too, moaning loudly with her mouth full and her brow furrowed with tension. All three of them were close, dancing along that knife-edge of release.

"Who's gonna be first?" Jandro smirked.

"Mari, duh," I scoffed. "Why, you wanna bet?"

"Nah." He folded his hands on his chest, awaiting the finale. "I know those two will make sure she gets hers first."

The air in the room grew thick over the next minute, while all the heat and energy and passion in the center of the bed reached a crescendo. Mari's thighs shook when the orgasm hit, her knees giving out until she lay prone between Reaper's legs. And still she sucked him with gusto, working his stiff length with her hands until he roared out his release. Shadow finished soon after, sheathing himself inside Mari with a final deep thrust and shuddering with a breathless groan against her back.

Jandro clapped slowly while the three of them stayed like that, barely moving in the aftermath.

"Stop that shit and open a window," Reaper panted, his hand tangled in Mari's hair, who rested her head on his lower stomach.

Shadow pulled out of her slowly, lifting her hair away to dress her neck in kisses. She shivered at the contact but otherwise didn't move.

"Falling asleep on us, baby girl?" I scooted closer to touch her ankle, and she shivered at that too. Our poor girl, so sensitive and orgasmed out.

"Mm no," she mumbled, but her fluttering eyelids and slack limbs said otherwise.

"Are you sore?" Shadow curled his body around hers, stroking a hand down her thigh. "We can start a bath for you."

Mari perked up at that, stretching her legs out long with a point in her toes and arch in her back. I could only sigh at the sight of her, so beautiful in everything she did.

"Bath sounds nice."

"Jandro." Reaper looked up at the VP who was opening the windows in the room. "What's for dinner?"

Jandro glared at him. "You're lucky your ass is gimpy, otherwise I wouldn't even entertain that question."

"Gotta milk it while I can." Reaper placed his hands behind his head.

"I'll help with food." Shadow placed a final kiss on Mari and rolled up from the bed.

"Thank you. At least one of y'all is useful," Jandro declared dramatically.

I slid into the spot Shadow just left, hugging around Mari's waist as I spooned her. "Guess that leaves me to help you with your bath."

"And me," Reaper said, grimacing as he sat up. "With what I can, anyway."

"With the two of you, what could go wrong?" Mari laughed as she kissed me over her shoulder.

"That's right." I grinned against her lips. "You were the key to preventing a zombie apocalypse by an evil god, so you definitely need a couple of dudes to help you with a bath."

"I'll take it as a perk." She grinned back, rubbing the stubble on my jaw. "Especially if it's from the men in this room."

"Good." I scooped an arm under her legs and hauled her against my chest. "'Cause we're the ones you're stuck with."

Mari wrapped an arm around my shoulders, drawing me in for a deeper kiss. "Perfect."

SHADOW

J andro and I were both pretty brain-dead after the sex, so we kept dinner simple—chicken tacos topped with random shit we found in the fridge. We all just stood around the counter, building the tacos as we wanted and then shoving them in our mouths. In other words, perfection.

"You think the governor's gonna throw another dinner party for us?" Jandro wondered after shoving his fourth taco down his gullet.

"Fuck, I hope not." I lost count of how many I ate, but I was in the middle of piling another one high with avocados and salsa.

"No?" Jandro looked incredulous. "We're even bigger heroes now, we saved the fuckin' world! You don't want to eat fancy, rich-people shit on the governor's dime again?"

"I don't want to wear too many layers of clothes and be forced to talk to boring people."

He laughed. "You got a point there." We were quiet for a moment while I chewed my food, but I felt the weight of his gaze for his next question. "Still sleeping good?"

"Yeah. Great, actually."

"Good, man. I'm glad to hear that." He turned at the sound of footsteps to see Reaper emerge from the hall—freshly showered and in a pair of sweatpants and a T-shirt.

"Yo." Reaper slapped Jandro's shoulder. "Leave me any food?"

"Yes, Your Highness," Jandro scoffed. "How's our queen?"

Reaper wandered toward the taco items. "Wrinkly from her bath and half-asleep."

"She gonna eat?"

"Maybe. You should lotion her up and ask her."

"You left her un-lotioned?" Jandro gasped in fake shock as he rinsed off his hands. "How dare you?"

"Gun's getting her started, but she'll love another pair of hands."

As soon as Jandro headed down the hall to the bedroom, I grabbed Reaper's favorite whiskey and set it on the counter. "You owe me a shot, President."

Reaper rolled his eyes but smiled easily. "How could I forget?" He finished preparing his plate of tacos and brought down two shot glasses from a cabinet. At my questioning glance, he said, "Hey, I ain't taking one alone."

"Fair enough." I finished the rest of my taco while he poured.

He slid one toward me and raised his, then paused. "I don't have the brain cells for a toast right now," he said before meeting my eyes. "But I'm glad it was you in there with me. And ah—don't." He raised a finger in warning when I opened my mouth. "Don't give me some shit about how you couldn't protect me or should have done more. You did your best, Shadow. You kept me just alive enough so that I could come home. I don't know if anyone else could have done that." He clinked his glass against mine quickly. "So thank you."

A mirthless smile came to my face. He knew exactly what I was going to say. So I said nothing, mirrored him as he raised his glass and poured the liquor down my throat.

"I'm glad you're alive and home," I said when we put our glasses down. "And I'm especially glad that… everything is in the rearview mirror now."

"Yeah," he breathed, leaning against the counter. "It's a hell of a fresh start."

"It is," I agreed.

Reaper ate his food quietly for a few minutes while I started cleaning up. Jandro didn't come back to get food for Mari, so I figured she was probably asleep now.

"Can I ask you something?" Reaper's voice took on a grave, serious tone.

"Of course." I turned to give him my full attention.

He swallowed before speaking and then nearly whispered, "The nightmares."

I moved closer to him, keeping my voice as low as his. "Yes? You're having them?"

"What do you do about them?" His expression was

raw, vulnerable like I'd never seen him before our time together in that dungeon. "Besides drink yourself to death. The old me would've had no problem doing that, but I don't want to deal with shit that way anymore." He smiled wryly. "Gotta make it to old age now, I guess."

"Yeah. We all do." I stroked my beard while I thought on his question. It wasn't at all surprising that he was experiencing nightmares from what he'd been through. I just didn't expect him to ask me for help this soon, or this openly. "It might be different for you, but hypnosis worked best for me."

"How does it work?" His hand inched toward the whiskey bottle. "How is it not just reliving the nightmare over and over?"

"It can be, if you're not careful." I sat across from him and nodded yes when he motioned for more to drink. "The first couple times for me were exactly like that. I almost stopped doing it because it didn't seem to work."

"Why'd you keep doing it?" Reaper poured for us into bigger glasses to sip from and slid one over to me.

"Doc convinced me to give it one last shot, and I'm glad I did." My fingers circled around the rim of my drink. "That time, I was able to separate myself from the memories. I was there, but I was also outside of them, like an observer to what was happening. He guided me through, and I was able to stay grounded, stay in control. And it got easier from there."

"Gotta be honest." Reaper sipped deeply from his drink. "That doesn't make a whole lot of sense to me."

"It didn't to me either, not until I did it." I took a small, pensive sip. "It helps to have someone there guiding you through it. They become an anchor to you, a safety net if something really ugly comes up."

"Could you do something like that for me?"

I hesitated in answering with another swallow of whiskey. "I can try if you want me to. But Doc had years and years of doing this. I don't want to lead you somewhere that makes you feel worse."

"Ah, how bad can it be?" Reaper polished off his drink. "You think Mari could do it?"

"Reaper, I..." I rubbed my palms together, searching for a way to answer in a way that he understood. "I know you're used to bearing down and muscling through things. I am too, but that's what led to me hurting Mari and you exiling me. I'm not saying that's what you'll do, but the stuff in your head isn't something you can just soldier through."

"I get that, Shadow. But you know I'm not one for the touchy-feely shit."

"It's not that simple. You never know how long this is going to affect you or in what ways. We'll probably be dealing with this shit for the rest of our lives, so you need the right tools. That might be hypnotherapy or...regular therapy, I dunno. I'm not qualified to help you but someone smarter than me is." I downed the rest of my drink, bringing the glass down harder on the counter than I intended. "I am here for you, though. We all are."

Reaper leaned his elbows on the counter and rubbed

his eyes. "Yeah I know, dude. And you're right. I need to not be a pussy about this and get some real help."

"Doc's colleague isn't far from here," I reminded him. "Dr. Ellis. She'll know what to do."

"Alright." Reaper placed his palms together, the curled fingers of his maimed hand nestled between them. "I'm glad I could come to you, Shadow."

"Me too."

"I think it helps a lot already, you know." He glanced up at me. "Knowing you've been through something similar and made it out the other side. I know Mari and the guys would never think differently of me, but..."

"They weren't there." I nodded in understanding. "Having Mari, Jandro, everyone really, is more support and care than I ever dreamed of. But what we went through...it's not an experience many people share."

"No." Reaper proceeded to pour another round of drinks for us. "And while I wish your upbringing was never inflicted on you," he paused to put the bottle away, "I don't think I'd be ready for help if it wasn't for you." He made a face as he lifted the glass to his lips. "That makes me sound like an asshole, doesn't it?"

"No," I chuckled, raising my own glass. A passing thought of my mother's ghost entered my mind and left just as quickly as it came. "I've made peace with my early life, I think."

"Really?" Reaper's eyebrows lifted in surprise.

"Yeah, we have a fresh start, like you said. I'll still have nightmares, I'm sure. The setbacks will still come. But I'm ready to move on."

"Well cheers to that, man. I'm proud of you." Reaper touched his glass to mine. "And hey." He looked at me intently. "When that stuff happens, you're not alone, alright?"

I smiled before taking my drink. "Neither are you."

MARIPOSA

Reaper's strength and mobility recovered beautifully over the next few weeks at home. Governor Vance wanted to immediately have an award ceremony and dinner party at City Hall, but thankfully everyone else insisted on rest first.

And that time relaxing at home with my men was absolutely glorious. We slept in and took naps. We took the bikes out and rode with no destination in mind, just for the thrill of it. In the evenings, we all went to bed together, my favorite part of the day.

My parents, eager for their own private time together, moved into one of the new duplexes a short ride away from us. Jandro regularly took over eggs for them and our other neighbors.

I still worked at the hospital because there was plenty to do and I couldn't *not*. But our patient load was slowly decreasing, and at my guys' insistence, I kept my hours reasonable.

By the time the governor's assistant, Josh, stopped by

to talk about the celebrations again, we had run out of excuses to say no. Everyone begrudgingly agreed, with Reaper stipulating that it had to be early in the evening so we could throw a raging after-party at our house. Just as I thought, he was not pleased to learn we threw a party in his hospital room after he got out of surgery.

"That's cruel," he insisted, pulling on a suit jacket that he had no business looking so dapper in. "Throwing a party in my room while I'm dead to the world and can't participate."

"We were hoping it would wake you up." I lifted my hair so Jandro could fasten my butterfly necklace. "But your ass had to keep sleeping for another two weeks."

"Did you at least funnel beer into my mouth?" Reaper turned down his collar and pulled apart the top three buttons on his dress shirt. Fuck, why was that so hot?

"We should have." Jandro decided to forgo a jacket for the event, rolling his shirt sleeves up past his elbows instead. The tailors altered his shirt a bit too small and it pulled snugly at the width of his chest and biceps.

Down girl, you can have him any time. None of them are going to war tomorrow. Or ever again.

"Slick wanted to flick playing cards at your face, but I didn't let him." Shadow too decided to go jacketless, since it was still daytime and warm outside.

He undid the shirt button at his throat and was in the process of rolling up his sleeves, exposing the forearm tattoo of me as a pinup girl. Okay, how the *hell* was I supposed to get through this event without dragging a pair of them to a dark corner for a quickie?

Gunner grinned at us from the mirror as he combed his hair. "I'll admit, I was really tempted to draw dicks on your face."

As usual, he was suited up nicely, everything tailored to perfection, from his jacket to his tie and waistcoat. That would only make it more fun to remove every piece later on in the evening.

I have been in the middle of at least *a threesome, if not a moresome, nearly every single night for two weeks, how can I still be this insatiable?*

"If I'm at a party, I need to be the drunkest one there by the end of the night," Reaper went on. "It's a cardinal rule."

"You were heavily drugged, if that counts?" I offered, winding my arms around his waist.

"Hmm." He lifted an arm to wrap it around my shoulders and pull me into his side. "You got a point there, sugar."

"Can we go already?" Shadow grumbled, fiddling with his sleeves some more in the mirror.

"So eager to chat and mingle with politicians again, are you?" Gunner teased him with a slap on the back.

"The sooner we go, the sooner we can get this over with."

"And then we can start the *real* party." Jandro rubbed his hands together gleefully. "I got the smoker going with a few racks of ribs already, they'll be perfect tonight."

Reaper squeezed my shoulder. "Who all is coming over?"

"I invited everyone we know," I said, swiping a final

coat of mascara over my lashes. "I imagine most of them will be at the ceremony too."

Once the five of us were ready, we left the house in the waiting SUV that the Governor sent to pick us up. He sent along five armed soldiers on motorcycles to escort us, which was, honestly, excessive, but it was more for show than anything. People lined up on the streets to wave and watch us drive by.

"I don't know whether to be flattered or uncomfortable," Reaper said through his teeth as he waved back.

"Just smile and go with it." I patted his leg.

Someone hit a button that lowered the windows and people screamed louder as they got a clearer look at me sandwiched in the backseat.

"Oh no." I hid my face in Gunner's shoulder, suddenly bashful at all the attention.

He just laughed at my reaction, smiling and waving like he was born for the spotlight. "Just go with it, baby girl."

I peeked up and saw that it was mostly girls and young women walking alongside the vehicle, craning their necks to get a glimpse inside the window. When I waved at them, the brightest smiles broke across their faces as they returned the gesture. They didn't know exactly what role I played in ending the war, but that was okay. If I gave them something to aspire to, I would take that honor proudly.

The crowd continued all the way up to the City Hall building. The perimeter was roped off to keep people at a distance, but our escorts still surrounded us as we walked up to the front doors.

"No offense, guys." Jandro grinned good-naturedly at one of them. "But I think we've proven we can handle ourselves."

The guard next to him smiled back. "The governor insisted. And we're honored."

Once inside, we were immediately crowded by members of the governor's cabinet. Everyone wanted to shake hands and congratulate us—mostly my men—personally.

"You must be so proud of your brave, er, husbands, is it?" One older gentleman clasped my hand tightly and leaned in *very* close.

His hand was firmly detached from mine as I was pulled back protectively against a tall, solid chest. "We're proud of *her,*" Shadow corrected. "She saved our lives."

"Give them space, you damn vultures!" A commanding voice cut through the buzz of curious questions and everyone crowding us slowly parted to reveal Finn and Lis at the end of the foyer.

They made such a beautiful couple—Finn in his formal general's uniform and Lis in a modest, floor-length dress and a few of her statement jewelry pieces. She held on to her husband's arm, the two of them beaming at us as we made our way to them.

"Mari, you look beautiful!" Lis held her arms out to me and pulled me into a tight hug. "Thank you for not giving up on him," she said when my cheek pressed to hers. "Thank you for loving my son."

There were no words that felt adequate enough to answer, so I just squeezed her back.

She pulled away, smiling and taking my hands.

"Your parents are already inside. We saved seats for everyone."

We moved slowly toward the ceremony room, which looked like an old-fashioned theater with a stage and red curtain. Lis and Finn guided us to the front row where my parents waited in an otherwise mostly-empty section.

"There she is." My dad beamed, patting the seat next to him. He looked more like the man I remembered every day with that warm brightness in his eyes and his hair growing back.

I hugged both of my parents before sitting down. "Are you guys coming tonight?" I lowered my voice to a whisper as people began to fill seats.

"We'll stop by but might leave early." Dad smiled apologetically. "This old man gets tired once the sun starts going down."

"So do these," I said, gesturing to my four men. "But they still try to party like kids."

My husbands came over to say hello and hug my parents before the lights started dimming in the auditorium. The governor and his daughter walked onstage to the sound of applause. I looked past my mom when I stood to clap, noticing the three reserved seats on the other side of her were still empty.

"Mom," I whispered, leaning over quickly. "Who was supposed to sit there?"

She looked at the empty seats and frowned. "Those biker friends of yours, I think. The three men who are always together."

So the Sons of Odin were snubbing the governor by not attending. Interesting.

Kyrie kept a pleasant expression on as she stood next to her father onstage, but I didn't miss how her eyes kept shifting to the three empty seats.

Governor Vance's speech was extremely flattering and long. I felt self-conscious from all his praise at first, then I quickly grew bored to the point where I was zoning out. I didn't know what the official story was that he was told about New Ireland, but from his speech, I got the sense he believed we saved the territory from a dictator using slave labor. That was close enough to the truth.

The governor stepped aside after his long monologue and invited Finn to the stage. Reaper's father walked up to shouts and applause and smiled charmingly from behind the podium. He looked the part of a diplomat, handsome and charismatic.

In Finn's speech, he praised the Jerriton troops who came to our aid and took a moment to speak the names of the fallen medics, soldiers, and Steel Demons who lost their lives over the course of the conflict. He even mentioned Dallas and the Sons of Odin club members who were lost before Four Corners ever became a target. That floored me, and I reached across the seats to squeeze Reaper's hand.

"I also want to extend my utmost gratitude to Andrea Marks, the widow of Dallas Marks, who went into New Ireland undercover to gather information for us." Finn's eyes scanned the room for her. "She acted selflessly to honor her husband, who gave his life selflessly so that his family could have a peaceful future. Four Corners is forever in your debt, Andrea."

Those of us in the front row stood and applauded loudly for her, with Finn's soldiers quickly following after. I spotted her a couple rows back, wiping her eyes and smiling as Tessa hugged her.

"To Javier and Emma Wilder," Finn continued, looking straight at my parents. "Not only are these two brave survivors of the New Ireland compound, they gave us the keys to save over two hundred more lives and secure a victory over this enemy. My wife and I have gotten to know you both personally over the last few weeks, and we are honored to call this kind, inspiring, beautiful couple, our family. Thank you for what you've done, and that includes," he leaned over the podium, grinning, "giving me the most incredible daughter-in-law I could ask for."

A ripple of soft laughter and applause rose from the crowd and my face burned hot.

After they each spoke, Finn and Vance took turns calling people up for awards and medals. Some were called individually, others grouped together, like the specific units who went into battle. Andrea walked onstage with her two children to accept her award. My parents went up together while holding hands. Because the Sons of Odin weren't present to accept their award, Shadow, as Grudge's assumed next of kin, accepted it in their stead.

We'd been sitting for a while and the guys were fidgeting, getting antsy. Once all the awards but ours had been given, a beaming Governor Vance strode up to the podium with his chest puffed out.

"And for the heroes who need no introduction, who

not only saved our modest territory from annihilation, but also who is most precious to me." He paused to look at his daughter who, for a moment, flicked her eyes to the ground as if she was uncomfortable. In actuality, Kyrie may have never been rescued if the Sons of Odin hadn't devised the plan. T-Bone and the others insisted they didn't want credit for that mission, but it was owed to them.

A couple seats down from me, Reaper also shifted uncomfortably. I knew he didn't feel the same way now, but he had been against the mission back then and didn't feel right with being awarded for her rescue. The Sons' absence was jarring, and I hoped they would still attend our after party.

"Our gratitude is beyond measure," Vance continued. "Words and recognitions fall short of describing what the Steel Demons MC has done for Four Corners. I speak for everyone in this room, in this territory, when I say I'm honored to have met you all. May the legacy of your strength, bravery, and compassion live on for generations." He paused once more to wipe his eyes. "Reaper, Jandro, Gunner, Shadow, and Mariposa. Please come forward and accept our highest decoration, the Four Corners Cross."

The room exploded into applause as everyone stood up for us. Even I had gotten a little teary-eyed at his speech and needed a moment to compose myself before I stood. The applause never stopped, not even as each of my men accepted the medal around their necks one by one, including handshakes with the governor, Kyrie, and hugs from Finn. Once my guys were fully awarded and it was my turn, Governor Vance stepped aside and Kyrie walked up to the podium. Only then did the applause die down to silence, but everyone remained standing.

"Mariposa Wilder," Kyrie said into the microphone. "For your dedication as a medic and for saving countless lives, it is my greatest honor to present you with the Caduceus Excellence in Medicine Award."

"What?"

The squeaked-out word was lost in another round of thunderous applause. None was louder than my men clapping across the stage. I started to actually cry, taken aback with a hand on my chest. Kyrie placed the ribbon over my head with the medical award, and then her father followed with the same medal my men wore.

Kyrie pulled me into a hug, quickly whispered, "Thank you," into my ear, and then the remainder of my time onstage was a blur. Only the familiar scents and touches of my men grounded me again as they guided me back to our seats. The next thing I knew, it was time for the dinner party.

"Ah, thank fuck," Jandro muttered as we and the other guests were ushered into the dining room.

Unlike last time, today's meal was more of an informal cocktail hour than a multi-course, sit-down dinner. There were several tables with various foods to snack on, several wet bars, and pub tables to sit at. It would allow us to chat and mingle enough to be polite, then exit whenever we wanted. Maybe the governor and his staff had picked up on the fact that we weren't terribly formal people.

"Shit, I forgot Vance had good fuckin' whiskey." Reaper turned to me, playfulness lighting up his eyes. "How many am I allowed before we blow this pop stand, sugar?"

"Hm." I tapped on my chin. "Two."

"That's it?"

"We have plenty to drink at home and a whole evening to celebrate."

"I can have two whiskeys in five minutes, that's barely pre-gaming."

"Fine, three."

Reaper kissed my cheek. "I'll make 'em last." He smirked at me before heading to the nearest wet bar.

"Do you want a plate of food?" Jandro eyed one of the nearby buffet tables while Gunner checked out a selection of wines at another bar.

"Sure, not a big one though." I squeezed his forearm. "Saving room for your barbecue."

Jandro kissed my opposite cheek. "That's my girl. We'll share a plate."

He went off to get in line, leaving only me and Shadow together.

"Holding up alright, my social butterfly?" I hugged an arm around his waist.

Shadow huffed out a laugh, draping an arm around my shoulders. "I'm fine, lover. How are you?"

"Oh, good. Still reeling a little from having a bonus award sprung on me at the last minute, but otherwise fine."

He squeezed my shoulder affectionately, turning me into him to kiss my forehead. "You deserve it."

"I was just doing my job."

"One that few other people can do as compassion-ately and effectively as you can."

Kyrie walked up to us just then, a glowing smile on her pretty face and two champagne flutes held out in offering. "Congratulations you two! How about a toast?"

"You've done too much for me already," I laughed, but accepted the drink along with Shadow.

"Oh, it was nothing." Kyrie snagged another flute from a passing waiter on a tray. "It just felt wrong to not recognize what you did in the medical field as well as in battle."

"Thank you," I said, at a loss for any other words.

"It was my pleasure." She smiled and lifted her glass. "To peace and prosperity."

The three of us touched glasses and drank. Shadow and I exchanged a look when Kyrie threw back her entire champagne flute instead of just sipping it.

"I hope I'm not intruding but, um..." She passed her empty flute to a nearby waiter, her face flushing red. "Do you happen to know why the Sons of Odin didn't attend the ceremony? Is everything alright?"

I resisted the urge to glance at Shadow again. "I don't know, I'm sorry. We last saw them on a ride two days ago. They seemed fine, but maybe something came up."

"There's a chance we'll see them tonight at our house," Shadow offered. "You're welcome to come over too."

"Oh, no." Kyrie waved her hand, blushing harder. "I couldn't, I don't want to intrude."

"We're having a party, you won't be intruding," I told her. "It might be a rougher crowd than what you're used to, but we'll all be there. Come alone or bring a friend, everyone is welcome."

"That's so sweet of you, Mari." She laughed nervously. "But I dunno."

"No pressure." I reached out to touch her arm. "If you'd like to come, we're happy to have you."

Kyrie quickly but politely made her exit after that, leaving Shadow and I to sip our champagne and ponder.

"Does she…like the Sons?" Shadow looked at me curiously.

I grinned impishly over my glass. "I dunno, have I been dying to rip your clothes off all day?"

His eyes widened briefly in surprise before the grin took over his handsome face. "Is that so?"

"I've never spoken truer words in my life." I played with the buttons on his shirt, sliding my fingers into the gaps between them until he grabbed my hand.

"Why are we having a bunch of people over at our house again?" His voice grew low and husky, meant only for me.

"I can't seem to remember the reason for that."

"Me either." He placed a slow, smoldering kiss on my palm before releasing my hand with a sigh. "These last two weeks have spoiled us."

"I know, love." I stroked his beard. "But tonight will be fun."

"It will be," he agreed. "I've been itching to do some tattoos."

"Oy, come here and eat!" Jandro motioned to us from a table piled with several plates of different finger food.

Gunner had one arm on Jandro's shoulder while he drank directly from a bottle of wine and talked to one of Finn's lieutenants. Reaper also sat at the table on, most likely, his second glass of whiskey. He also had a cigar and was talking to one of Governor Vance's cabinet members. A few other important-looking men hovered around the table, waiting for a chance to talk to one of the saviors of the territory.

"Shall we?" I took a step in their direction, my hand in Shadow's as I looked back at him.

"With you, always," he said warmly, following after me.

THIRTY-THREE

MARIPOSA

W e mingled for another hour before saying our goodbyes. Once in the car, the guys became a flurry of removing ties, unbuttoning shirts, and rolling up sleeves. I knew they loved me, but in that moment, I was absolutely certain they were trying to kill me.

At home, everyone changed into casual clothes and we rushed around the house like bees in a hive to prepare for our guests. Did any of them take me up for a quickie? No. Wholly unfair, honestly.

After changing into a casual sundress, I helped Jandro prepare food while the others cleaned the house and ran out to stock up on alcohol. Shadow also set up a small tattoo station in a corner of the dining room.

The usual suspects arrived first—Andrea, Tessa, and their children, quickly followed by Noelle and Larkan, and then Slick, who held hands with a pretty young woman I'd never seen before. She smiled nervously, leaning into him for support as they walked in through the living room.

"Mari, this is Katelyn." Slick puffed his chest out, turning to beam at the girl he was clearly smitten with. "We started talking a few weeks back, she finally let me bring her around to meet everyone."

"It's so nice to meet you." I reached for her hand, utter elation in my chest that Slick had found someone. "Please make yourself at home."

"Call me Kat, and thank you. I've heard a lot about you," she blurted out, her face reddening. "One of my friends, Erica, is a medic under you."

"Small world." I smiled at her. "Erica might come over soon too. Slick, you know the drill. Help yourselves to anything. And Kat, don't pay attention to my husbands' hazing of him. It's really out of love."

"It's not that bad anymore." Slick chuckled, leading her by the hand toward the kitchen.

"Slick, ya dumb fuck! I told you not to kidnap pretty girls!" Jandro shouted, not a moment later.

"Worked out for you, didn't it?" Slick retorted.

"Ohh, he's a big man now!" Gunner taunted.

I barely had time to laugh at the situation before Noelle pulled me into the hallway. "I'm so fucked, Mari," she hissed under her breath.

"Why, what's wrong? Wait, hang on." I pulled her into the nearest bedroom and closed the door behind us. "What is it?" My heart pounded, worry spiking.

"I'm fucking pregnant!" she whisper-yelled.

"Wha—oh my God!" My palms flew to my mouth and then wrapped around her in a hug. "Congratulations!"

"Don't tell me that yet." She pulled loose from me

and smacked a palm to her forehead. "I found out this morning and I'm...still in shock, I guess."

"That's okay, that's normal." I placed my hands on her shoulders in an attempt to calm her down. "This wasn't planned, I take it?"

"No, it wasn't planned! He usually comes *on* me but lately it's been all, you know, end of the world and shit, and it feels nicer when...aw fuck, you get what I'm saying?"

"Sure I do." I rubbed her arm in sympathy. "But this is the consequence of doing that."

"I know! Ugh, I'm such an idiot. I should have gotten one of those birth control things from you."

"Yeah, a little too late for that. How's Lark feeling?"

Noelle worried her lip and scratched one of the bright tattoos on her forearm. "I haven't told him yet."

I bit back my smile. "You should probably do that."

"I know, I know. I've just been trying to process this all day. I probably will tonight, since I guess I can't drink anything and he's gonna be suspicious."

"Noelle." I hesitated on my next question but squeezed her arm in support. "Do you want this baby?"

She squeezed my hand as a blissful smile took over her face. It was the calmest she'd looked since dragging me into the hallway.

"I do, Mari. I want it because I made this baby with *him*. I never really thought about it before because I assumed it would never happen. But it's...scary how much I want this baby." Her worried expression returned. "What if I fuck it up? I drank and smoked before today, what if something's already wrong? Oh fuck, what if Lark doesn't want it?"

"Calm down, honey. Take a breath." I placed my hands on her shoulders again, breathing deeply so she could copy me. "Come to the hospital tomorrow and I'll do an ultrasound. You're probably fine. Lots of people don't abstain from vices early in the pregnancy because they don't know. But we'll monitor you and make sure, okay?"

Noelle nodded, her throat still working in nervous swallows.

"As for Lark, honey, you have absolutely nothing to worry about. That man *loves* you. He will be overjoyed, you know that."

"You're right, you're right." Noelle laughed sheepishly. "I'm just freaking out."

"That's okay. It's a big change."

"Mari?" She clasped both of my hands in hers. "Will you deliver the baby for me? Like you did with Tessa?"

"Noelle," I gasped, tears springing to my eyes. "Of course I will, I'd be honored."

"I don't want anyone to do it but you." She squeezed around my fingers. "You were so amazing with her, and I don't trust anyone else as much."

"I wouldn't miss it for the world," I promised, squeezing back.

She released my hands and hugged me, her laughter and smiles now more joyful than nervous. "Guess I should tell my baby daddy what we made, huh?"

Larkan was hovering at the end of the hallway when

we left the bedroom, concern darkening his face. "You okay, baby?" He held an arm out to Noelle.

"Yeah, babe." She slid under his arm, hugging around his waist with a beaming smile. "We were just having some girl talk."

They kissed and turned toward the kitchen, still wrapped up in each other. "What do you want to drink?" I heard Larkan ask, but they were too far away for me to hear Noelle's answer.

A heavy knock came at the front door and I rushed to open it, finding three tall men with wiley smiles on their faces.

"Sons!" I shrieked, jumping up to hug T-Bone who caught me against his chest.

"Little lady." He greeted me with a warm kiss on the cheek before setting me back down on the ground.

I hugged Grudge and Dyno, then halted the trio before they could get too far inside the house. "Where were you guys today?" I lowered my voice to a conspiratorial whisper.

T-Bone's charming smile disappeared, replaced by a frown and a shifting glance at his two partners. "I'm sorry we missed the ceremony. We made other commitments earlier today."

It was clear he wasn't going to say anything else, nor did the other two care to add details.

"Fine." I smacked a palm on T-Bone's chest, earning a smile from him again. "But I'm glad you guys are here."

"We wouldn't miss the *real* party," Dyno scoffed. "Where your boys at? Making fools of themselves?"

"Oh, I hope not yet," I groaned. "It's still way too early for that."

Grudge broke off from his men and embraced Shadow in the dining room. The two men clung to each other tightly and slapped each others' arms. We'd seen the Sons regularly since bringing Reaper home, but those two always greeted each other like they hadn't seen each other in months. It was sweet to see a deeper appreciation of the friendship and bond they shared.

Seeing Grudge and Shadow reminded me of the slip of paper in my bedroom. I had just gotten it from the hospital and planned to show them together. I excused myself quickly and headed back down the hallway. My heart pounded as I retrieved the folded piece of paper from the desk drawer, the beat doubling in speed as Shadow looked at me with such love and adoration as I approached.

"Hey, lover," he said, reaching for me.

I let his protective, unbreakable embrace fall around me and planted a kiss on his mouth before producing the paper. "Do you guys still want to know?"

Grudge's eyes widened at the paper and then at me. Shadow squeezed my waist, the pulse in his neck accelerating. "Is that...?"

"The results from your blood tests, yes," I confirmed. "I picked them up from the lab yesterday. I haven't looked at them yet. I figured you guys should be the first to know."

Shadow took the results from my hand, loosening his embrace as he held it out to Grudge. "Should we do this together, brother?"

"Mm." Grudge jerked his chin down in a nod and grasped the other end of the paper in his fingers. They unfolded it together and I waited with my breath in my chest.

The two of them peered at me after a few seconds. "I don't know what any of these mean, lover. What is X-DNA?"

"Oh sorry!" I laughed, taking the paper from them. "Allow me to translate." After a quick scan of the results, a smile overtook my face as I looked up at them. "I knew it!"

"Mari." Shadow's warning growl of my name was low and playful, lighting up heat between my legs.

"You two are half-brothers," I said. "You share the same Y-chromosome, which means you have the same father. Your X-chromosomes don't match at all, which means you have different mothers."

Grudge made a noise like a scoff, glancing away for a moment until Shadow thumped him on the back. "I know, brother. He was most likely an evil son of a bitch, but he's hopefully dead now. And if he's not," Shadow clapped his shoulder, "take comfort in knowing we are huge disappointments to the old man."

"Heh." Grudge looked back at him with a lopsided smile, gesturing between the two of them and then pantomimed counting on his fingers.

"That's right. We could have a whole bunch of siblings out in the world." Shadow's jaw tightened, returning his gaze to me.

"Maybe, maybe not." I perched myself on his thigh. "But family isn't determined by blood."

"Mm-hm." Grudge nodded in agreement.

"I'm glad we know for sure, but you're right." Shadow nuzzled my face, planting a kiss on my cheekbone. "Nothing has changed. And life is so fucking good."

———

THE PARTY WENT on late into the night. I had only sat with Shadow and Grudge for a few more minutes when we heard Larkan's shout of, "Whoooo! I'm gonna be a daddy!" reverberate through the house.

That victory cry kicked off the real party atmosphere. People cheered, shouted congratulations, and the alcohol flowed through everyone's good mood. Someone brought out a guitar and couples started dancing in the backyard. Reaper and Shadow weren't dancers, but I had a blast being passed back and forth between Jandro and Gunner. Slick and his new girlfriend stayed huddled to themselves for the most part, but she did manage to drag him out to dance for a couple of songs.

When I headed inside for a quick restroom break, I spied a tipsy, pink-cheeked Finn with his shirt off, getting tattooed by Shadow.

"What is this?" My voice was high and probably a little too loud from my own tipsy state. "What are you getting?"

"My old lady's name, of course." My father-in-law smirked.

"Oh my God!" Shadow had indeed sketched "Alisa

Forever" with a pen on Finn's chest and was currently in the process of outlining it. "How sweet. Does she know?"

"She will soon." Finn laughed.

"You crazy kids," I teased him.

"I don't recommend it until you've been together a minimum of thirty years," he added with a grin.

Time passed in a blur. I drank and danced some more, kissed my men, and laughed with my friends. It felt so, so incredibly good to have fun for essentially no reason. Yes, we were celebrating being alive but now we knew tomorrow would come. And the day after, and the next week, next month. Next year, and many more years. We were celebrating a future we never thought we would see.

At some point I kicked off my shoes and danced barefoot, the grass cool and soft on my aching soles. Spinning away from Gunner, I left our makeshift dance floor in search of a drink and place to sit to catch my breath. Reaper pushed a glass of water into my hands, then was quickly pulled away by some guy calling his name.

I was plopped down on the back porch, chugging my water, when a large man took a seat next to me.

T-Bone cleared his throat awkwardly. "We're taking off, Mari. Thanks for having us."

"What, already?" I set my water down to wrap my arms around his bicep. "You're not leaving yet. I won't let you."

He let out a rumbling chuckle but firmly removed

his arm from my hold. "We've got an early ride tomorrow."

"Oh yeah, where are you guys going?"

T-Bone swallowed, taking a long time to answer and looking unusually serious. "Mari, we're leaving Four Corners. For good."

"What?" I rocked away from him, taken aback in the moment, but in reality, it wasn't all that surprising.

"Yeah. I'm glad the Demons have found a home here, but it feels like we've outgrown the place. We'd been thinkin' on it for a while, but after Grudge's whole hostage situation...it's just time for us to move on."

"I hate to hear it, but I understand." I placed a hand on his forearm. "After everything you've done, I'm sorry you weren't treated better here."

"Shit happens." He shrugged. "We'll find a place where our funky little threesome can live like kings."

The question, *What about Kyrie?* hovered on the tip of my tongue, but I decided against voicing it. Their decision was made, and while I didn't hold out hope that she would attend our party, it was clear that she had wanted to see them. I had thought the feeling was mutual, but it wasn't my place to get involved.

"You guys better visit," I said instead.

"I promise we will, little lady." T-Bone lifted an arm to wrap it around me in a side hug. "This isn't goodbye forever."

"Our house is always open to you," I told him, returning his squeeze. "Our food, our liquor, everything."

"Your prettiest husband?" He chuckled into my hair.

I slapped his chest. "No! Gunner's mine."

We laughed together, saying another friendly good-bye, until he reluctantly stood to break the news to the others.

I watched, a mixture of wistful and happy as T-Bone hugged my guys and tried to sneak a grab of Gunner's ass. The Sons of Odin were amazing allies and friends. We wouldn't be partying tonight if it hadn't been for their help. But not all paths continued in the same direction.

While T-Bone mingled with my guys, I stood from the porch and headed inside to find the other two. Grudge and Dyno were sprawled on a couch, drinks in hand and talking softly to each other.

"T-Bone told me," I said at their glance up at me.

They sat up straighter, faces apologetic. "Mari…" Dyno began.

"No, it's okay." I took a seat on the coffee table in front of them. "I understand, just…" My fingers clasped together as I tried stringing my thoughts into words. "Just be careful out there. Take care of each other. Especially him." I angled my head to indicate T-Bone, who was still off talking to my guys.

Gunner told me what happened when he and T-Bone were out in battle together against Blakeworth. He started that huge fire and went apeshit when they got captured, trying to goad Blakeworth officers into cutting out his tongue.

From how he reacted when Grudge was taken hostage too, it was clear T-Bone could be a loose cannon when those he loved were threatened. The jovial, flirtatious man still harbored a great deal of pain. Dyno and Grudge were likely the only ones keeping him grounded.

"We will." Dyno nodded solemnly, understanding my meaning.

"I'll miss you guys," I sighed, and leaned in to accept their embrace when their arms opened up.

They left our house soon after and my chest tightened at the roars of their bikes starting up. I listened until the sounds of motorcycles faded, and the Sons of Odin rode off to start the new chapter of their lives.

THIRTY-FOUR

REAPER

The party began to wind down not long after the Sons left. Their departure shifted the atmosphere to a more sobering one, that tomorrow we'd be living in a Four Corners without T-Bone's boisterousness, Dyno's sly remarks, and Grudge's observant silence. I owed those guys everything, which made our goodbyes especially bittersweet.

Until they broke the news, my spirits were higher than they'd been in months. The party was just like the ones we threw back in Sheol. I nursed a good buzz for hours, got a belly full of food, and shot the shit with my favorite people. It was the perfect way to end one chapter and start anew.

Then once the Sons left, everything felt a little more wistful. The music in the backyard stopped, children started blinking heavily, and people started settling on our chairs and couches after dancing the night away.

I spotted Mari on the back porch, leaning against

the exterior wall as she watched Jandro and Andrea's kids playing fetch with Hades.

Mari smiled when I approached her, leaning into me when I slid an arm around her waist and pulled her back toward my chest.

"All alone, Mrs. President?" I nudged a kiss by her ear, our fingers intertwining on her waist as I hugged around her.

"Never." She kissed me quickly over her shoulder. "Just enjoying a moment of quiet."

I squeezed tighter around her hands, rubbing my finger over the stone on her ring. "You alright?"

"Yeah, I'm okay." She rested the back of her head on my shoulder. "Just didn't expect the Sons to take off so suddenly, I guess."

"Ah, they'll be back." I kissed the top of her head, then rested my chin in the same spot. "They might not see this place as home but they know we're family. Besides, T-Bone will miss hitting on Gunner too much to stay away *that* long."

Mari's laugh was bright and playful as she spun to face me, winding her arms around my neck as she stood on tiptoe to kiss me. I held her flush to me with a heavy grip on her waist, kissing her back deeper than all the short, flirtatious pecks we shared during the party.

"I want you," I groaned out when we parted for a breath.

A coy smile tugged at her lips. "I've wanted you all day."

My palms slid to her ass, squeezing and pulling her forward with not a fuck given about who saw.

"I want you to myself," I clarified.

Sharing her was great, but the five of us had been damn near inseparable for the last two weeks. I still only had partial use of my left hand, but overall my strength and mobility were coming back quickly. Certain positions and movements didn't hurt anymore, but the moment Mari and I would get started, the others couldn't resist touching or kissing her.

Not that I could blame them, especially in the aftermath of everything. It felt like we were on vacation, a honeymoon even. I'd never push the guys away, but it had been months and months since I had my wife to myself. I didn't need it all the time, but fuck me, I needed her now.

Mari's smile only grew wider at my request. "Then what are you waiting for, Mr. President?"

A spark lit up my chest. My doubts of her feelings for me were long gone...mostly. I knew she wouldn't have stayed at my side every day during my coma, wouldn't have been so hands-on with my physical therapy, and endlessly patient once I came home if she didn't love me. She apologized too many times, needlessly and tearfully, for how she treated me before I got captured. I believed she was sincere, I truly did.

But it was hearing that confirmation from her lips that she wanted me, and me alone, that smothered that last, lingering seed of doubt.

I tugged her inside the house without another moment of hesitation. The beautiful sound of her laugh followed me through the hallway to the bedrooms. I went for the nearest door, not caring whose room it was.

The five of us had fallen into the habit of spending every night together anyway.

Mari closed the door behind us and headed for the untouched bed, but I tugged her back to my side.

"Not there. Come here."

I smothered her mouth with a kiss, driving my tongue past her lips to taste every part of her I could reach. My hands gripped her ass like a lifeline, encouraging her to rock and grind against my dick that was already fighting to get out of my jeans.

Mari stretched up on her tiptoes, one leg nudging around the outside of my thigh, and I picked her up so that she could straddle my waist. Her legs now secure, I turned to perch her ass on top of the chest of drawers against the wall.

The casual dress she wore, which had spun around her so hypnotically as she danced, now rode up high as her legs spread to accommodate me between them. My touch dove under the fabric, finding the warmth of her bare skin as I followed the curves of her hips and waist.

"I like this dress," I murmured, mouthing my way down the side of her neck.

"The dress or the easy access?" She reached for my jeans, pulling apart the snap and the zipper with quick efficiency.

"Both." I pulled a strap down her shoulder, lingering a kiss on the new stripe of exposed skin. "You looked beautiful tonight. Happy."

"I am happy." Mari's fingers returned to my neck, scratching through my hair as she kissed me with a smile. "Are you?"

For once in my life, I didn't need to think about the answer. Just getting by, living to another day, used to be enough. It satiated me until the next big fight, until I counted every Steel Demon patch and reeled from however many we lost. Not losing anyone was once a blessing, a rare gift that was fleeting and unreliable.

Now I knew, with as much certainty as possible, that everyone at this party would still be here tomorrow. Mari would still love tomorrow. Jandro's stupid rooster would crow at the crack of dawn, and then...the day was ours. The future, our lives, belonged to *us*.

"Yes," I said through a tightening in my throat, my forehead on hers. "I am."

We kissed while I pulled down the other strap on her dress and bunched the fabric down around her waist. She gasped into my mouth as I rolled her breasts in my hands, drawing me in closer with her legs. Together, we gathered up the fabric of the dress to keep it out of the way. From the top down and the bottom up, my wife was so beautifully, obscenely exposed.

"Oh, look at you," I groaned out at the sight of her damp panties, pressing my hand between her legs. "So wet for me already?"

"I've missed having you to myself too." A moan escaped her as I rubbed, giving her that friction she wanted so badly. "I love the other guys and never want to turn them down, but—" Her breath stuttered in her chest while I kept rubbing, sweeping the edge of my hand over her lips and clit through the damp fabric.

"But what, sugar?" It was a command, not a question. One that made her hooded eyes pop open at the bark of my voice.

"I've missed how *you* fuck me. You and no one else."

A growl tore from my throat, my fingers hooking into the edge of her panties to pull them aside. I stroked once, twice through her slick folds, just to make sure she was ready before freeing my cock and notching it against her.

"Ah, good," Mari sighed, grinning at me. "I thought you'd make me wait."

"I'll still make you come until you can't remember your name." I pressed forward, her slippery heat embracing my blunt head. "I just want to feel all of it on my cock."

Her thighs squeezed around my hips as I pressed inside, and my head fell to her shoulder with a groan. She was the best feeling—familiar, soft, warm, and just so good. When the memories of the Sha's dungeon made me unsettled and on-edge, she brought me back.

My hips drew back and when I pressed forward again, my thumb circled over her clit. And there my hand would remain until she couldn't take it anymore.

My hand motions were fast, faster than my thrusts, the pressure of my thumb consistent and unrelenting. Her first orgasm built up faster than she could catch up, her moans turning to pants, then gasps and yelps when the release hit. She gripped the edges of the dresser for purchase, her pussy squeezing and stroking around me so beautifully.

"Good girl." I eased the pressure off her clit slightly,

my circling motion just a touch slower. "Shall we do that again?"

"Bastard," Mari huffed with a laugh. "I want more of this." She grabbed my waist and pulled me forward, causing me to sink to the hilt inside her and pulling a deep hiss from my chest.

"I'll fuck you twice as hard for every orgasm I get from you," I told her. "Deal?"

Her head fell back with a bright, breathless laugh. "How could I forget how terrible you are?"

"You wanted me," I reminded her, leaning forward to suck a pert nipple into my mouth, dragging my teeth on the stiff peak until she cried out.

She came again quickly with a lighter touch, still sensitive from her first one. Her pussy fluttered around me again, and it was such sweet relief to fuck harder like she wanted.

"Good girl," I praised again, biting a rough kiss on her shoulder. "How about another?"

Mari came for me three more times before she slumped back in exhaustion, her elbows propped on the dresser and her skin dewy with sweat.

"Come here, sugar." I pulled her to me and kissed her once before allowing her head to rest on my shoulder. Bracing one arm against her back, I brought the other to her hip.

She was limp and utterly spent, leaning on me as I finally released the white-knuckled control and fucked her wildly. My cock felt like solid iron after being teased and stroked by her orgasms, so ready to take my woman and burst into her perfect pussy.

Mari looped her arms around my neck, soft moans crooning directly into my ear. Her hips rocked forward, meeting the rough crashes of my thrusts and letting me plunge to new depths that had me seeing stars. But before I finished...

"One more," I rasped into her neck, returning my hand to where our bodies joined. "Come for me one more time, sugar."

"Reaper, I can't," she whined, but she still responded to my touch. A shiver raced over her skin, and still she chased the weight of my hand on that sensitive bundle of nerves.

"Oh fuck yeah, that's it," I urged her with my mouth against her rapid pulse. "Take it sugar, it's all yours."

Her hips stuttered with the build-up of pleasure, movements growing frantic and needy as she raced toward release. The shift in our hard-crashing rhythm staved off my own orgasm *just* long enough. She found the edge and hurtled herself off, the hot spasms of her pussy taking me with her.

My hands slapped the dresser as my body became boneless, the heady rush of my orgasm too good and all-consuming. Our hips kept moving, creating a feedback loop to extend each other's pleasure. And oh fuck, how I wanted to stay here, flush inside her and bliss every-where in my body.

"Would you marry me?" I mumbled on our slow, lazy descent back to earth.

Mari's legs relaxed around me, but her pulse was still racing as she panted out a soft laugh.

"I thought we were already married." She leaned

into me, resting her temple on my shoulder as she placed soft kisses on my neck. The sensation made me shiver and she hugged around me tighter.

"If we weren't already, would you?" I brushed a kiss along her forehead, then nudged my face lower to look at her eyes. "If I asked you for the first time now, after everything that's happened, would you still?"

She cupped my cheek, staring at me for a moment before answering confidently, "Yes. I would." She caught my mouth in a kiss and I poured all of the elation and relief building in my chest into that kiss. "I'll marry you again, if that's what you want."

"Hm." I ran my fingertips up her naked back, in no rush to see her clothed again. "A ceremony might be nice. With all the guys."

Mari leaned away, her blissed-out expression sobering. "Would you want to marry *me* again, after all this?"

I let out a scoff. "First of all," I tapped my index finger to her nose, "I ask these questions, young lady. Not you."

She huffed, a smirk pulling at her lips before I leaned in again, just short of a kiss.

"Second of all," I whispered. "Yes. My answer to you will always be yes."

"I want that in writing." She grinned. "In your vows."

"Don't get any crazy ideas, missy."

We laughed, kissed, and held each other lazily, lingering in our precious alone time until she mentioned that we should probably check on the party. I grumbled out a reluctant agreement and we quickly got decent before leaving the bedroom, holding hands on our way out.

The air was cooler out here, soothing to my heated skin as we came out of the hallway together. About half of the people who'd settled into the living room had taken off. Slick had his new girlfriend in his lap in *my* armchair, making out like fucking kids.

"Get a room and use condoms," I yelled as Mari tugged me away toward the kitchen.

"Whoo, I'm gonna be a daddy!" Larkan yelled from somewhere in the backyard for the seventeenth time that night.

"Or you'll end up like that guy," I added.

Mari slapped my arm. "Leave them alone. You're going to be an uncle!"

"Yeah." Truth be told, I was excited for Noelle and Lark. *It'll be our turn soon*, I thought.

Mari wanted to become a doctor and I didn't want to impede those plans, but I also really, really wanted to raise a family with her.

We'll talk about it soon. There's no rush, I assured myself.

"Where have you two been?" Jandro and Gunner were putting leftovers away, eyeing us across the kitchen counter. Behind us, Shadow's tattoo machine buzzed as he worked on someone.

"We went off to fuck, what do you think?" I snatched a rib from a plate, sucking the meat off the bone while Mari snorted and slapped a palm to her forehead.

The guys didn't bat an eye, although Gunner laughed at her embarrassed reaction.

"We have too much food. Here, send people off with these." Jandro shoved foil-covered plates at us.

"Are we kicking people out?" Mari loaded several of the plates into her arms.

Gunner yawned. "Yeah, I'm beat. Don't think I've ever danced, drank, and socialized more in my life."

"You got plans tomorrow?" I started loading up on to-go plates as well.

"No, and don't give me any." Gunner leaned his elbows on the counter and rubbed his eyes. "Let me sleep in 'til noon tomorrow, please."

"Jandro?"

"Nah, auto shop's closed for the next week while they repair the building." Jandro wiped his hands clean, casting me a curious glance. "Why?"

I nudged Gunner with my elbow. "Let's go to your fabled hot spring for a couple days. Camp out, just the five of us. And the animals, I guess."

"I'm down, but let's go late."

"Sure, sleeping beauty. We'll let you get your rest." I turned to face the other end of the room. "Shadow, you down for a hot springs trip?"

"Yes," he grunted out, not looking up from his tattoo.

"What are we doing?" Mari had just returned from handing out food and seeing our guests off.

"Hot springs tomorrow, for a few days." I reached for her waist, bunching up the fabric of her dress as I pulled her forward. "Just you and us."

"Yes! Later is good. I'll do Noelle's ultrasound in the morning." She lifted to her tiptoes to hug and kiss me again. Her skin was still deliciously warm, lips swollen and flushed from the love we just made.

"Sex, food, and booze mandatory." Jandro pantomimed checking off a list. "Clothing optional."

"Dare you to ride there naked," Gunner challenged.

"Oh boy, just watch me. You see this tan?" Jandro smoothed a palm down one arm. "The sun loves me. Now for you, that's something I don't recommend."

"What are you trying to say?" Gunner demanded in mock offense.

Mari unwrapped from me with a soft laugh and a shake of her head at their antics. That dress swished from her legs to her hips as she went over to Shadow. He paused his tattoo immediately, looking up at her with a smile. She leaned over and kissed him, nestling into his side and the big arm that came around her waist.

A clicking of nails on the floor drew my attention to the large black dog in front of me.

Hades licked his lips and sat like a good boy, dark eyes wide and innocent, no doubt begging for some left-over barbecue. It felt weird to think of him as Hades now that I knew the god no longer inhabited this animal. But calling him by another name didn't sit right either.

I knelt down to the dog's eye level, scratching the sides of his face as he licked his lips hopefully.

"I know you're not in there anymore," I said. "But I know you're always present, so I hope you can hear me."

On instinct, I paused to wait for a reaction, but there was none. Not a flicker of that ancient intelligence in those wide puppy eyes.

"I'm grateful," I went on. "Thank you for the valuable lessons you taught me. For choosing me, even though I fought against you many times. Thank you for protecting Mari and just...helping us to have this second chance."

The dog only stared back at me, ears lowered and those puppy eyes losing hope that he would earn a treat after all. With a slightly sheepish laugh, I returned to standing and went to grab a piece of rib meat.

Then I felt it.

The weight of a hand on my shoulder and a whisper in my mind.

You did well, my reaper.

Epilogue

MARIPOSA

THREE YEARS LATER

I stared at the objects on the bathroom vanity, eyes moving over each one in disbelief.

Three different pregnancy tests. All positive.

"*Mariposita?*" Jandro called out from the other side of the bathroom door. "You alright? You've been in there a while."

I was too shocked to answer in words, but a nervous giggle left my mouth. The first test I took on a whim and did not expect those results. The other two I took this morning, a day after hiding the first one yesterday. One could be a faulty test, but *three* positives?

"Mari?" Jandro began to sound genuinely worried. "If you don't answer me, I'm coming in. And you're not allowed to get mad."

"I'm okay!" I called back, finding my words finally. "You can come in."

He hesitated before opening the door slowly, poking

his head in with a curious expression. "Not interrupting anything, am I?"

I laughed and felt the first rush of emotion as the reality hit me. "Come here, look at this."

Jandro looked concerned again, as I was on the verge of crying. "What's going on, babe?" He came up next to me at the counter, looking down at the three tests laid out on the surface. "Are those..."

"Yeah," I laughed, sniffing and wiping away tears.

He looked at me wide-eyed, which was all the confirmation I needed. "They're all..."

"Yeah," I confirmed, full-on laughing joyously now. "It's really happening."

"Holy...shit!" Without another word, Jandro snatched up the tests and ran out of the bathroom with them. "Hey guys! Yo, dickwads, stop what you're doing! Important announcement! Family meeting right now!"

I followed him out to the sound of Reaper's grumbling—it was already ten AM and he still hadn't broken out of his morning grumpy mode. "What the fuck requires so much excitement in the morning?" He was in his favorite armchair with coffee and a newspaper, bare feet scratching Hades stretched out on the floor in front of him.

"Hang on, Groucho, everybody needs to be here for this." Jandro stuck his head out of the sliding door to yell at Shadow in the backyard. "Get in here, big dude! We got something important to tell everyone."

"Where's Gun?" I spun around in the living room, noting my golden man's absence.

"He rode out to grab shit from the farmer's market,

he'll be back any minute." Reaper set aside his paper and coffee and stretched with a groan in his chair, grinning at me. "Come here, sugar."

I happily obeyed, climbing into his lap to nestle against his chest. My lips rested near his throat and I kissed his warm skin there.

Reaper let out a small groan of satisfaction as his arms came around me. "What's the big news?"

"Not telling." I nipped the edge of his jaw. "Not 'til everyone's here."

"You won't make an exception for me?" he purred, lips grazing my cheekbone. "Your favorite husband?"

"Is that what you are?" I grinned and brought a hand up to his jaw, running the stone of my ring against his coarse stubble.

"I'm pretty sure I earned the title last night." His mouth trailed to the shell of my ear, nipping playfully.

I laughed, squirming in his hold. "Aren't you a confident one, Mr. President."

"I sure as fuck am when you call me that, Mrs. President."

The slider to the backyard opened then, Shadow's imposing figure filling up the space as he stepped inside. Freyja followed after him, headbutting his ankles at every opportunity.

Shadow wiped his face on a towel hanging over one shoulder, his bare upper body glossy with sweat and muscles taut from the exertion of his workout.

"What's the big news?" He bent over and picked up Freyja, flipped her upside down like a baby—*A baby!* —and cradled her against his chest.

"We're just waiting for Gunner to get home," I said, my heart pitter-pattering at the sight of his firm, supportive hold on the cat. "And then we'll stop keeping everyone in suspense."

We heard Gunner's bike roaring up the driveway a few minutes later and opened the garage door to see a bunch of grocery bags and produce boxes bungeed precariously to the back of his bike. On his handlebars, Horus chirped happily and preened his feathers.

"Jesus, Gun. Did you buy up the whole market?" Reaper asked.

"Nah, they just had a ton of good deals. I figured we could store any excess in the chest freezer. Baby girl, I got that goat cheese you like." He nodded at Jandro. "And before you ask, yes, I got a whole box of cabbages for your girls, *papi pollo*."

"Gun, don't worry about that stuff right now." Jandro waved a hand at him. "Come inside and sit down. We've got something important to tell everyone."

Gunner's smile dissipated, his expression concerned as his eyes floated over all of us. "Is everything okay?"

"Yes!" I told him with a beaming smile, reaching for his hands. "Come on, everybody's here now."

Everyone sat in the living room, their attention rapt on Jandro and I. "You want to do the honors, then I'll present the evidence?" he asked me.

"Sure." I couldn't stop grinning, my joy and excitement impossible to contain. "I'm pregnant!"

"What?!" Gunner gasped, his jaw dropping.

Reaper clapped his hands and punched the air victoriously. "Yes! I fuckin' knew it!"

Jandro took my three pregnancy tests from his back jean pocket and laid them proudly on the coffee table.

"Wait, how did you find out first, asshole?" Gunner threw one of Hades' dog toys at him.

"He barged in on me in the bathroom," I said.

"Bullshit, I gave you plenty of warning!"

Shadow was the only one who remained quiet, if even sullen at the news. He stared at the tests on the table, a slight furrow in his brow.

"Hey." I scooted toward him on the couch, taking one of his hands. "How are you feeling about this? It's okay if it's not all good. This is about to be a huge change for us."

His odd-colored eyes flicked up to me as he squeezed my hand. "I'm happy that you're happy, I'm just...concerned. I don't know anything about being a parent. Especially a *good* parent."

"None of us do, man." Reaper leaned over and slapped his shoulder. "But we'll be fine. We're all gonna struggle through it together."

"The child-raising part worries me, but it's not just that." Shadow swallowed, his gaze fixed on me. "I've read that pregnancy is very uncomfortable, even dangerous sometimes, for a woman. I don't want your health in jeopardy, lover."

"True, you're not entirely wrong about that." I leaned into his side, letting his heavy arm wrap around me. "But a few things to consider—one, pregnancy is temporary. I'll only be carrying for nine months. Two, it's different for everyone. It could be very easy for me, difficult, or anywhere in between. And if it is difficult, I have my medical training and I know my body. I'll also have Dr. Brooks and Rhonda to monitor me throughout the whole thing."

"And you'll have us," Jandro reiterated. "We'll do everything we can to make it easier on you."

"When you're not being a massive pain in my ass, you mean?"

"Well yeah, naturally."

Laughing, I turned back to Shadow and kissed the scar on his cheek. "Does that help alleviate your worries?"

"A little," he said, still looking concerned. "Even once the pregnancy is over, there is still the whole caring-for-infants thing."

"Yeah, that's the terrifying part," Gunner laughed. "But hey, there's four of us, and we already know the kid has an amazing mom. That puts us ahead of the game already."

"We're all gonna screw our kid up, just to varying degrees," Jandro said.

Shadow glared at him. "Is that supposed to make me feel better?"

"Well, no one is gonna screw the kid up worse than Reaper, so—"

"Fuck you, 'Dro." Reaper tossed a throw pillow at him.

"Most importantly." Gunner reached across Shadow's lap to squeeze my leg. "How are *you* feeling about this, baby girl?"

"I feel…" It took a moment to find words for all the sensations in my body, all the thoughts running through my head. "I'm *so* excited! I can't wait to meet this baby and to see all of you become fathers."

"You haven't stopped smiling." Jandro leaned over and planted a big kiss on my cheek. "You're glowing already. This happiness is such a beautiful look on you."

"I'm a little nervous too," I admitted. "I didn't expect it to happen so soon."

My birth control implant was removed about three months ago. I thought it would take much longer for my hormones and monthly cycle to return to normal. The guys and I talked right before I removed it and, while we weren't exactly *trying* to get pregnant, the five of us decided not to actively prevent it either.

"The timing is perfect." Reaper beamed from his armchair. "Your parents just finished moving into their house, my dad's retiring next month, Noelle and Lark's new place will finish being built soon. Everyone will be on deck to help out, sugar."

"I might have to take a break during med school." I frowned, trying to mentally calculate timelines over the next few years. The first semester started in two months. I'd finish it before the end of my pregnancy, but would be too far along to start the second semester. I'd have to take it off and go back in the summer, and even then, I'd probably only want to be in school part-time.

With four husbands, two sets of grandparents, and plenty of friends close by, finding childcare wasn't likely to be an issue. But as much as I wanted to further my education and become a doctor, I also wanted to experience motherhood and watch my child grow up.

"I still think they should just give you the MD,"

Gunner scoffed. "After all the lives you saved in this territory, I don't get why you still have to go school."

"Because I don't know everything, Gunner." I leaned in front of Shadow to stick my tongue out at him.

"I don't believe that for one goddamn second." Gunner leaned toward me, grinning as he cupped my face and kissed me. "I love you so much, baby girl," he whispered, lips grazing mine. "And I can't wait to meet this baby too. Everything will work out. It always does."

"I love you too." I smiled against his mouth before kissing him and leaning up, nudging my head against Shadow's shoulder. "And I know it will. Especially when we have each other."

Shadow rubbed the nape of my neck, brushing a kiss across my forehead. "I'm fucking terrified," he admitted. "But I'm yours forever, and I'll do my best."

"You'll be amazing." I nuzzled the side of his face, a mental image of him holding a tiny infant making my heart soar. "Because you already are. I love you."

"I love you endlessly," he said before kissing me.

I turned to Jandro, who was practically bouncing in his seat. "Fuck, I'm so excited!" He yanked me out of Shadow's arms to squeeze me against his chest. "We're gonna have a fucking baby! How many more do you want after this one?"

"Jesus, slow your roll!" I laughed, smacking his shoulder. "Let me get through this pregnancy first."

"I gotta write to Angie and tell her. Our nieces are going to have cousins. Oh, I bet they'll want to come visit!"

"Slow down, *guapito.*" I licked his neck, still laughing. His excitement was adorable and infectious.

"Can I speak Spanish to the baby?" His hand rubbed over my stomach. I didn't look any different yet but his gaze was already fixated there, where our bundle of love was growing.

"Please do." I scratched the back of his head, then kissed his ear. "*Te amo, mi amor.*"

"*Te amo mas, mi Mariposita.*" He kissed me, then lowered a kiss to my belly. "*Y te quiero mucho, mi bebe.*"

I let him talk softly to my belly for another minute before heading to Reaper's chair, where my first husband patted his lap in invitation.

"My little sugar cube," he cooed, running a hand over my belly as I climbed on. "Jandro's right, though. I probably will screw you up more than the others."

"Don't say that." I ran my fingers through his hair, finding it peppered with a few more grays in recent years, as I brought his gaze up to mine. "This baby is going to learn about all the amazing things you did for your family, to save and protect us. They'll learn how to be a leader, to be confident in the decisions they make, all because of you."

Reaper's green gaze locked onto mine, such bright and expressive eyes that I fell in love with. I hoped at least one of our children inherited those eyes from him.

"You're never wrong, so who am I to argue?" He smirked, arms wrapping me up and holding me close. "I love you, and I'm so grateful to the gods that you're my wife."

I knew he meant every word, especially about being

grateful. Ever since waking up from the coma, he looked at the world with a renewed sense of gratitude. And I knew he would teach that to our children as well.

"I love you so incredibly much." I snuggled close to kiss him, the outside world melting away as I curled up with my first husband, the first love of my life.

My men, my loves. We beat the insurmountable odds stacked against us just for this, so we could raise a family with hope, joy, and the normal fears and worries that came with it. Our children would never experience the horrors that all of us had to endure.

And that made every single battle, against enemies and ourselves, worth fighting for.

THE END

…OR IS IT?
Want a sneak peek into the Steel Demons' growing family?

Read more in ENDLESS - The Steel Demons MC epilogue novella.

PRE-ORDER ENDLESS HERE:
http://books2read.com/SDMC10

————

Can't get enough of Shadow?

From the Shadows contains three bonus scenes from

Shadow's POV not included in the original Steel Demons series.

Grab it for free here when you sign up for my newsletter!

———

Want to know what happened to the Sons of Odin? Their book is available now!
Click to start reading Their Property!

———

Ready for the next generation?
Faithless: Book 1 of Vengeful Gods MC releases December 2022!
PRE-ORDER FAITHLESS HERE:
https://books2read.com/VGMC1

Acknowledgments

Well, this is the hardest Acknowledgements section I've ever had to write. Here come the tears.

I've always been a writer (my mom will happily show you what I wrote at twelve years old). The story of the Steel Demons MC hit me harder than anything I've felt compelled to write in my life. I don't know when or if a story will ever hold the same kind of magic for me like this one did. This series was truly something special, and I'm so grateful I had the opportunity to share it.

Thank you to Brandy Slaven, Kathryn Moon, Aleera Anaya Ceres, Britt Andrews, Caroline Peckham, Susanne Valenti—just a handful of incredible indie authors who supported me while writing their own books. I'm honored to know you all and share readers with you.

A gigantic thank you to Izzy, Telisha, Erica, and Janet, the readers and friends who got to peek under the hood and helped me get these books ready for the world to see. You all are irreplaceable.

Mr. Ash, thank you for encouraging and supporting my two-year love affair with these crazy bikers. You're worth a dozen fictional harems and I love you.

There are too many incredible readers to name, but thank you, thank you, thank you, so much. I'd give you all SDMC patches if I could. Thank you for riding with this club until the end.

The Steel Demons' story is finished, but who knows? We just might see them again one day…

When one ride is over, another begins! For regular updates, exclusive teasers, and excerpts, join my reader group, Crystal's Coven.

See you all in the next book!

-Crystal

About the Author

Crystal Ash is a USA Today Bestselling Author from California. She loves writing steamy, heart-wrenching romance with tortured heroes, especially if they're in a reverse harem. Crystal's other loves include animals, mythology, and well-crafted alcohol, most of which can also be found in her stories.

When she's not writing, she's probably drinking craft beer with her husband or trying to coax her feral cat into accepting affection.

crystalashbooks.com

facebook.com/Crystal.Ash.Romance

instagram.com/crystalashbooks

amazon.com/author/crystalash

bookbub.com/profile/crystal-ash

www.ingramcontent.com/pod-product-compliance
Lightning Source LLC
Chambersburg PA
CBHW051320190726

48290CB00001B/249